The
# RAVEN'S
Gift

# The
# RAVEN'S
## Gift

## Don Rearden

PINTAIL

PINTAIL
a member of Penguin Group (USA)

Published by the Penguin Group
Penguin Group (Canada), 90 Eglinton Avenue East, Suite 700, Toronto, Ontario, Canada M4P 2Y3
(a division of Pearson Canada Inc.)

Penguin Group (USA) Inc., 375 Hudson Street, New York, New York 10014, U.S.A.
Penguin Books Ltd, 80 Strand, London WC2R 0RL, England
Penguin Ireland, 25 St Stephen's Green, Dublin 2, Ireland (a division of Penguin Books Ltd)
Penguin Group (Australia), 707 Collins Street, Melbourne, Victoria 3008, Australia
(a division of Pearson Australia Group Pty Ltd)
Penguin Books India Pvt Ltd, 11 Community Centre, Panchsheel Park, New Delhi – 110 017, India
Penguin Group (NZ), 67 Apollo Drive, Rosedale, Auckland 0632, New Zealand
(a division of Pearson New Zealand Ltd)
Penguin Books (South Africa) (Pty) Ltd, 24 Sturdee Avenue, Rosebank, Johannesburg 2196, South Africa

Penguin Books Ltd, Registered Offices: 80 Strand, London WC2R 0RL, England

Published in Penguin paperback by Penguin Canada, 2011

Published in this edition, 2013

1 2 3 4 5 6 7 8 9 10 (RRD)

Copyright © Don Rearden, 2011

The excerpt on page 1 is from *Intelligent Culture of the Copper Eskimos* by Knud Rasmussen,
published by Gyldendal, Copenhagen, 1932.
The excerpts on pages 3, 115, and 201 are from *The Eskimo About Bering Strait* by Edward Nelson,
published by the Smithsonian Institution Press, Washington, 1899, 1983.

*Publisher's note: This book is a work of fiction. Names, characters, places and incidents either are the product
of the author's imagination or are used fictitiously, and any resemblance to actual persons living or dead,
events, or locales is entirely coincidental.*

Manufactured in the U.S.A.

ISBN 978-0-14-318749-3

Visit the Penguin US website at **www.penguin.com**

ALWAYS LEARNING                                                                PEARSON

*For Dan and the Real People of the Kuskokwim River*
*and of course for you, Annette*

# ACKNOWLEDGMENTS

I have dreamt of the day I would write these words since *ellangellemni*, since I became aware that writing and stories would forever be a part of my life. And since this has been such a long dream in the making there are too many people to thank, and for that very fact I am so grateful.

Still, I must name a few important souls.

First I must thank the Yup'ik elders, tradition bearers, and families I have learned so much from, including the late George and Martha Keene, Dr. Oscar Kawagley, the Slims, Moseses, Ivans, Angstmans, Lincolns, Hoovers, Hoffmans, and Morgans (to name just a few).

Quyana to "Mikngayaq" Selena Malone for her photography skills and Yup'ik spelling assistance, and to "Piunriq" for always finding the right answers.

I owe a debt of gratitude to Yup'ik scholars and anthropologists Ann Fienup-Riordan, Alice Rearden, and Marie Meade. Without their work and the work of so many others dedicated to recording the elders' wisdom, too much would have already been lost.

To all those haunted by the initial drafts of this novel, I thank you for the advice, criticism, and optimism. Special thanks to Shane Castle, for the incredible insight and calling me dirty names on that first copy of the manuscript. To Ben Kuntz for the killer notes and for not letting me end the story a little past Haroldsen's. To Helena for her unending optimism and enthusiasm. To Sarah for catching, so, many, comma, errors. To Shannon for coffee walks, Arctic whaling, and zany poetic distractions.

I have had some incredible teachers along the way. I'd like to thank Ronald Spatz for pushing me and for teaching me to slow down. A heartfelt thanks goes to Sherry Simpson and Jo-Ann Mapson for always caring and always believing in my work.

Thanks to Jodi Picoult for the advice and for insisting I direct my writing efforts toward the novel.

Of course this manuscript would have died a quiet digital death in some file on my laptop if not for my amazing agents. So I offer a huge thanks to Adam Chromy for all his effort and expert advice and to Danny Baror for helping me catch a penguin and making this dream a reality.

And to Adrienne Kerr, my editor extraordinaire, writers dream of having an editor like you who understands and shares their vision. I can't thank you enough for your guidance and your faith in this story.

Thanks to Daniel Quinn for being my coach and for daring to save the world with *Ishmael*. With this story, I am doing my best to become *B*.

To my amazing family and to Annette, thank you for never doubting me.

Finally, *quyana* to the people of the Yukon-Kuskokwim River Delta for sharing with me the way of the human being.

# PROLOGUE

*Don't you hear the noise? It swishes like the beating of the wings of great birds in the air. It is the fear of naked people, it is the flight of naked people! The weather spirit is blowing the storm out, the weather spirit is driving the weeping snow away over the earth, and the helpless storm-child ... Don't you hear the weeping of the child in the howling wind?*

—BALEEN, COPPER ESKIMO SHAMAN, 1920s

# PART I

# The Bones of the Mammoth

*The bones of the mammoth are found on the coast country of the Bering Sea and the adjacent interior ... the creature is claimed to live underground, where it burrows from place to place, and when by accident one of them comes to the surface, so that even if the tip of its nose appears above the ground and breathes the air, it dies at once.*

—AS RECORDED BY EDWARD NELSON, 1899

# 1

He crawled on his stomach through the snowdrift and lifted his head over the edge of the riverbank, just enough to see the first few houses, charred black and dislodged from the wood blocks and tall steel pilings meant to hold them off the tundra's permafrost. Below the bank, the girl sat in a plastic orange toboggan, waiting. Her eyes stared back at him as white as the wisps of snow covering the thin river ice beneath her.

"They're all gone here, too?" she asked.

He stopped short of shaking his head and half slid down the hard frozen embankment, holding the rifle on his lap.

"I'm going to check it out," he replied. "Maybe stay for a few nights and rest. Let the ice firm up. Find shelter. Hopefully something to eat."

She pointed her brown fur mitten upstream. "The riverbank is not so steep a little ways up. You can pull me up there. By the school," she said, and then asked, "Are there any more tracks?"

He surveyed the light blanket of white covering the river, searching for the two strange snakelike lines he'd encountered at the river's edge three days earlier. "No," he said.

"Good," she said. "I don't like those tracks."

"Me either."

He reached down, wrapped the yellow rope around his waist and began pulling her up the river of ice. His feet were numb with cold. He slipped with each step, the fresh snow making the going slick and dangerous. He knew better than to be walking on the river ice so early, but they had to keep travelling. They had to beat the colder weather on the way, and he didn't feel safe if they weren't moving.

"Do you see the graves yet?" she asked.

He did. High up on the river's bank a cluster of leaning and listing white wooden crosses poked out from the long straw-coloured grass that the snow hadn't completely covered.

"That's where you can pull me up," she whispered, "between the graveyard and the school." She turned her head away from the village, as if she could see the sweeping flat expanse of white nothing. "You know, I never liked coming to Kuigpak, for basketball games, or for anything, really. Even now, I don't like it."

The cut in the high dirt wall of riverbank was right where she said it would be. He strained to pull her up the embankment, imagining what life had once been for her, the sounds of a basketball game, sitting at the edge of the court with her legs crossed, her head following the hollow twang of a bouncing ball against the gym floor, a player dribbling, driving toward a hoop, silence as the ball floated up, the swish of the nylon netting against the leather, the small gym choked with cheering, with life. He wondered why, of all villages, this one she openly disliked.

"You smell that?" she asked.

He stopped halfway up the fifteen-foot-high bank. He crouched and turned back toward her. She lifted her chin; her small nostrils quivered and her milky eyes seemed to search the grey sky.

"Not like that evil smoke," she whispered. "This is just wood, drift-wood smoke. I think there's someone good here, John! Someone safe."

He pulled the rifle off his shoulder and bear-crawled, with the sled in tow, toward the top. Just before he reached the crest he dropped down and pressed his body into the hard frozen mud, the rifle in his right hand, the toboggan line in his left. Her weight, what little there was, tightened the thin rope wrapped around his glove.

"It's coming from over that way," she mouthed, pointing to her left.

He chambered a round while his eyes scanned the few remaining chimneys of the houses on the north side of the trail that cut the lifeless village in two. The carnage was the same as in the other villages. The shack houses had been burned or pilfered and what remained made little sense. Out of the broken window of one house dangled a large black television, its cord running up and into the darkness beyond the window frame, as if somehow holding on.

THE JOB INTERVIEW took all of twenty minutes, with the questions geared more toward whether they were serious about teaching in the middle of Nowhere, Alaska, than whether they were competent educators. Gary Brelin, the personnel director, a handsome, fit runner type in his late forties, looked the two of them over, tugged at his earlobe for a moment, and scanned their résumés one final time.

"Impressive," he said. "Your reference letter from your mentor teacher nearly brought a tear to my eye, Anna. 'The kind of spirit all teachers should have.' For first-year teachers, you both have striking résumés. You know, we get three types who apply to teach on the tundra. Teachers no one else will hire. Teachers looking for an adventure. And then those who are running from something. You running from something?"

"I'm in it for the adventure. John here? We figured Alaska was the only place anyone would hire someone as goofy-looking as him," Anna joked.

Gary laughed. "Let me ask you, have you, as a couple, experienced anything like this, remote living, like Alaskan Bush life?" he asked.

"We've travelled abroad quite a bit," Anna replied. "And my husband likes to go on the cheap, so we know all about zero-star accommodations. We're open to adventure and cultural experiences. We're tired of the whole urban sprawl thing. Plus, this guy here isn't a fan of confined places. The open tundra will be perfect for him. I think it's in his blood. He's already part Alaskan."

John shook his head at Anna's attempt at humour. She often tried to make light of his not knowing.

Gary took the bait. "I saw you marked 'other' on the application, but I'm not supposed to ask about those things, of course. You're Alaska Native?" he asked.

John shrugged. "I don't know, that's why I just check 'other.' My father was a product of the war, I think. My grandfather was stationed somewhere up here during the Japanese occupation of the Aleutians. He stayed here for a while afterwards, doing studies for the Atomic Energy Commission. I never met my grandmother."

Gary nodded, as if this was commonplace. "Probably not Amchitka. I wonder if you were a Project Chariot baby?" He turned to Anna. "Does he glow in the dark?"

"Project Chariot?" John asked.

"A genius government idea back in the fifties to detonate a nuke to create a deep-water port in Point Hope. We actually dumped radio-active waste there, just to see what the effects would be, and as you might expect, the Inupiaq villagers there have some of the highest rates of cancer in the country. Amchitka, well you'll have to research that for yourself. Let's just say that in the late sixties the government detonated three nukes in Alaska, one of which was the most powerful bomb the U.S. has ever detonated. You will appreciate, as a history teacher, John, that our state has quite a colourful record." He stood up and stretched, then walked to the window and looked out at the sweeping postcard view of the wall of mountains that buttressed the east side of Anchorage.

"You've got to understand something," he said. "We've had the most qualified of teachers refuse to get off the airplane when they arrived in their assigned villages. The place you'll be going will look as familiar as the moon to you. Flat. Barren. Not like this, I can tell you that. The weather is usually brutal, and the housing situation, to be honest, is less than perfect. Pretty shitty, actually. The best part is you're going to be immersed within the Yup'ik culture. Really, it's one of the last places in America where children grow up speaking their Native tongue. Nicest people in the world, but like any indigenous population struggling to adapt to this world ..."

He turned back to them, sizing them up as if to pick teams for a dodge ball game in gym class.

"We've done quite a bit of research on the area," Anna said. "It fascinates us, really. The chance to live somewhere so exotic, in our own country—and help out some kids who really need it. We both love teaching. And he's excited to do some hunting and be outdoors twenty-four seven." She rolled her eyes. "That's in his blood too."

"If hunting is allowed. If not, that's fine," John added, not wanting to spoil the interview.

"Well, you're in luck, John. The Yukon-Kuskokwim Delta is home to one of the world's largest waterfowl refuges, and one of the last living subsistence cultures in North America—which, if you're a fan, equates to quite a bit of bird hunting and salmon fishing. So if you like fishing or plucking ducks, you'll be just a little north of heaven. Plus, you could be hunting so much you get sick of it. Last spring the National Guard unit in the area got a fifteen-month deployment to the Middle East. Over a thousand of the leaders and hunters in the villages are out in the desert somewhere. I suspect you'll be able to hunt for as many elders and hungry families as you want. Not a ton of game in the winter, though. The pickings can be pretty slim."

"And big game?" John asked.

Gary ran a hand through his hair and then stretched his lower back. "Big game hunting is another story. Moose and caribou take some serious travel, usually by boat or plane or snow machine—you guys probably call them snowmobiles. From most of our villages, you're looking at a hundred, maybe two hundred or more miles to reach big game hunting. But sometimes a big herd of caribou can just show up, and let me tell you, that's a magical thing to witness."

"The guns are already being sent north," John said.

"Should you accept." Gary looked back toward the mountains.

Anna gasped. She turned and squeezed John's forearm.

"Let him finish, Anna. Forgive her, she's excited. We both are. We've been talking about moving to Alaska for years."

Gary laughed. "You'll have to understand that you probably won't have running water in your house or apartment, which means you'll have to use what we call a honey bucket, which is—"

"A bucket with a toilet seat. We read about those, the classic Alaskan toilet! We can live with that, Mr. Brelin."

"Gary, please," he said with a smile. "As I was saying, Anna, you'll need to realize that all of your food will have to be purchased here in Anchorage and then flown into the village. The stores in the villages, unfortunately, carry little more than junk food, really, so you'll want to plan out your meals. This will be a different winter for us with those troops gone. I suspect we'll be fine, but there will be some adjustments for villages and families, I'm sure. Speaking of government BS, there's a wheelbarrow full of paperwork, of course, but I'd like you to really discuss whether or not you can handle a nine-month commitment like this. Teaching in the Bush has put the best of marriages to the test."

Anna and John stood up and they both shook Gary's hand.

"Anna, John, it's been a pleasure talking to you, and I look forward to offering you a contract by the end of the day. Here's my number here at the hotel. I can pretty much guarantee this as a life-changing experience for you two. My wife and I started as teachers out there, with two young children. Raised them on the tundra. I can't imagine living anywhere else, really, but then again, this sort of life isn't for everyone. Thank God for that."

"Thanks, Mr. Brelin," Anna said.

"Anna, it's Gary, please call me Gary. Last names don't mean much in the Bush. Your students will call you Anna, just like they call the superintendent Billy. I'll see you two this afternoon."

ALONE, WITH ONLY the light of a candle for company, John tried to study a detailed topographic map book of Alaska he'd found in the library. The scale was too great, but he could at least see what he thought might be the best route if no one came to help. He didn't want to believe there would be no relief, but if no one came he was going to try to walk out. He'd trek up the Kuskokwim River to McGrath, then across the Iditarod Trail toward Anchorage. A thousand-mile trip, at least.

His finger traced the route, following the wide river as it slowly narrowed, meandering hundreds of miles toward the little town of McGrath. He paused at Kalskag, noticing the Yukon River seemed to almost touch the Kuskokwim there. He was pondering the trip up that river, toward Fairbanks, when he heard the first shot.

He closed the book and held still, flat on his back. His pistol and rifle within reach.

Another shot. Then another. They sounded close. Then distant. He listened until his ears rang, waiting for the next. The shots continued through the night.

After a while he slept, and in his dream a pale, baby-faced man with piercing blue eyes and an evil smile, wearing a black cowboy hat, a long black oilskin duster, and black leather boots, roamed the village killing survivors. He carried two silver-plated six-shooters with pearl handles that glinted in the moonlight.

2

The shattered windows of the house had been covered with cardboard and blue plastic tarps to keep in the heat. The smoke drifted west toward them, grey as the sky. He kept the sight of the rifle on the door and waited. The girl rested beside him, seeing nothing, but somehow keeping watch. They had crawled beneath the house with the hanging television, right at the edge of the riverbank, to keep from being spotted.

"Maybe someone's inside and will help us," she said.

"Maybe," he replied.

When the word came from the girl's mouth it sounded something like hope.

"If we find someone else, someone who needs us. Will we help them?" she asked.

"I only wish we could find someone like us," he said.

When he saw the door open he raised his glove to his mouth to tell her to be quiet. As if she would see the gesture. But she heard the hinges squeak and the footsteps on the stairs and she pressed herself down in an effort to sink into the frozen dirt and to never be seen. She took several quick stabs of breath. Her nose searched the air.

He followed the man down the steps. The red bead on the metal sight at the end of his barrel slowly moved across the stained and tattered tan Carhartt jacket that covered the man's chest. He knew this man was not the skier. The man paused at the bottom of the stairs, wiped his nose on the back of his hand, and looked out at the village and then the river. He thrust his hands into his jacket pockets and began walking in their direction.

"What's he doing?" she whispered.

"Coming this way."

"Don't shoot yet. Wait," she said.

She took short, shallow breaths through her nose. He wondered how she could smell anything there, under that house, surrounded by the skeletons of old broken sleds, bike parts, and three half-flattened basketballs. His nose couldn't get past his own smell. The stink of sweat and hunger. Of a body eating itself.

She took another breath and held it. She reached over, grabbed his forearm and squeezed. John didn't need to see her face, but he looked, and the sadness that pulled at her cheeks said enough.

"Cover your ears," he whispered.

He waited until the man was only twenty yards from them. The tan jacket hung open, his brown chest a thin line of ribs, the stomach wasted and stretched drum tight. His black hair hung along his face in greasy strands, his brown eyes hiding somewhere in the shadows of his skull.

The girl screamed with the concussion. The shot reverberated against the hollow shell of a house above them and the man crumpled into the snow. She held her hands over her ears and buried her face in her chest.

He chambered another round as he swung the rifle back toward the house with the smoking chimney and waited.

"Quiet," he said.

"But my ears hurt."

"I know. I know," he whispered. "I'm sorry."

THEIR UNSIGNED CONTRACTS and the other papers were spread out on the floor. Anna rested on her stomach, her naked body across the bed, with her feet dangling off. Her head and arms hung over the edge. She was enthralled at the contents before her.

"It's almost like they want to scare us away. That's fascinating to me, don't you think? All this fuss about no running water, the brutal weather, the National Guard deployed—who cares if the nearest Starbucks is over four hundred miles away? Isn't that the point?"

He propped himself up on his elbow. "I'm sure they just don't want to have some yahoos who think they're going to be teaching in, what was the name of that stupid TV show? The one with the doctor in Alaska from New York?"

"I can't think of it. I know what show you're talking about. *Northern Exposure!*"

He nodded. "That show was ridiculous."

She sat up. "Are you staring at my crotch?"

"That's such a harsh word for something so divine. Plus, isn't crotch staring a rare privilege of my role as husband?"

She sat up and pulled a sheet over her body.

"You can take the girl from the Catholics, but you can't take the Catholic from the girl," he joked.

"Funny. I'm going to shower, and then we'll call Gary and sign those babies. We'll go eat somewhere nice, to celebrate our new jobs!"

"I'll join you," he said. "We better start practising those short military showers. If the only water supply is at the school, this could be our last shower together for a while." He paused, and then said, suddenly serious, "Anna?"

She stopped halfway in the door to the bathroom. "Yeah?"

"No more about me, okay? People don't need to know everything," he said.

"If you're part Eskimo then you're part Eskimo, John. It's okay to be a half-breed," she said in a weak attempt at humour.

John looked down at one of the brochures; an old Yup'ik woman wearing a traditional fur parka stared back at him. "I just don't want it broadcast to the world, okay?" He stood up and turned his butt toward her. "Besides, no Eskimo has an ass this white."

AFTER SEVERAL MONTHS he ventured outside the school for the first time. He'd spent days watching and listening for any sounds. Everyone in the village was either hiding out, had fled, or were, like so many others, dead.

He didn't go far. Just out to get his bearings, get some air, and see if things were as bad as they looked from his peephole above the village.

They were worse.

Before the sickness, the weathered plywood houses stood without paint. Beside the houses rested the rusted carcasses of boat motors and old red three-wheelers and four-wheelers with flat tires, white five-gallon buckets, shredded blue tarps that covered sheds and flapped in the wind. Even then everything possessed a worn appearance, as if the hand of a god brushed and burnished each item in just the right spots so that outsiders would know the irrelevance of time in such an ancient land.

That was before, and what was left was a nightmarish arctic waste-land. Many of the houses were looted and abandoned, or shot up. Windows broken. Snow machines and four-wheelers scorched or taken apart, the last vapours of gas from every tank in the entire village emptied, the tanks tossed on their sides and scattered about.

His survey was quick. He crept along the edges of buildings, his rifle in hand, and the pistol in his right parka pocket. He wasn't sure what he was looking for, just mostly deciding how he would leave the village at night with his supplies to make sure no one spotted him. If there was anyone left to spot him.

Nothing looked the same, which was an odd relief because, as he slipped from building to building, he didn't want to think of Anna, of them together, their walks through the village. He wondered what had made people burn some of the houses. To stop the sickness or cremate the dead? He thought about checking inside the ones that weren't burned, to see if he could find any more supplies. That would be risky, and he wasn't ready for that yet.

Something darted beneath one of the buildings and for a moment he was sure he'd spotted the bright red Bulls cap Alex always wore. He knelt to the ground, rifle ready, and peered around the edge of the building. Nothing moved. He wondered if he encountered one of them, one of his students, if he could do it, if he could pull the trigger.

The movement caught his eye. Low and stealthy, something beneath a house thirty yards away. He lifted the rifle and waited. More red emerged, and then a slender white and black–tipped nose. A skinny fire-red tundra fox flitted away.

He let out his breath and watched the fox dart from house to house. The rail-thin creature would lift its snout into the air and sniff, and then shoot over to a set of stairs and slowly creep up them. It avoided the burnt houses, and suddenly he realized the fox was looking for something in those houses too, and he took a mental note of which houses the fox avoided and which ones he tried to enter. Never staying long, but seeming to search each one in the row of the ten or so houses methodically. The fox feared nothing, as if he knew the village was now his; he would occasionally stop, lift a leg, and piss, staking his claim.

At the last house, the fox climbed the steps, slowly put his head in the door, and stopped. He turned and bolted down the staircase and toward the river in a streak of red. That was the house John told himself he would avoid at all cost. The fox was telling him something.

Countless months later he would enter that house and find the blind girl hiding beneath a mattress in a back bedroom.

# 3

The shot dropped the man mid-step. His body fell, splayed out on his side, his right foot in front of the left, his hand slipping from the side pocket of his jacket. Dirt and grease covered the exposed hand, and the black under his fingernails and around his lips had a look of either dried blood or gangrene. John wasn't sure.

"What's he look like?" the girl asked.

"Dead."

"No, describe his face to me."

"I'm not doing that," he said, "not now. Someone might still be in there. We need to get inside and warm up."

He started to follow the man's tracks that led to the house. He watched for ski tracks and pulled her in the toboggan behind. He doubted the dead man had been alone and he wondered why the man left the house unarmed in the first place. She put her mittens down against the ground, and when he felt her resistance, he stopped pulling. She turned toward the dead man, her blind eyes staring out at him.

"Tell me just one thing."

He stopped, not wanting to completely leave his back exposed to the house. To make sure no one was coming, he scanned the thin grey line of horizon surrounding them and then back toward the river ice at the edge of the village that stretched over a mile wide and ran north and south as far as he could see like some giant frozen highway.

"I want to know. I want to know if he's my uncle," she said.

"He's not. Come on."

"Does he have burns on his skin?" she asked. "Raised, thick? On his neck? Here?"

She slid the brown beaver fur mitten to the left side of her face and down her own neck. He dropped the sled rope and walked around her to the dead man, nudged him over with his boot, and tilted his head so he could see the brown skin of the neck. A thin string of half-frozen blood ran from the side of the man's mouth, down his collar, and into the snow where it pooled in icy red clumps.

"Not him," he said.

"Would you lie? I don't want you to lie to me. I don't care if it's him. He used to live in our village. Our village council kicked him out because of something he did and he had to move here. It's okay if it's him. I won't cry. Is it?"

"It's not," he said.

"Are you sure?"

"It's not him."

"This man smells like him, though—like one of them, but like my uncle, too," she said. "The outcasts smell different. Not a bad smell, just different. Wrong. Like a flower that's rotting. Sweet, but not a smell you want around you," she said and rubbed her nose with the back of her hand. "That smell comes through their skin, like stinky alcoholic drunks. They can't hide what they've done. It's in their pores."

He couldn't smell the hunger, not like the girl could, but he imagined he would be able to see it in the lifeless holes they used as eyes. Their teeth wolf-sharp, their hungry mouths slowly taking over their faces.

Or maybe it was what someone couldn't see. He imagined a person lost some little part of their soul when they consumed another. But he hadn't looked into a mirror, so he could only imagine what his own brown eyes looked like.

THE JET FLIGHT from Anchorage, "from civilization," Anna joked, revealed to both of them right away that the world they were headed to was different. They left from the farthest end of the terminal four hours after the scheduled departure, walked out on the tarmac with the other passengers, who were carrying boxes of diapers, bags of fruit, paper sacks of fast-food cheeseburgers and fries, video game consoles, stacks of DVDs, and cartons of eggs. The route to the aircraft consisted of a walk down the jetway, down a flight of stairs, and then out on the tarmac, around the wing of the jet, and then up a tall, narrow rolling staircase near the jet's tail.

"This is something, isn't it?" Anna said. "You can take the window. Can't say I've flown on a full-size jet with only a dozen rows of seats. You?"

He pushed his backpack into the overhead compartment and pulled a pillow down.

"Want one for your back?" he asked.

"What do you think is up there?"

He looked toward the bulkhead in front of their seat. A mutely coloured carpeted wall separated them from the cargo taking up three-quarters of the jet.

"Our food, I hope."

He took the seat next to the window and she settled in beside him.

"This is going to be some adventure," she whispered. "Strange being packed in like this. You going to be okay?"

He nodded.

"You excited?" she asked, and he nodded again. "I'm a little scared, myself."

"Why?" he asked.

"What if they don't like us?"

He stifled a laugh. "Not like us? Has anyone ever not liked you? The most lovable person on the planet."

She smiled and kissed his cheek. "You always know just what to say. Thanks."

A rotund woman, breathing heavily and sweating at her temples and on her neck, squeezed into the aisle seat next to them. She buckled herself in and gave a giant sigh.

"Damn bush travel," she said. "They can delay and delay our flights, but then when it's time to go, you'd better be ready. I got sick of waiting and decided to go fabric shopping. They weren't going to let me board." She added, "I quilt."

Anna smiled.

"You must be new teachers."

They both nodded.

"I thought so—you have that new-teacher look."

"Like a new-car smell?" John said. "What look is that?"

"Well, people new to the Bush have that half-terrified, half-excited look in their eye, but mostly it's the shoes that give a rookie away. Look around. It's fall out there. No one's travelling in town shoes."

She pointed to Anna's feet, white canvas slip-ons, and then her own white-toed rubber slip-on boots. "See? Mine are tundra boots. I'm Cathy, by the way. I'm a nurse in Bethel."

"I'm Anna, and this is my husband, John."

"Nice to meet you," Cathy said. "I didn't mean nothing by picking on your shoes, it's just that it's August and that means fall's just a day or two away. It's our rainy season, usually. Lately though, with all this crazy global warming stuff, it's been different. Even warm. Who knows? Might be seventy and sunny tomorrow. Don't count on it, though. Might be forty and blowing rain sideways so hard you can't stand on your feet. Then snow tomorrow! What village are you headed to? Or are you teaching in Bethel?"

"New-nah-jew-ak," Anna said. John could tell she was trying to pronounce the name the way Gary had taught them. He loved how hard she tried to get everything right.

"Oh, that's a nice little village," Cathy said.

The jet taxied down the runway and lifted off. John watched out the window as the Anchorage skyline dropped away beneath them. They banked left over the inlet with a rapid ascent skyward. Soon the plane levelled out as they approached what appeared to be an endless mountainous void. No roads. No lights. Just mountains and glaciers stretching off forever in every direction. Their new nurse friend's mouth kept running.

"I work at the hospital in Bethel. It's the hub, really, serves all the medical needs of an area about the size of Oregon. And we get it all. This summer, I was in the ER when we had a case of botulism poisoning. Here's some trivia for you. In all of America, there are two places with the antidote for botulism on hand. At the CDC, that's the Centers for Disease Control in Atlanta, Hot-lanna, as my sister calls it, and in beautiful downtown Bethel. Ain't that something? We're like a CDC hot zone practically, all kinds of exciting diseases, new and old. We've always got government scientists and know-it-all doctors up in our business with their half-baked studies and new protocols."

She leaned in toward Anna and lowered her voice. "See, the Natives like to eat this fermented concoction of rotten fish heads. They bury salted fish heads in the ground and let them get just rotten as can be and then eat the heads! It's like a delicacy to some of them, the elders now mostly. I would avoid it if someone offers it to you. I've seen what botulism poisoning looks like, and I can tell you that sickness is something awful."

She paused and asked the flight attendant for a diet cola.

"Yup, you're headed somewhere special," she continued after opening the can and taking a long sip. "I'm not a huge fan of the Native foods, as you can tell. But these people, they're the best sort of patients from a nurse's perspective. Sure there are problems, you'll hear plenty about that, but you'll never meet kinder folks. How long have you two been married?"

"Two years."

"That's great. Do you have a layover in Bethel?"

"We've got an in-service there, before we go to the village. We'll be there two days," Anna said.

"That's super. Do you want to grab lunch one of those days? I'd love to take you around, show you the town, and grab some Chinese food."

Anna laughed. "Chinese food? I thought we were going to the tundra!"

"Girl, Bethel has cuisine from all over the world. We might be the so-called armpit of Alaska, but we have some of the best restaurants you'll find anywhere. Look at me! Would a chunk like this lie about food? We've also got cab drivers from Albania, Korea, Yugoslavia—you name it."

"Taxi cabs?" Anna asked.

"Honey, you haven't lived until you've ridden in a Bethel cab, that and get a bingo game or two under your belt. I'll give you the full scoop on all the must-do things in the thriving metropolis of Bethel at lunch."

"Thanks for the offer," John replied, "but I'm sure they'll have food for the in-service. We'll be pretty busy."

Anna elbowed him.

"What John means to say is that we'd love to sneak out of in-service and go with you. We're in this for the adventure."

"Just so long as it doesn't involve botulism," he added.

She elbowed him again. He turned away from their conversation and stared back out his window.

Jagged peak after peak passed beneath them. He wondered if any of the summits below were named, and whether anyone had travelled that impossibly rough and desolate terrain. It wasn't just miles that would be separating them from their old life; it was an ocean of impassable ice-covered mountain ranges.

He stared down at the land below him and soon the mountains

began to shrink. The jagged peaks and glaciers melted into the earth and a watery moonscape replaced the mountains. Rust-coloured lakes with thin winding rivers speckled the foreign world racing beneath them.

HE WATCHED FROM ABOVE as three young men entered the principal's house carrying weapons. When they didn't come out, he waited for shots. He watched all afternoon and into the night for the young men to leave. He hadn't heard or seen the principal since the village called the curfew.

He was worried about someone coming back into the school and thought about returning to his hiding spot, but he had to wait to see. So many times Anna had begged him to go to the principal's house and demand that the balding man find a way to get them out safely, but he didn't. He knew better. She was already getting sick by then, and he couldn't risk breaking the quarantine and getting the principal and his family sick, or get shot in the process. He imagined the men inside the house, ransacking it, looking for food, supplies, or worse.

The classroom window had a light glaze of frost. With his fingernail, he scratched her name. ANNA. Then he licked the ice beneath his nail. He was thirsty and hungry. He hadn't cracked into any of the school food hidden in the attic, and he had moved all that he could from their house before the fire. So long as someone didn't burn the school down, he would be okay. Enough food, if rationed carefully, to last him at least six or eight months, maybe longer.

The letters faded and he scratched them again. Motion caught his eye. The three young men walked slowly. They were empty-handed. They moved down the stairs to the boardwalk, and then out onto the moonlit snow in front of the principal's house and knelt down on the ground. He heard a gunshot, and one of the men fell forward. Another flash and shot came from inside the doorway. A second man fell. The third got up to run, and made it halfway across the wooden play deck when the shot hit him in the shoulder and spun his body. Another shot and the man slumped to the play deck. He crawled half a dozen feet, dragging his legs through the snow, leaving a long dark gash of black in the snow before he collapsed, dead.

John pulled back from the window, suddenly aware that the shooter might see him. He hoped his motion hadn't been too sudden.

Using his headlamp, he made his way quietly through the piles of overturned desks to the hallway. He crept down the hall and into the gym. In the dark gym only a slice of moonlight cut through an opening high at the far end. He made his way across the gym to the ladder. He climbed the ladder to the small door, eased himself in, and pulled the ladder up.

He knelt down on the wrestling mat and thought of the way the first man had dropped to the snow and the hollow shots. Pop. Pop. Pop.

# 4

He waited until almost no smoke could be seen coming from the chimney before they approached the steps. His toes had gone completely numb with cold and his index finger, the one he'd held on the trigger, felt as if the skin had frozen solid. He couldn't stop wondering where the man he shot had been headed. But the possibility of warmth and a house to sleep in, even for the night, made the risk of entering akin to the risk of travelling on the river when the young ice wasn't quite thick enough. The other houses would have already been ransacked, and if the man was the only living person left in the village, then what was worth salvaging would be inside.

"I'm going now. You sit there," he said.

"You think I'll run away?"

She laughed once and slapped her mittens against her withering legs. The echo of that strange sound, the chuckle and the slap, hung in the air of the village like a half clang of a church bell.

He walked up the front steps, through the weathered plywood-covered porch, and kicked the door open. At the same time he threw himself against the doorframe, fully expecting the blast of a shotgun or the high-pitched pop of a small-calibre rifle. When nothing happened he swung the rifle at hip level and stepped through the door.

An old Yup'ik woman sat in front of an open woodstove, poking the small flame with a broken broom handle. A soft blue light came in through the weathered blue tarps that covered the windows. He didn't shoot, but he didn't take his finger from the trigger either.

"You going to kill me, like that man you just shooted?" she asked.

"Should I?"

"What's wrong with that girl out there? She got those sicknesses? Why she blind?"

He raised his rifle slightly and watched her thin, brown wrinkled hands.

"You shouldn't a kilt that man," she said. "He was trying to do goot."

"He was one of them," he said.

She pushed a few more small twigs into the stove and shut the door halfway. She turned and knelt down on the floor, her legs tucked beneath her. She wore wide round glasses with thick lenses and black electrician's tape on part of the frame.

"We're all people just trying to live. Now, tell that girl to come inside. Cold out there. She is safe here. The hunter gone for a while. No bad ones allowed in my house," she said.

"What hunter?" he asked.

She stared at him for a moment and then removed her glasses and cleaned the thick lenses with a thin green scarf protruding from the pocket of her jacket. He wasn't sure whether she understood him or was ignoring him.

"What about him?" he said, gesturing in the direction of the man he'd just shot.

"He's not the hunter, and that one out there is dead, if you're any kind of goot shooter."

"Where was he going?" John asked.

She sucked at her lips, and said after a short silence, "That girl should come inside now. Cold out there, you know? Unless maybe you want her to freeze so you don't have to take care of her?"

"Where? Tell me where he was going, or I'll shoot you, too." He raised the rifle again, to prove he was capable, but she wasn't even looking. He lowered the barrel to the floor.

"You only shoot the bad ones," she said. "I know. Get more woods for tonight's fire. Bring that girl inside. You go get woods down by the river for us. That's where that man you killed was going, to find driftwoods for an old woman's fire."

He started out the door and the old woman called after him. He stopped. "The hunter?" she said. "I don't know nothing more about him than you."

"WHAT SORT OF PLACE IS THIS?" Anna asked as their taxi, a ramshackle green Suburban with cardboard covering the holes in the seats and one door wired shut, bobbed its way down the roller coaster of a road, a narrow paved stretch with ridiculous undulating heaves.

"It's so ... so wide open. The sky seems so huge. And it's flatter than I imagined," she said, peering out at the land surrounding them, and then turning her face up to see the sky.

"Except for the road," he said. "This is crazy. Hold on."

The vehicle flew down another dip, up the other side, and bounced hard enough for him to hit his baseball cap on the roof. He winced and rubbed his scalp.

The cab driver, a white older man with his yellow hair slicked straight back, and one gold tooth, peered at them in the rear-view mirror. The man obviously wasn't Korean, but the black lettering on the Suburban's door read KOREAN CAB.

The radio beeped. He pushed a button and took the receiver. "Twenty-four."

The radio speaker squawked and a sultry woman's voice said, "Twenty-four? Post office, Swanny, airport."

"Roger," their driver said. "You sound sexy today, Rose."

"Screw you, Del."

The tundra gave way to houses and buildings, seemingly placed at random intervals, with long silver aluminum pipes connecting them like metal feeding tubes.

The cab swerved across the other lane and pulled into the parking lot of the post office. He hit the horn with two short blasts.

"Sorry about that," the driver said. "New-teacher time of year, ah? Where you cats from?"

"I'm from the Midwest," Anna said. "He's from Wyoming."

"Midwest, ah? My first girlfriend was from Chicago."

Anna chuckled and squeezed John's leg. "I'm happily married, Del," she said, "but I'll keep you in mind if I need an upgrade."

A Yup'ik woman with short jet-black hair emerged from the post office. In one arm she carried a baby, in the other a large parcel. Three kids trailed behind her.

"You guys will have to scoot together," the driver said.

Anna slid across the seat and the family climbed into the Suburban. The three kids piled into the seat beside them, and the mother and the baby sat in the front. Anna made a funny face at John, and he knew what she was thinking, always the overprotective one. No car seat for the baby.

"Swanson's Store," the mother said. The kids stared at Anna and John without saying a word. "Don't stare, you!" the mother commanded. The kids looked away, then looked back. John winked at the boy and he smiled. "Sorry," the mom said, "we just moved to Bethel from the village. They're still getting used to so many kass'aqs. That's you guys. I'm Molly." She reached back and offered her hand to Anna and John. They shook. Her hand was soft, warm. John wondered if he'd squeezed too hard because she turned her eyes away from him. "These are my kids: Val, Mik-Mik, Marylynn, and baby."

"You guys are cute!" Anna said, patting the girl beside her on the head. John hoped she wasn't already breaking some cultural rules.

"She's ugly like a ling fish!" Mik-Mik said.

"You're a stinky blackfish!" Marylynn retorted.

"No name-calling," their mother said. The kids fell silent again.

The cab pulled back on the roller coaster road. Anna tapped the driver on his shoulder and asked, "Hey, what's the deal with those giant tanks? Are those fuel tanks?"

Off to the right of the road sat a complex of huge white containers, at least a dozen of them. It reminded John of pictures he'd seen of oil complexes in the Middle East.

"They don't drill oil here, do they?" Anna asked.

Their driver laughed. "Here? No way. I wish. We wouldn't be so damn poor then. That place, we call the tank farm. It's our local fuel supply. All of our gas and heating oil for the whole town and all the river communities is stored there. They bring it up the river on a fuel barge. The last barge will be here in a few weeks, before freeze-up. My new taxi, a sweet 2004 Buick, will be on this next barge. That's the jail, and that is YK, the regional hospital, right there."

He pointed off to a yellow space-age building on his left. Like almost all the buildings it sat high off the ground on stilts of some sort, except this one had rounded walls and windows that looked like portholes.

"It looks like a submarine!"

"Yellow submarine, they call it. Like the Beatles song. Classic. They're just starting to remodel and repaint it. Locals are sorta pissed. We like to be a bit different here in Bethel."

Molly laughed with him as the cab hit another giant heave in the road.

"Yeah, different, for sure," she said. "So many kinds of people. Everything is *so* expensive. I wish we could have just stayed in the village. No jobs there, though. Too depressing."

The cab took a hard left and pulled into a dusty parking lot and stopped.

"Here's the cultural centre," he said.

John started to unload their bags while Anna went to pay the driver, who stayed in his seat.

"How much do we owe you?" she asked.

"Fourteen dollars."

"What? It says seven."

"The trip from the airport to town is seven. You and him equals fourteen."

"I told you things was a rip-off," Molly said.

"Hell," the driver said, "if this is your first time in Bethel, the ride's on me."

"Really? Thanks," Anna said. "What about them?"

"Yeah. My ride better be free then, too. I'm new to Bethel, too," Molly said.

"Yeah right, lady."

"We're paying for them, then," Anna said. "How much?"

"Twenty-five," he said.

"What?"

"Five of them."

"Pay him," John said as he pulled his backpack from the rear seat. "They said they'd reimburse us."

"But twenty-five?"

"Just pay him for us," John said.

"No, I'm paying for *them*."

She ducked back in the taxi, paid the driver, shook Molly's hand, patted the kids on the head again, and closed the door extra hard. As the cab drove off, she tucked her wallet back into her satchel. "The least I could do was help her," she said.

"You're generous to a fault, you know?"

"There are worse faults to have, Johnny," she said, pinching his butt.

He stretched and took a deep breath of the air. It smelled heavy, wet; a cool, swampy dampness hung in the breeze. A few mosquitoes began to gather around their heads and she swatted at them. Houses and buildings were the only thing between him and infinite horizon on all sides of the town.

THE NIGHT BEFORE he found the girl, the night before he planned to start walking, he tore the shrink wrap off a ream of notebooks and took the top one, a red-covered lined one, and opened it to the first page. He took a No. 2 pencil, pre-sharpened, from a box of office supplies in the corner, and tried to write. He didn't know why he felt like picking up the pencil, or what compelled him to do it, but when he had the paper there in front of him he couldn't do a thing. No words. Nothing came to him.

He set the graphite tip to the page. Just enough moonlight came through the small attic window that he could still see the blue lines on the paper. The pencil didn't move. Each exhale of his breath hung around his head and disappeared, only to be followed by another.

He imagined that the pencil would start moving, as if some unseen hand would wrap itself around his and write. He would call out to the spirits and become a human Ouija board, and he would have the answers he needed. They would tell him it was okay through the scratch scratch of the pencil against the notebook paper.

The pencil didn't move, and he was too scared to call out because he knew no one would answer.

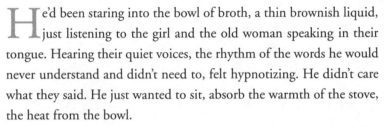

# 5

He'd been staring into the bowl of broth, a thin brownish liquid, just listening to the girl and the old woman speaking in their tongue. Hearing their quiet voices, the rhythm of the words he would never understand and didn't need to, felt hypnotizing. He didn't care what they said. He just wanted to sit, absorb the warmth of the stove, the heat from the bowl.

"She wants to know why you won't eat," the girl said. "And she wants to know why you won't let me have soup."

He stirred the broth with a plastic spoon and looked once again at the blackened pot sitting on the woodstove. The head of a duck peered out at him from the brown bubbling liquid.

"I don't think we should eat it," he said.

"Why? We need to eat something other than that canned fruit," the girl said.

He poured the contents of his bowl back into the pot. The soup and a few chunks of dark brown meat fell in with a plump. His stomach grumbled.

"I'm not eating it, and neither should you," he replied.

She lifted her bowl to her nose and inhaled a single long, deep breath. She held it, as if she was savouring the smell and drawing strength from it.

"But it smells so good," she said. "It smells okay. She caught it this summer. Cooked it up just for us. We eat when someone offers food. It's rude not to eat her soup."

The old woman responded to her concern. "*Assirtuq.*"

"She says it's good."

"Of course she does," he said.

"You think it might make us sick?" the girl asked.

"Yes," he said. "It's duck. *Duck.*"

The old woman reached over and squeezed the girl's arm. She spoke for a second in Yup'ik, and the girl raised her white eyes toward him.

The girl said quietly, "She says you can't let fear eat you like it did all the others."

"What do you mean?"

The old woman sat up from her place beside the woodstove and moved toward a stack of blankets in the far corner of the one-room house. He noticed the wooden panelling had all been stripped off. Probably burned for firewood. All that was left were the wooden supports, a thin stuffing of pink insulation, and the outside plywood covering. The inside of the house became the inside of whale's stomach, the flimsy wooden house frame becoming giant rib bones with the walls closing on him. He took a deep breath and tried to relax.

"Have you seen the hunter?" he asked.

The old woman turned back and looked at him. She pulled the bundle of blankets to her chin. "You should listen to your hungry stomach," she said.

"I've got to eat it," the girl said, moving her spoon in small slow circles. "I miss real foods, our Native foods. I'm starving for them. I don't care if this is duck."

"Go ahead, then. Eat it."

"What about you?" she asked.

"I'll be fine. Who is he, the hunter? The man on skis. Was he here?"

The girl took a small spoonful and held it in her mouth. He

swallowed hard, and turned away from her. The old woman threw a wool blanket toward them.

"Here," the old woman said to him, and then turned to the girl and asked something in Yup'ik.

The girl shook her head and said, "*Qang'a.*"

"What did she ask you?"

"She wants to know if I sleep with you."

"With me, or near me?"

"To her there is no difference," the girl said.

"What did you tell her?"

The girl didn't answer. She set her spoon on the floor where she sat and lifted the bowl to her lips.

"She knows English, why doesn't she just ask me these things?" he asked, and then turned to the old woman. "Why won't you just talk to me?"

The old woman pulled the blankets over herself and turned her back on them, her words floating across the room, quiet, barely audible, and to him, completely foreign.

The girl finished licking the rim of her bowl clean and then ran two fingers around the inside and caught the last of the duck soup. She gave a long satisfied sigh, followed by a soft burp, and said, "She says, because you won't listen anyway."

HE SAT IN THE BACK of the conference to avoid the crowd and pored over a heavy three-ring binder containing the school district's new high school curriculum. Anna sat toward the front of the large room, chatting with other new teachers. She did the socializing for them, and he had no problems with that set-up.

The next session was the one he looked forward to, a break from all the school district's goals and priorities and all the new educational buzzwords. The schedule simply called the next in-service topic *Camai!* He knew this word worked as a simple greeting, pronounced

juh-my, from the morning welcome from the district's superintendent. The words *Introduction to Yup'ik & Cup'ik Culture* formed the
session's subtitle.

Two Yup'ik women, dressed in brightly coloured hooded smocks
took the stage. The speakers chirped with feedback as the younger of
the two held the microphone to her mouth and smiled at the audience.

"*Camai.*"

"Juh-my!" the crowd responded, with far too much enthusiasm.

"*Quyana tailuci.* Thank you all for coming. That first word, *quyana*,
is the first word you should all learn. In Yup'ik it means thank you.
Pronounced goy-yan-na. I'm Nita and this is Lucy. We work at the
District Office in the Yup'ik Immersion Program. Today we want to
take some time to tell you a little bit about our culture and share with
you some teaching ideas to take with you when you go out to teach
in the villages."

Anna turned back and gave him the thumbs-up, as Nita passed the
microphone to Lucy and turned on the computer projector beside
them.

"As Nita's getting our slide show ready, I thought I would tell you
about the clothes we're wearing. These are called *qaspeqs*. Mostly
women wear them, but sometimes men, too, for special occasions.
They are great in summer when you're picking berries or cutting fish
because the hood keeps the mosquitoes out and this big pocket on the
front can hold all your snacks."

"And you can see Lucy packs plenty of strips in her pocket," Nita
said, as the lamp lit up the screen behind them, projecting a giant
frowning face of a young boy holding a green can of soda pop.

"That's my grandson," Lucy said. "He was mad I wouldn't let him
drink that pop."

John laughed with the crowd at the presenters' subtle joking. He
noticed that the locals and the teachers who had been around awhile
were quick to understand and enjoy the humour, while he and the rest

of the new teachers laughed with sincerity but also a slight awkwardness. The teachers didn't want to offend during a lesson intended to help keep them from offending anyone.

Nita pointed a remote and a new photo appeared. Onscreen a giant fish hung from what looked like driftwood racks, the wood weathered white and grey.

"This is probably what you're feeling like right now," Lucy said, grinning. "Like a fish out of water?"

The crowd laughed.

"That looks like dinner to me," Nita said.

The crowd laughed again.

The slide changed again, this one with a small boat brimming with freshly caught salmon, their scales glistening in the sun.

"The kids most of you will be teaching come from a subsistence background. This means that their families live maybe seventy to ninety percent off the land. As you might have guessed from these photos, salmon and other fishes are a huge part of our diet."

"So when I teased Lucy about having strips in her pocket, I was talking about fish strips, or dried fish—fish we smoke or dry during the summer and eat year-round."

The next photo revealed rows and rows of fiery red salmon strips hanging from what looked like a series of clotheslines, stretching along a steep riverbank. The photo after that showed three young Native men, buzz cuts and camouflage, holding M16s and grinning ear to ear. "We have the highest percentage per capita of military members in the country," said Lucy. "Their deployment just started, too. Going to be really hard on us here, but we're so sad for them over in that awful desert."

The next photo revealed two young boys, shotguns slung over their shoulders, walking at the river's edge, each of them carrying large dead birds. He thought one looked like a Canada goose; the other was some sort of large black duck he'd never seen before.

"I must be hungry," Nita said. "These pictures are making my stomach rumble."

The crowd chuckled. She smiled back.

"We hunt, fish, and gather pretty much all year round. The rest of the time we're getting ready for the next season. Always getting ready, we say. Right now people are putting up silver salmon, and the men who aren't overseas are already thinking about moose-hunting season."

"That's in September," Lucy added, "when many of your students will leave upriver with their fathers. Some of them will be gone for one to two weeks. They will travel hundreds of miles to get to the moose."

"Because sometimes," Nita said as the slide changed to an old woman cutting a leg-sized salmon on a sheet of plywood, "sometimes we get tired of eating only birds and fish."

The teachers didn't get the give-and-take of cultural exchange, the ins and outs of verbal and non-verbal communication. The two women delivered their view of their own culture, and just from their presentation alone, the humour, the subtle joking, John felt more at ease and sat back in his chair.

Anna wheeled around and smiled a broad grin when a picture appeared of Lucy's grandson straddling a dead seal. He wished for a moment he had sat beside her, so he could give her hand a squeeze.

HE DISCOVERED THE BLIND GIRL and her bundle of dried grass the afternoon before he planned to start up the river by himself. Finding her set back that plan, bringing the worst part of winter closer. At first he just told himself he'd sit by and wait for her to die. At first. Then, when her thin, leathery brown face began to come alive, to smooth and slowly fill in the hollows beneath her eyes and in her cheeks, the plan had to change.

That first night he almost shot her. He held the barrel of the black Glock inches from her skull with his finger just resting on the trigger guard. Blind. Starving. Dehydrated. She was already long past dead.

He knew from her heavy breaths that she hadn't slept soundly for a very long time. How long, he couldn't guess. One month? Two? How long had she been alone? How did she manage on her own, blind and malnourished?

He waited there beside her for hours on that first night. The pistol didn't move. His finger didn't move. He wanted to kill her for her own sake. For his own sake. She would be nothing but a burden. She would exhaust his supplies and require more energy than he could spare. She would drain him and the two of them would starve or freeze to death.

As much as it made sense to just squeeze the trigger, he couldn't do it. He told himself that he would wait one day. If nothing changed by the next night, he would spare her the agony. One day, he told himself, he would give her that, but really, he knew. He knew he didn't have what it took. He knew that already.

Even if the trip across the impossible expanse of snow, ice, and tundra would most likely kill them both, he couldn't leave her to the cold, the empty cupboards, or the people she called the outcasts and their hunger.

Each sunrise brought no warmth. Most nights the two of them would bundle up in their sleeping bags and burrow inside a tarp to escape the incessant and violent winds. Each breath of winter air bit and crystallized the moisture about his nostrils.

The girl meant another human's breathing to listen to at night. But mostly the girl provided a reason to go on, even if just for another day.

Then there was that eerie thing about the day he found her. How he stopped, as if some invisible bony hand grabbed him by the throat and began pulling him toward the one house in the village he hadn't checked. The house he'd seen the red fox avoid. He told himself he was looking for extra matches, canned goods, or rifle shells, but instead, in the last house, in the last bedroom he would check, beneath a stained mattress, wrapped in an old, heavy grey wool blanket, he found her.

"It's okay," he told the small black spherical hole in the rifle barrel that sprang up when he pulled the mattress off her. He raised his hands, until he saw she couldn't see him, the light reflected off her dull white eyes. He lowered his hands and she pointed the .22 at his skull.

"Let me smell your mouth," she cried.

"What? I'm not going to hurt you. It's okay. My name is John. You're going to be okay," he said. "What's your name?" he asked.

He leaned toward her and she took three deep sniffs of his breath and lowered the rifle. A thin, colourless line of foam gathered at the edges of her cracked and blood-scabbed lips. Her white irises searched the space between his body and hers.

"Please," she whispered, "please help me." She reached for him. "*Kaigtua.* I'm starving."

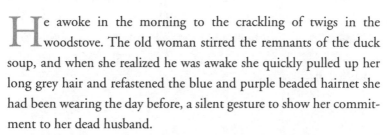

# 6

He awoke in the morning to the crackling of twigs in the woodstove. The old woman stirred the remnants of the duck soup, and when she realized he was awake she quickly pulled up her long grey hair and refastened the blue and purple beaded hairnet she had been wearing the day before, a silent gesture to show her commitment to her dead husband.

After pulling his boots on he stood and stretched. His back ached from the hard plywood floor. He probably could have found a sleeping pad or mattress in one of the other houses, but to find one that wasn't soiled with death, one that the girl could sleep on, wouldn't have been worth the effort. A stack of her grass sat in a pile beside her. He wondered when she'd removed the grass from the sled, and how he hadn't heard her. The yellow strands were woven together tightly in a long, flat braid, but he couldn't tell what she was trying to make.

The stove creaked as the fire started to heat the metal sides. The old woman stirred. He held his hands out and warmed himself in front of the stove's open door.

The woman took out a small white enamel saucepan with a broken black plastic handle and set it on the stovetop. She poured water from an empty coffee can into the pan and set the coffee can aside. From a tan plastic grocery sack she took a handful of thin green sprigs like pine needles and dropped them into the water.

He reached for the coffee can beside her and ran his fingers across the label: Rich. Dark. Satisfying.

"A cup of joe would be the bee's knees about now," he said.

She stirred the mixture in the small pan, using the same wooden spoon she'd used to mix the duck soup.

"We'll have tundra tea when this done cooking. Too bad, I got no coffee."

She caught him looking at the spoon.

"This soup is not what make you sick," she said. "People didn't die from birds. The earth didn't make this disease, you know. Yup'ik people been eating birds forever. Yup'ik people been seeing bad sicknesses since when *kass'aqs* come here. Not the ducks. Not the birds that did this to the people. I've seen these kind of diseases before. When I was little *piipiq*. Smallpox, measles, influenza—so bad mostly everyone all on the river and the tundra villages die. My sisters tell me that when my mom died from smallpox, at night in our sod house, they let me sleep by her so I stop crying. Even they try to have me *aamaq* on her breasts to make me stop crying during the darkness."

The water in the saucepan began to boil, a light green mixture, with the little needles floating and churning. She poked her spoon at it, filled the carved wooden depression, and brought the steaming liquid to her lips. She blew gently, and then sipped it.

"Mmm. Almost ready," she said. "You ever tried our Eskimo tea? Labrador tea to you, maybe."

"No."

"You first-year teacher, ah?"

"Yeah."

She pointed the wooden spoon at his wedding band.

"She teacher, too?"

He nodded.

"It will get easier. Not better. Just easier," she said. "My first husband die young. He go through the ice, and I never remarry for a long time, until maybe I was twenty."

"How old were you when you first got married?" he asked.

"Maybe twelve. They marry early back then. I hardly knew that man at first, but he was a good man. They never found his body, and I said I would wait for him to come back. He never did, and then someone else try marry me."

She took the saucepan and poured the contents into three green plastic coffee mugs. She handed one to him and called to the girl.

He sniffed at the tea. The steaming liquid had the light scent of gin, or of a juniper berry, but when he sipped it, the warm fluid puckered his lips and numbed his tongue. He ran his tongue against his top teeth to scrape the taste off. He took another sip, this time prepared for the bitterness. It warmed his throat and slithered down into his hungry stomach.

"Girl, have tea," the old woman said. She pointed the spoon at his ring again, and said, "She not want you to walk heavy without her."

The girl sat up and took the warm mug from the old woman. She held her nose to the rim and inhaled deeply. She smiled. The first real one he'd seen from her.

"*Quyana*," she whispered.

"Ii-i," said the old woman. She plucked a branch out from the saucepan and sucked on it and dipped it into her cup. "I don't know who that hunter is. But I seen him. He wears a mask and white clothings. He think he is invisible like a snowshoe hare. He was going downriver. He never stopped here, just waited for a bit across the river, watched this way for a while, like he maybe hunting something, and then went floating away on top of the ice."

"Why do you call him that?" the girl asked. "The hunter?"

"That's what he is," she said. "He's a hunter. He hunting for someone, maybe those bad people, maybe all human beings left. Even us. But he not a real hunter from here. We don't think when we hunt.

I don't say, 'I'm hunting caribou. I want caribou.' I just go out and hope the earth will provide. A real hunter don't think about what he hunts. Otherwise the hunted know he's coming and they know what the hunter wants and they know how to get away.'"

THAT FIRST NIGHT in Bethel, Anna and John roamed the streets. They held hands, but let go to cover their mouths against the plumes of fine dust that would billow up from the pickups, cars, and ATVs that raced past them. The intersections, some gravel, some paved, allowed for an odd sort of lawless short-cutting, with vehicles often leaving the roadways to cut off a meaningless amount of distance.

"What did you think about today's festivities?" Anna asked.

"The in-service? I don't know. Guess I just want to get out there and see the classroom and get ready. This is just a strange distraction." John squashed a mosquito on his forehead. He looked down at the small spot of blood on his finger and wiped it against his jeans.

"I liked the whole culture presentation. I'm not so worried now," Anna said.

A cherry-red monster-sized truck roared by them. The muffler and bass boomed.

"That's obnoxious," Anna said. "It could shake those houses off their little stilts!"

"I would have thought we could escape that crap."

"They can't have trucks like that in the village, can they?" Anna asked.

John reached down and picked up a flattened plastic soda bottle. "I hope not. I don't think they have roads."

"Look," Anna said, stopping and pointing to a reed-filled pond alongside the road. Two young Yup'ik boys stood inside a large white plastic box. "What are they doing? What is that?"

"It's a fish tote, for commercial salmon fishing probably. I think they're going to try to float in it."

The boys pushed off from the bank, each of them attempting to paddle with sticks. The white box began to tip and the boys lurched to the far side. Water poured in as the box began to sink. The boys crawled over the edge and jumped to shore. The box sank until it sat just at the surface. The boys threw the sticks at it and meandered away.

"Are they just going to leave it there?" Anna asked.

John gestured to a blue van, its tires flattened, the windows broken out. "Looks like things get left where they die out here on the tundra," he said.

HE WATCHED THE GIRL eat the last bit of creamed corn. Of the remaining supplies, the creamed corn was the easiest to part with, and probably the easiest for her to stomach. Even starving, he hated creamed corn.

At first he didn't want to share any of what little food he had left. It didn't seem possible that she had lived as long as she had, and he'd read plenty of stories about people who survived against incredible odds, only to die almost immediately after being rescued. If she ate up a bunch of his food and then just died, he would have just wasted months and months of calculated and torturous rationing. He would also have to rethink his food supply for the beginning of his trip.

When she was finally able to sit up and feed herself again, she would tell long, rambling stories that helped him understand how she'd managed by herself. Alone. Blind. Starving.

"My dad was a *nukalpiaq*, a good hunter and fisherman. A good provider," she said. "And my mom dried more fish than anyone. Not just salmon and whitefish, but pike and smelt, blackfish, and lush fish too. Our whole entry was full, and two freezers full of strips and caribou or moose meat. Before they got sick, he started protecting and hiding the food. He even hid salmon strips in the walls. He showed me where. Said people might go hungry and crazy if help never comes.

He said when he was young the elders would tell scary stories about the old days when things like that happened."

He held another spoonful in front of her mouth and she lifted her head, opened, and let her dry lips close around the spoon. He scraped the bottom of the can and gave her the final bite.

"It's hard for me to understand how you survived so long," he said. "How did you get water? And what about summer? The mosquitoes?"

"For water, I would go as long as I could. Until my mouth burned. Until my tongue bled. When there was snow, I would sneak out at night and scoop some up in a bowl, and after breakup and the ice melted I would sneak down to the river at night. Sometimes I would drink out of the river like a dog, I was so thirsty. I even think about it now and my mouth gets dry. Mosquitoes must have felt sorry for me. You?"

"They almost killed me. Then I found a bug net."

"Lucky."

She reached for the water, sitting in a red plastic cup beside her. He helped her hold the cup to her lips. She finished and sighed deeply. The sound of her relief scared him.

"Before my dad got sick. He took all the food out of the freezer and tipped it over. He hid the meat behind it. Said he wanted it to look like people already stole everything. Left a couple old chunks of bad meat. 'They will get like dogs,' he said. 'They will take what is in front of them and leave the rest for me.'"

Tears slipped from the edges of her white eyes and froze to her cheeks.

"Maybe he knew I would live and you would find me. He told me when everyone was gone to hide in the back room under a flipped-over mattress in the daytime. 'Eat just a tiny little bit,' he said, 'and use your other way of seeing. You'll be saved.' That's what he told me."

"Where did you put them? Their bodies? There were no bodies in your house."

More tears. She didn't say anything for several minutes. He wished he could take the question back, and in his own mind tried not to see the flickering flames on the quilt he had wrapped around Anna. He imagined the blind girl dragging her mother, her father, the brothers and sisters—down the steps and somewhere out on the tundra in the dark of night.

"He took them out to the cemetery, one by one," she finally whispered. "Until it was just us. Me and him. Then he said he had to try to keep me safe. He was really sick, and I told him to stay. I would take care of him. Keep him warm and he would be okay. But I could hear him loading his guns and he kissed my forehead and said, '*Tangerciqamken*,' I'll see you, and he left. I heard a gunshot, not long after he left. Then another. Then another. Then more. One or two shots. Then nothing for a long time. Then three together: pop, pop, pop."

# 7

He opened the backpack and began pulling out the contents while the girl and the old woman watched. He set each item on the floor, thinking about the individual weight and usefulness. He could pull quite a bit in the sled, but if he had to carry the pack, he'd need to really think about what would get left behind.

"She wants to know if you're going to leave me with her," the girl said, licking the end of one long, flat dried stalk of grass.

"Why would I do that?"

She turned to the old woman and asked a question and the woman responded with a question.

"Because the bad months are coming, and she wants to know where you'll take me."

"Where does she think I should take you? Why are you translating for me again?" he asked, and then directed his question to the old woman. "Where should I take her?"

He pulled a knife from the pack and gently set it on the floor. His grandfather had given him the knife. He had always liked the feel of the moose-antler handle.

"You think I should leave her here with you?"

"Why doesn't she come with us?" the girl asked.

"Not a chance," he replied.

"We're going to leave her by herself? The man … the hunter," she said, and set the grass braiding on her lap and sighed.

He took a water-filter pump from the bag. His wife had given it to him after their run-in with Montezuma's revenge while backpacking through the Yucatán. With the sickness he'd now been exposed to, he wouldn't need to carry the filter any further.

The old woman sucked at her lips again and said, "This is my village. My body should stay here, so my *anerneq* stay here, too. My spirit belongs here. I'll take care of this girl if you leave her. We can hide from the hunter, but then no one's left to take care of you. Without her, you won't make it very much ways upriver. Even she's blind, she knows better than you. And besides, that man will find you." The old woman picked up the girl's work and inspected it. She took the girl's hand, said something to her, and the girl began unravelling the grass weaving.

"Thanks for the optimism," he muttered. "Why are you undoing all your work?" he asked the girl.

The old woman spoke to her again in Yup'ik and the girl nodded. She continued to unravel the braids of grass.

"She said the only imperfections should be intentional. Only the creator can make perfection."

"Yeah, well, the creator made a perfectly good mess this time," John said.

He emptied the last can of fruit cocktail from the bag and tried to ignore how the heft of the gallon USDA-stamped can caused his stomach to burn with hunger.

"Maybe you'll stay one more night," the old woman said. "Tonight, you'll finish the soup. Rest. I'll tell you how to get upriver a ways. Then maybe tomorrow you leave."

"I think we'll get moving this afternoon," he replied.

"Maybe it will storm tonight," the old woman said. "You'll be warmer *maani*. Here. Maybe you got a few more days before it starts to get real cold."

"Maybe she's right," the girl added. "Plus, I feel stronger today, from the soup. You should have some tonight."

He took another inventory of his stuff, eight extra rifle shells, a flint for fires, his grandfather's knife, the water filter, the tarp, some string, ten feet of rope, duct tape, remnants of a first-aid kit, the gallon can of fruit cocktail, a gallon can of tomato paste, a gallon of red plums, and a 9-mm Glock with two clips and a spare box of hollow-point bullets.

He took the Glock, slid it into his parka pocket, and stood up.

"I'm going to go look around, get some wood for tonight. We'll stay, but I'm not eating duck soup."

HE COULDN'T SLEEP that first night in Bethel, so he slipped out from their bed-and-breakfast and walked across town toward the river. Midnight in the middle of August and he walked down the street needing no light to guide him. A haze of pink sat on the horizon to the north, bathing the town in a flat, pale glow.

"Damn!" he said in amazement when he reached the grassy slope that led down to the river. The enormous body of water swept silently and quickly past the town. At the farthest point he guessed the river was nearly a mile wide. He leaned his weight back against a guardrail and just stared out across the water.

A short open-bow aluminum skiff skipped across the glassy surface, the high-pitched motor buzzing downstream. He imagined the family of four, perhaps somehow related to him, sitting on the benches inside the skiff, headed toward the village he would soon be calling home, too. Long after they disappeared from his sight, the wash from the boat lapped at the row of white and grey boulders protecting the city from erosion like a crumbled castle wall.

Farther upstream, a quarter-mile-long row of wide steel pipes rose from the water's edge like a line of giant limbless redwood trees. He guessed the wall of pipes was part of the city's attempt to keep the monstrous river at bay. Downstream he could see a steep bank, towering twenty or thirty feet above the river.

As the greenish brown water rolled past he wondered how it could be that he'd never even heard of the Kuskokwim River before. All those waterways he'd learned as a kid. How could a river so impossibly huge be so invisible to the outside world?

A lone hooded figure walking upstream toward him caught his attention. The person seemed to be struggling, carrying something heavy and working to keep from stumbling on the boulders. The person stopped for a while and rested and then continued the trek upriver. Curious, John started down toward the river's edge.

"Mind if I ask what you're carrying?" John asked as the woman approached. She had long black hair stuffed into a hooded jacket that seemed as if it was made of a mosquito net, the type he'd used on the trip in the Yucatán. She sat down on one of the rocks and gently rested a bundle beside her. Whatever she'd wrapped in the blue denim jacket, she felt it was precious enough to hide or protect.

"Not if you're going to tell on me, or arrest me," she said half-jokingly. "I'm too old to get arrested."

"Don't worry about that," John said. "I'm just a teacher."

"Me, too. Retired last spring. We're leaving town in the morning. I had to go treasure hunting one last time." She zipped open her hood and wiped the sweat from her face. "My last night on the river and look at the beauty I found."

John approached as she unwrapped the jacket to reveal what looked to him like a gnarly piece of black driftwood attached to a rock.

"It's a mammoth tooth," she said. "Look here, these sharp things are the roots, this smooth rounded part here the molar. Feel this chewing surface. Funny, isn't it?"

John ran his hand over the bumpy surface. He leaned down close and tapped his fingernail against the rock-hard enamel. It was an enormous tooth. The biggest he'd ever seen.

"Here," she said, "heft it. At first I thought it was just a piece of dirty driftwood, but then when I pulled it up from the mud, then I knew it was a mammoth tooth. I've found a couple others, but this one is in the best condition yet. I can't believe these roots, they're like T. Rex teeth." She handed John the tooth and he nearly dropped it.

"Whoa. I wasn't expecting it to weigh so much!" John turned the tooth over and over in his hands. "This is amazing! You just found this along the river?"

"Down past all this erosion protection. I started looking where the river is cutting into the bank. People have been finding tusks and bones of mammoths and other ancient creatures there for years. Nights like these I like to imagine what it must have been like when those critters ruled this land. Mammoths, dire wolves, sabre-tooth tigers. These used to be their stomping grounds. Amazing eh?"

The woman took the tooth from him and wrapped the jacket back around it.

"That's quite the going-away present," John said.

"I'll pass the torch of treasure hunting to you," she said, starting up the grass slope. "If I could give you some advice about living here I'd say this. Don't just teach and go home at night and hole up in front of the TV like most people do. Get out and learn about life here. This place will teach you more than you'll ever teach your students."

"Thanks," John said, sitting down on one of the boulders. "Good luck getting that thing through security."

The woman crested the slope and disappeared. John turned back to the river and sat for a while. He crawled over the rocks and found a spot where he could sit with his hand touching the cool surface. He splashed the water and wiped his wet fingers across his face, the rich soil from the mammoth tooth gritty and cold against his skin.

AS SOON AS THE GIRL was well enough, the questions started. She usually waited until night. Sometimes asking them while her fingers danced between the lengths of dried yellow grass she pulled from the thick bundle she carried, or when her fingers were too cold to weave the grass strands together the questions would come from the depths of his wife's old sleeping bag. He wondered if she spent the whole day holding them in her head, thinking of different things to ask, just so that they could talk about something at night when they tried to sleep.

Her questions passed the time, especially when their stomachs cried out, almost in response to the nightly howling of the few packs of sled dogs that had been turned loose or managed to escape and had so quickly remembered the instinct of their wolf cousins. Avoid man. The dogs avoided being seen just as he avoided most of her questions. But still, the questions lurked, especially the ones he ignored.

Some he would answer, the ones that didn't burn. The ones that made sense. The ones that didn't require a lie. Or a half-truth.

"Why didn't we get sick, too?"

That was one of those questions that loped around his mind at night. He'd been asking himself. Until the question didn't really matter any more. Any speculation, about his background, his life before moving to the village, any previous sickness or exposure, presented few possible answers. What traits or characteristics did he share with a blind Yup'ik girl? She was at least ten years younger and had never even travelled beyond the broad tundra plain of the Kuskokwim River Delta. Once he started asking himself her questions in his head, he would just shut her out completely. "That's enough," he'd say. "No more questions. We need to sleep."

"Why didn't anyone come for us? Did they want us all to die?" she asked, feeling for her bundle of grass and running her fingers through the stalks, searching by touch for the perfect dried blade.

Another question that brought only more questions. Her questions would kill him, slowly squeeze at his heart, until he could no longer breathe, engulfed by that suffocating feeling of the walls closing in, and of the world becoming too small.

Some nights after the muscles at the side of her jaw went slack, and her breathing steadied and they readied themselves for the nightmares that would surely come, the questions would continue. They would hang in the air like campfire smoke on a cloudless night. Her endless questions would overlap in her soft voice, in her cries, and sometimes mingle with the voices of others. His mom. His grandpa. His students. A janitor. An old friend. Anna.

Where will we go? Can we make it walking? Why didn't you float out during the summer? Why do I feel like someone else is out there? Maybe coming after us? How did you find me? What was it like in the Lower Forty-eight? Why did you find me? Why don't you leave me behind? How many people do you think died? Was it everywhere? Did they want us to die? What made people act like the outcasts? Will you leave me? Do you miss her? Do you miss her? Do you miss her? You won't let me starve to death again? Okay? Please? Do you miss her? Do? You? Miss? Her?

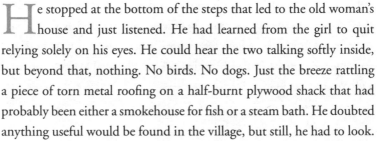

## 8

He stopped at the bottom of the steps that led to the old woman's house and just listened. He had learned from the girl to quit relying solely on his eyes. He could hear the two talking softly inside, but beyond that, nothing. No birds. No dogs. Just the breeze rattling a piece of torn metal roofing on a half-burnt plywood shack that had probably been either a smokehouse for fish or a steam bath. He doubted anything useful would be found in the village, but still, he had to look.

He'd start with the school, the heart of every village: the sanctuary for kids, the public meeting place, the dance hall, the non-stop basketball court, and the community dining room. If he were to find anything of use, it would be there.

The school, a boxy green building, stood on skinny metal pilings with chain-link fence wrapped around the base to keep kids from playing under it, something he'd learned the villages started doing after losing more than one structure to bored kids playing with matches.

The unbroken windows and the small drift of snow building up at the front door didn't make sense. He stopped and inspected the grated steel walkway that led into the building. The heavy door wasn't open wide, broken, or pried—it was closed. He could see no sign of tracks. He listened until the silence made him uneasy. A quick glance at the wide river and at the open tundra behind the school was enough to tell him no one was coming. He looked again closer, for someone wearing all white and staring back at him.

He gave the door a tug, and it opened silently.

He stepped inside and let his eyes adjust to the darkness. He looked for something to prop the door open for light and found a plastic garbage can. He shoved it into the doorway and turned back to the foyer.

He expected a ransacked, vandalized shell of a building. He expected something that looked the way he felt.

As his pupils expanded in the darkness, he put his hand into his pocket and rested it on the pistol.

The hallway was clean. No broken glass. No scattered papers or books. No signs of violence.

He took a deep breath as he read the sign on the entrance wall: WELCOME TO KUIGPAK ELITNAURVIK! HOME OF THE WOLVERINES.

He took another deep breath. The air in his nostrils didn't smell like death. It smelled like a school.

THE ALASKA COMMERCIAL COMPANY STORE made up the town centre of Bethel, but he only guessed this by the twenty half-wrecked taxis and, oddly, one Hummer stretch limo idling in the pothole-laden parking lot. Anna went for a walk on the tundra with some other teachers, and so he figured he'd get ready for their morning flight into the village. On the advice of several seasoned village teachers, he popped into the city's main grocery store to stock up on a few fresh vegetables and other necessities just in case it took a week or two for their boxes of canned goods to arrive in the mail.

"It's always good to have too much food," a balding, middle-aged principal said when Anna asked, during one of the in-service Q&A sessions, if there had ever been a food shortage. The two supply sources, by barge for only a few months in the summer and by air year-round weather permitting, seemed inadequate, so Anna's question was fair.

Lucy, also on the panel, said that in Yup'ik history there had been several famines, and in bad fish years, when the salmon didn't return, bad things had happened and people took extreme measures to survive.

With the session's dialogue replaying in his mind, he entered the store half expecting a warehouse-style market, a place for people from the surrounding villages to come and load up on bare necessities. Instead, he entered what appeared to be a modern one-stop shopping centre. At first glance, the place looked like a Wal-Mart of sorts, with everything from vegetables to full-size ATVs all stuffed into one building. The first major difference he noticed from any other store he'd ever been in was the prices.

$7.99 for a small bag of potato chips.

$8.99 for a gallon of milk.

$13.99 for a gallon of orange juice.

"Holy shit," he whispered to himself as he stood in front of small display of semi-fresh fruits and vegetables.

Cucumbers $6.99—each.

He reached out and touched a watermelon as big as a volleyball. The red and white sign beside it read:

AC VALUE PRICES
WATERMELON $12.99 PER LB.

He found himself wondering how anyone could afford to eat.

After ten minutes of idle walking, he grabbed a grocery cart and started meandering through the aisles. He wasn't shopping for specials. Just the basics. Just enough to get them by until their boxes arrived.

As he shopped he smiled at those who passed him. He couldn't get over the diversity of the town. For lunch they'd dined at Demitri's, and he ate one of the best gyros he'd ever eaten, the night before the tastiest Mongolian beef he'd ever had, and by the next night he was going to be one of three white men living in a Yup'ik village in the middle of nowhere with almost nothing other than canned or frozen food to eat.

He stopped at an extensive Asian section and just stood staring at the selection in amazement. The shelves carried cans and jars labelled in Japanese, Chinese, and Thai. Nothing about this place called Bethel made sense. He picked up a bottle of fish sauce and wondered what Yup'ik cuisine tasted like. If it was anything like Thai or Chinese or Indian or Vietnamese, he was going to love it.

"Excuse me. You're a new teacher?"

He looked up from the bottle and realized he'd been oblivious to the old Yup'ik man standing beside him, the grocery cart nearly shoulder-height to the man. The man wore a green flannel shirt, aviator sunglasses, a faded blue baseball cap with ARCTIC AIR printed in white on it, and jeans tucked into black rubber boots.

"Yeah. I'm John. John Morgan."

The old man took his hand and gave it a single quick shake.

"Charlie," he said. "I was at the cultural centre today, same as you."

"The in-service?" John asked.

The old man raised his eyebrows. A non-verbal, he'd just learned, used as an affirmative answer.

"That woman who asked about famine ever happening here—she your wife?"

"She is. She was just wondering how food gets to villages. She didn't mean anything by it. She's just inquisitive."

"Long time ago we had no food. Me, I was just barely old enough to walk, but I remember my stomach burning real bad. I remember we had only old dry berries and rotten old salmon with mould on it. The elders said it was punishment, that we were starving because we left the old ways behind."

He waved his arm around at the store and then hefted the red plastic AC Value basket in his hand. In it, a blue box of Sailor Boy Pilot Bread, a can of hickory-smoked Spam, and a *Weekly World News*.

"Nowadays," he continued, "maybe I'm almost an elder and maybe

I think this way's leaving us behind. They teach you what the word
*Yup'ik* used to means?"

John shook his head. "No, not yet," he said.

"Maybe they'll learn you someday. Good luck out there, John."

The old man gave a slight nod of goodbye and disappeared down
the aisle, his red plastic basket swinging at his side.

SINCE HE'D DISCOVERED the girl his dreams were unlike any he'd
ever had before. Not the normal dreams of daily life, of interactions
with other teachers and students, not scenes from his youth, and not
of Anna.

Instead, his dreams contained the atmosphere and darkness of a
world without light. A combination of some horrific vision of what
might be happening to the outside world, filled with the creatures and
images from the girl's stories of the ancient Yup'ik world.

He would find himself enveloped in a stark, bleak, lifeless void. He
would walk down empty black streets in desolate and dingy towns.
Sometimes towns he'd travelled to, sometimes just generic towns from
books he'd read or films he'd watched. In all the dreams he walked. Just
looking, listening, searching for life, sometimes looking for a letter
from his grandfather that would explain everything.

And sometimes there were signs of struggle. Blood. Smeared tracks
and tiny handprints. A small creature, half-human, crawled about in
the shadows, devouring survivors before he could find anything more
than a crimson trace.

Not in a single dream did he walk down along one of the frozen
paths between the village houses, carrying his rifle, afraid of the life he
might find. The dreams seemed to have nothing to do with him now,
except for the desolation and that heavy feeling that the world was as
empty and soulless as those small towns. He expected to encounter
any one of her monsters or the blue-eyed gunslinger he'd dreamt of
before, but perhaps even they were dead.

The dreams differed only in how they ended—with each dream stopping so abruptly it would rip him from his sleep. Heart contracting in his chest. Fists clenched. The grit of freshly ground bits of molars and incisors sticking to his dry tongue. And each time the girl would whisper, "It's okay. Don't cry. It's okay, John."

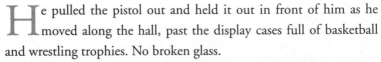

# 9

He pulled the pistol out and held it out in front of him as he moved along the hall, past the display cases full of basketball and wrestling trophies. No broken glass.

The building, aside from having no lights or heat, looked as though school let out for the day, the janitors vacuumed the blue hallway carpet and shut the doors. Of all the burned and wasted buildings he'd been in, he'd seen nothing so normal. He hadn't been in a school building, village store, house, or fish camp that hadn't been picked clean.

He peeked into the main office area. Also clean. A phone, off the hook. From the soft winter light coming in through the window he spotted a yellow plastic flashlight, standing at the edge of a bookshelf. He tested it. The light snapped on, and he stared at the glowing bulb for several seconds before he shut it off. A working flashlight! He opened a few desk drawers and found more batteries. A pack of gum. Some Aspirin. He pocketed it all.

He would check all the drawers more carefully, but first he had to look through the kitchen and storage rooms. If no one had cleaned the office out, there still might be food somewhere.

He stuffed the flashlight in his pocket with the gum and Aspirin and started toward the gym. He held the pistol out in front of him, still not sure what to think about the untouched school.

The kitchen would be off the side of the gym, which, as in all the village schools he'd been to, would also serve as the cafeteria, the largest, darkest part of the building, the last place, really, he wanted to enter, but the possibility of shelves loaded with canned fruits, vegetables, and even a canned chicken or two made his stomach tighten. He stopped at the heavy double doors to the gym and turned on the flashlight.

He pushed the latch to open the door, but it wouldn't budge. He tried again. He looked around for something to pry the door with, but the empty hall offered no ideas. As he walked back to the office he poked his head into the classrooms. They too were in order. A locked gym almost made sense.

Back in the office he opened drawers, looking for keys. All he could find was a Phillips screwdriver, not enough to break the lock on the door. In a small room off the side of the main office, he sat down at what he figured was the principal's desk, rummaged through the drawers, and then tried to think where someone might hide a master key for the school. He felt around under the desk, imagining he might find a key taped underneath. Nothing.

He sat, resting for a moment. Thinking. Then he saw the legal notepad. The black pen that had written the scrawled message sat, with the cap off, to the side of the three words:

*For the children.*

THE MORNING OF THEIR FLIGHT the rain came shooting sideways from the west with gale-force winds that shook the mud-covered school district Suburban delivering them to Gary Air. The vehicle pulled up to an oblong office building attached to a hangar on a road with half a dozen other small airline companies.

"Don't suspect you'll be flying out today," the driver said through a full blond and grey beard that John guessed he'd been cultivating for the last decade. The driver pulled up to the door of the airline and stopped. He turned the wipers off and slipped the vehicle into Park.

"If you get stuck, tell 'em to call Ross—they got his number. He'll find you a place to stay tonight."

"Thanks," John said.

"Stuck?" Anna asked.

The driver turned to the back seat, where Anna sat, tightening the knot on her raincoat hood. "You can expect to be stuck or delayed at least every other time you fly around here, if 'n you're lucky. I hope you get out. But if you don't, well, that's how it goes. You're *stuck*."

"Thanks again," John said, and he stepped out into the torrent.

Inside they stood at the counter, a chipped Formica construction that looked as if it had been taken from an old kitchen and slapped on a plywood frame. A Yup'ik boy, fourteen or fifteen, sat behind the counter playing a hand-held video game. He wore a black knit AND1 stocking cap pulled down tightly around his head.

"We're flying out to Nunacuak today," Anna said.

The boy didn't look up from his game. "Maybe not today," he said.

"Do you work here?"

He paused his game and looked up at them. "Not today, if the weather's staying like this."

"We're supposed to leave at nine, I think?"

"I'll get a weather update at ten. There's coffee."

He pointed to a coffee pot with a stack of white plastic cups sitting beside it. The phone rang. He went back to his game and picked it up on the fifth ring.

"Gary Air," he said curtly. "Weather delay. Maybe we're not flying. We'll know more at ten or eleven."

He hung up the phone and went back to his game. John shrugged, leaned his pack against the wall, and started for the coffee pot. He stopped at the small table that held the pot, cups, creamer, and sugar packs.

"Did we send any coffee filters?"

"I don't remember," Anna said. "Coffee is your ball of wax."

"Crap. I don't remember either. You think they sell coffee filters out there?"

"You could use an old sock."

He poured himself a cup, took a sip, and grimaced.

"Tastes like *his* sock," he whispered, thumbing toward the kid behind the desk.

And so they sat all day, drinking coffee, listening to the kid play video games and tell callers to check back in another hour to see if the planes were flying. The two of them knew they weren't going anywhere.

The wind splattered the rain in sheets against the finger-marked window that looked out to the soaked black tarmac. A fleet of planes, mostly Cessnas, spanned a quarter mile of asphalt-covered tundra.

"I'm kind of scared to fly in one of those," she said.

"I don't think you'll be flying in one today."

"Why aren't you ever afraid of dying?" she asked.

"Who said I'm not?"

"Well, those little planes look spooky. I wish there was another way to get out there."

"We could find someone to take us in a boat."

"No, thanks. Not in this weather. Where are we going to sleep tonight? Here?" she asked.

"At this point, I don't really care. I just want to get there already."

He took what must have been his hundredth sip of coffee. She reached over and took his hand.

"Can you believe we're doing this?"

"Waiting for our first Alaskan storm to go away?" he asked.

"No, this. This move. It's crazy, isn't it? Are we crazy?" she asked, running her hand through her hair and pausing to look for split ends.

Anna always second-guessed herself. Sometimes it annoyed the hell out of him, but on this day, as he stared out past the planes, past the runways, and out to where the impossibly flat tundra just blurred into a wall of wind and rain, he tried to think of something reassuring. He took another sip of coffee, and bit at the plastic foam. "Yeah," he said, "pretty crazy."

"You think so? I mean—are we making a mistake? Should we have taken normal jobs?"

"Only crazy people want normal jobs," he said. "We wanted something different in our lives anyway, right? Get away from the mortgage, two point five kids and a flat-screen, right? Figure out if a quarter of me belongs here. I'm getting hungry. You?"

"Don't change the subject," she said. She traced a finger around a small greasy handprint on the window. "I'm excited," she whispered, "but I'm also scared. I mean, what if the kids hate me? What if they can't understand me, or I can't understand them? What kind of teaching materials am I going to have? Christ—there are a million questions slamming around my skull."

"I'm wondering if we can order up some of that Chinese food, like the kid there did."

"Don't be a jerk. Everything can't just always be so simple for you. So cut and dried. Food. Sex. You must wonder what it's going to be like."

"Sure I wonder," he said. "But I can imagine and wonder and worry all I want and it's not going to do me any good, us any good. What's that saying about wishing in one hand and shitting in the other?" He paused and smiled. "Did you say sex?"

She punched him in the shoulder. "Tell me one thing you wonder about—then you can ask the kid about ordering some food. We might as well enjoy dining out while we can, but I'm sure it's going to cost a small fortune."

"Well, I wonder about friends," he said. "Will people like us? Will they want to hang out with us? And I guess I wonder if anyone will take me hunting."

"I should have known it would come down to hunting. Why do you wonder if we'll have friends? Why wouldn't we make friends?"

"Would you quit worrying? You're going to be fine. You'll be the life of the village. We'll have to do what that one old bag said and make a signal that lets people know when it's okay to visit because we'll be so popular."

"That's the dumbest thing I've ever heard. Tell me one thing you worry about, too," she said.

He scratched his chin as he tried to unravel his thoughts. "I guess I'm worried I won't be brave enough to step outside of my comfort zone, but part of me is really excited to maybe learn about where I might have come from. There's a whole new world that I could be a part of, and that's exciting and worrisome all at the same time."

"How so?" she asked.

"That world just might not want me."

"It will, John. I know it will."

He set his coffee cup on the windowsill and scratched the thin stubble on his chin. He hadn't shaved in a few days and the sparse bristles added something to the sense of adventure awaiting them.

SOMETIMES, WHEN THE GIRL grew tired of asking questions, she would just talk while twisting and braiding the three strands of yellow grass over and over and he would watch and listen. He never told her to shut up because he didn't like the silence of the night either. Once in a while, especially on those nights before they left Nunacuak, he would just say, "Shh," and just listen for a moment or two. He didn't want to become so lost in her tales of life before the sickness that he wouldn't hear someone or something approaching.

The night before they left the village to start their trek up the river, as they curled up in the sleeping bags, she told him something he wished he'd never heard.

"I lost my vision when I was just little," she started, and he should have stopped her there, but he didn't. "And I don't really remember how. But I remember what things used to look like. I remember going down to the river and throwing old black cherry Shasta cans into the swirling water. They never told us not to litter back then, so we didn't know better. My brothers used to like to throw cans in and shoot them with rifles. I loved watching the cans spin on top of that green water as they sank and the water exploded around the cans with each shot. I still see things like that in my head, you know. I see my memories, but once my eyes failed, they stopped seeing. I don't remember if they got blurry or if they just went white one day. I remember the clinic flew a woman out here, an eye doctor, a pretty half-Japanese and half-*kass'aq* woman is what my little brother Yago told me, and she held my face and looked into my eyes and said it was too late, 'Sorry. I'm just so, so sorry,' she kept saying, and I remember how sad she sounded, I think because if they could have sent me into Anchorage, maybe even to Bethel, in time I might have never went blind. I remember her hands on my face, though, they were warm and soft, and she told me I would learn to see in other ways."

The girl stopped for a while, then continued. "And I did. You know? You know how I can smell and hear things you can't? But sometimes I still think that I see things, too. Even with my eyes open in the summer, I can stare right into the sun and not see the light, but still, sometimes I think that I see things. Shadows mostly, but that doesn't make sense. If you stared into a black room, you wouldn't see something move, would you? I remember hearing someone in a movie say once that being blind is like being in a cave. If you were in a cave, would you know someone is out there waiting for you, hunting you?"

"Quiet for a moment," he said, pretending to listen, but only hearing the wind outside. He didn't want to imagine shadows moving in the darkness.

"Before the sickness came, I saw something. I never told anyone this. I was sitting on the steps of our house. Plucking feathers from a crane my brother caught. I saw a flash of white and I looked up in the sky. I saw two lines of white light like geese or ducks in a V in the blue sky. Then the white started to fall apart, crumble sort of, and then fall like rain and the light burned my eyes as it fell, so I closed them and when I opened them up my eyes worked again, but only for one blink. As soon as I blinked them everything went black again."

The girl said nothing for a while, and he thought she'd fallen asleep.

"I want to tell you what I saw when I blinked, okay?" she asked. "Are you still awake? I want to tell you what I saw when I blinked, okay? Are you still awake?"

He was, but he couldn't say anything.

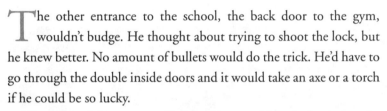

# 10

The other entrance to the school, the back door to the gym, wouldn't budge. He thought about trying to shoot the lock, but he knew better. No amount of bullets would do the trick. He'd have to go through the double inside doors and it would take an axe or a torch if he could be so lucky.

Thoughts of the man on skis kept him searching the horizon as he started down the steps toward the small brown outbuilding that held the school's generator and, if it was anything like the school's maintenance building in Nunacuak, a small shop. If that building had been left alone like the school, he'd find what he needed to get through the door.

The sound of crunching snow startled him. He turned, with the pistol drawn. The girl stood at the edge of the school building, her left hand bare and gripping the silver metal fencing that enclosed the school's underbelly, steadying herself.

"I didn't mean to scare you," she said.

"You didn't scare me. What the hell are you doing out here?" he asked as he tucked the pistol back into his parka pocket.

She started toward him. Her feet moved slowly through the snow, each footstep a little more confident than the last.

"I told her I wouldn't let you go in the school. She says you need to stay out of there."

"Go back and wait with her. Go."

When she was within an arm's length of him she stopped, and then took one final step. "I'll go in with you," she whispered. "You can't go in there alone."

He took hold of her sleeve and turned toward the outbuilding. She lifted her arm and took his hand.

"Come on," he said, gently squeezing it. Her fingers were cold, but the inside of her palm felt warm against his.

To the west the wide grey sky had a dark line of blue near the horizon, threatening another snow squall. He hoped it wouldn't bring too much precipitation. A heavy snowfall would mean slow going without skis or snowshoes, and the new layer of insulation would guarantee the river ice wouldn't thicken.

"This isn't the school," she said.

"It's the maintenance building."

They climbed the steps and stopped at the open door. A light skiff of snow covered broken glass and debris on the corrugated steel floor. Nothing like the orderly school.

"What did she tell you about the school?"

"She said no one goes in there."

"Sit down here." He picked up a black metal folding chair and set it beside the doorway. She sat down and he surveyed the small room. The workbench had been flipped over, the toolboxes rummaged through. Tools covered the floor, but nothing useful jumped out at him. No hammers, crowbars, not even any long screwdrivers. Someone had probably picked through anything that could be used to get wood loose for fires or break into other places. Except the school. Of all places, why had they left it unmolested?

"What are you looking for?" she asked.

He turned toward her and saw what he needed. Leaning against the inside of the door jamb was a long steel ice pick, taller than the girl, with a yellow piece of rope tied to the handle and a thick, double-welded chisel four inches wide at the base.

"I think you just helped me find it."

"What?"

He hefted it and thumped the pick against the floor. She reached out and wrapped her hand around it. She smiled.

"A pick? You going ice fishing? My dad had one just like this. You wrap this rope around your wrist, so it doesn't break through the ice and plump! Gone. Here."

She took his hand and slid the rope loop around it and closed his fist on the icy metal. She held her warm palm over his and then quickly took it away.

"We'll need this on the trail," he said.

"Are we going into the school now?" she asked.

He took her by the sleeve and helped her out the door, down the steps, and toward the school's entrance. The long pick slung over his shoulder like a lumberjack's axe.

"You want me to take you back?" he asked.

"No. But I'm scared," she said. "First the hunter and now this."

She stopped just inside the front doors and would go no further. He waited for a minute for her to say something, and when she didn't he started for the gym.

"It doesn't feel right," she whispered.

He stopped, and slowly set the point of the ice pick to the thinly carpeted floor. He turned back to her.

"You want me to walk you back?"

She shook her head. "Why isn't the place wrecked up like everywhere else? Why does it feel so normal?"

"How can you tell it's not?"

"I just can," she whispered. "It feels like it did when I came here before the sickness. Except cold. Something isn't right. Trust me. I can just feel it. Maybe we should listen to her. We shouldn't be here, John. This is a mistake."

"Well, we're here, and there might be food. I have to check. We can't rely on dinner to fall from the sky."

He lifted up the pick and continued toward the gym. He could hear her boots on the carpet behind him, her hand running down the side of the hall. At the door to the gym he stopped. If the pick didn't work he would tear the building up looking for a key. He hoped he had enough energy to pry the double doors open.

"Stand back a bit. This is going to be loud for you," he said.

He pushed the wedge end of the pick between the two doors where he hoped the latch met on the other side. He gave one hard push to get the point in as far as he could get it and then rocked his body against the bar. The right door popped open a crack and a rush of air hissed past him into the blackness of the gym. The girl stepped back and covered her ears. He pushed the heavy steel pick into the crack and pried again. The gap widened a little more, and he heard the familiar clink of chain links.

"Come on. Come on," he said.

This time he slammed the bar in and groaned as he pushed against the door. It gave slightly, just enough for him to see the chain links on the swing-arm handle. He remembered the yellow flashlight in his pocket and pulled it out. He held it to the crack but couldn't see into the thick darkness in the gym.

"What's in there?" she whispered.

"I can't tell."

"The door's chained, too?"

"Yeah. From the inside."

"How are you going to get in?"

"I need to think for a minute."

He pulled the pick out and slipped his arm into the darkness. He grabbed the chain, gave a quick pull, and knew it wasn't going anywhere easily. He slid it toward him and tried to do the same on the push bar for the left door. Then he pulled his hand out quickly, as if something or someone on the other side was about to grab it. He pulled on the door and it gave a little more.

The girl stepped to the entrance and felt the edges of the opening. He could feel the air sliding past them into the gym, but she was still trying to smell what was on the other side. She checked the size of the gap.

"Can you get it a little wider?" she asked. "I could try slipping inside."

From her voice he could tell she was scared. Scared, but trying, in her own way, to help.

"If I can find something to cut the chain," he said.

"Just try. Open it a little more and I'll go in. Maybe the kitchen won't be locked. I can pass food through the door here. I'm not afraid. I'm not."

She stuck her hand in through the crack and rattled the chain to prove her point, or to prove something to herself.

"We can try. You'll have to take your parka off."

He needed some sort of fulcrum to lever against, so he slid a metal waste can near the opening. She pulled off her parka and stood beside him. He rested the pick against the can, slipped the point into the crack, and threw his weight against the bar. The gap widened slightly. He slammed against the bar again, this time pushing and holding his weight against it.

"That's as far as I can get it," he said.

She stepped past him, felt the edges, rested her head against the closed door, and pushed it forward toward the crack. She pulled with her hands. John strained and pushed the bar harder to give her more room. Her head slipped through and then she began pulling her shoulders through. He hadn't seen her sideways like that, her body so slender, a skeleton, covered with a threadbare red T-shirt and thin black jeans tied about her hip bones with a blue nylon cord of some kind.

Her hips slid through the crack. He let off the bar a little.

"You okay?" he asked.

She whispered back to him through the crack, "I don't like it in here. It's cold."

"I know, but you're in. You need to go across the gym to the kitchen. See if it's open." He shoved her parka to her through the gap. "Take this."

"I think they're in here, John. I can feel them."

She put her hand back through the crack. He took it.

"Just go across the gym to the kitchen. Go."

He let go and she pulled her hand back.

"Go," he said. "You'll be okay."

He could hear her footsteps move slowly away from the door, and then the screaming started.

THE WEATHER BROKE at four in the afternoon. The wind died. The rain stopped, and suddenly the sun came through and the dull grey day transformed. In minutes the phones were ringing and the boy had his hands full. Taxis began pulling up, unloading people carrying shopping bags and cardboard boxes full of groceries.

A slender young man sauntered in carrying a can of Coca-Cola and tugging at the carefully creased brim of his baseball cap. He pulled an aluminum clipboard off a nail in the wall and turned and pointed to the two of them.

"You two are headed to New-num-chuck," he said with a slow southern accent. "I gave up trying to pronounce these village names a year ago, 'bout the time I got here. You ready? Grab your gear and let's start flapping. I'm Randy."

The two of them stood up, grabbed their bags, and followed Randy out the door. As they walked out on the tarmac, Anna mouthed to John, "How old?" He smiled and shrugged.

Randy stopped at a blue and white Cessna 185. He opened the back and looked at their bags. He lifted each one carefully and then started stuffing them in. "You can hop right in that seat there, Missy. I'll need the big guy up front with me, in case I need to take a nap mid-flight. From the looks of it you guys never flown in a small plane before."

They both shook their heads.

Randy took Anna's hand and helped her step up into the plane. "Me neither."

Before they had any more time to be nervous about their young pilot, they were taxiing down the runway. John sat in the co-pilot's seat staring at the controls, while Anna looked from side to side out the windows. Bethel stretched off in the distance on one side of the runway, and on the other the lake-pocked land seemed to have no end. The little plane picked up speed, and Randy pulled back on the yoke. The plane lifted off the runway and banked hard right, the earth falling away beneath them, flattening and stretching out all around them for as far as his eyes could see. John's stomach dropped as they gained altitude.

Randy pointed at a pair of headphones hanging on the console. John took them and slipped them on his ears. The pilot's voice crackled over the headset.

"Ever laid your eyeballs on anything like that?" Randy asked.

He pointed at the horizon, a panorama speckled with lakes and rivers that extended in every direction. "See that drive-in movie screen–looking thing? That's White Alice, Cold War radar, meant to catch invading Russkies. Quite a view from the top of it. Almost like flying. Out there, to the west, that's the Bering Sea. You can just barely see it. That shimmer there, that's the sea. Off to the left here—that giant bitch of a river, that's the Kuskokwim—a mile wide in some places and well over five hundred some miles long. Those mountains out that way, south, are the Kilbucks, the Alaska Range on the other side—nothing but mountains forever that way. Nothing but bare open tundra to the north for a long, long ways. You can sort of see the Yukon River over there. That river's even bigger than this bugger. You're really in the middle of nowheres."

They flew along the edge of the Kuskokwim. John looked back at Anna. She grinned and widened her eyes to show her excitement.

"Whatcha think?" Randy asked. "Pretty damn desolate, eh? First time I saw it, I just kept saying to myself, Why, there ain't nothing here. Ain't no reason anyone, even Natives, oughta live in a place like this. Now look at me."

John nodded. He didn't know what to say. So he just smiled.

"It's great flying, though. I get plenty of hours, and don't have to worry about running into too many mountains."

John spotted a cluster of plywood shack-like buildings at the river's edge.

"Is that a village?" he asked, pointing at the decaying structures passing beneath them.

"Fish camps," Randy said. "The folks here set up camps in the summer and prepare salmon. Those are smokehouses and camps. There's one village, right there. Yours is a couple more down."

He pointed to a settlement at the confluence of a small river and the huge greenish-brown swath of the Kuskokwim. The two rivers mixed together like a thin stream of creamer in coffee. "That's Kwik-pak, as I like to call it. Had an old girlfriend from there. I can't even pronounce its real name."

The houses stretched in two rows away from the river. A small runway sat west of the village, and John guessed that the larger structures were the school buildings. The entire layout of the village seemed to be organized around the school. What surprised him most, at least from the air, was the starkness of it all. A few big satellite dishes, a few winding paths through the village, with a pickup or Suburban, boats along the river, but that was it. A few dozen homes packed together within a hundred yards of each other with no backyards, lawns, or individuality. From the air, the place looked half planned, like some strange form of Alaskan urban sprawl but without the garages, fences, or pools.

The village had hardly passed them and Randy pointed at the horizon. "There she is," he said. "You're twenty minutes by air, probably forty minutes by boat or snow machine from Kwik-pak. An hour or two to Bethel."

John leaned back to Anna. He covered the microphone on his headset and yelled over the plane's engine, "We're almost there!"

The land travelled beneath them faster as they dropped. John tried to take in as much as he could. The giant river meandered off to the south, and the desolate-looking tundra reached out forever to the north. As they drew closer to the village, he could tell it had that same organized look, except at one edge, closest to the river, the houses looked older, more shack-like. The two rows of houses paralleled the river, and the runway sat just north of the village. Randy dipped a wing and banked in hard. John's stomach lurched.

"Like to give 'er a once-over before I land, just in case some kids are playing on the runway or if there's another plane," he said.

Randy banked again at the far end of the village and dropped toward the strip of gravel. John was too enthralled to be scared as the ground raced up at them. This village looked smaller than the last. He could easily make out the school, and could see a red three-wheeler pulling a trailer bouncing its way toward the runway.

"Looks like someone knew you were coming," Randy said, pointing, and then quickly pulling his hand back to steady the plane as they hit once, bounced, and touched down.

"Welcome to your new home, folks," Randy said, pulling off his headset and spinning the plane around at the gravelled end of the strip. "Can't say I could ever live anywhere like this. More power to you for trying it out."

THE GIRL WONDERED OUT LOUD how the two of them survived a whole summer in the same village without running into each other. He didn't tell her that he'd only left the school a couple of times, that for weeks he didn't really even leave the comfort of Anna's sleeping bag.

"Last summer, when it got real hot, I had a dream. Like maybe I was delirious from not enough food and water. In my dream I could see. I saw a different world. Not our village, but maybe an old village. Like the ancient Eskimo villages in the books at school. Or the ones the elders used to talk about. The houses were the old sod houses with tundra growing on top of them, like they were half buried, and the people were all dressed in our old clothings. Some of them had parkas and fur leggings, and some of them were almost naked and dirty with soot from the seal oil lamps. It looked like spring, like it was when I was plucking ducks and geese, except that the people were mostly dead or half-dead. Their faces were skinny and streaked with that dark black soot. So many dead, their bodies stacked in piles like wood for a steam bath, and *kass'aqs*, they were getting out of a long wooden boat and coming up the riverbanks carrying torches and crosses. White crosses. That's what I saw. White crosses. And one man, he had only caribou-skin pants, he was fighting with them, trying to make them go away.

"I wonder why I dreamt that. Even though I never saw your face, I think you were him, John. You were trying to make those men with the crosses leave. The Native man I saw was you. I remember the voice in the dream, too. It was your voice. Even though I never heard your voice before, I know it was you," she said.

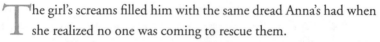

# 11

The girl's screams filled him with the same dread Anna's had when she realized no one was coming to rescue them.

"Get back!" he said. "You've got to move your hands!"

He tried to pull her hands away from the gap between the two doors. Her fingers tore at the metal. The girl stopped clawing and pressed her face to the crack, one milky white eye shooting her fear out toward him.

"John, get me out! I can't be in here with them. Get me out …"

Her voice trailed off and she began a moan-like wail that sent shivers through him.

"Stand back. I'm coming in."

He took the ice pick and slammed the sharp edge into the jamb. He slammed again and again. Sparks splintered into the dark gym. Nothing.

"We shouldn't have come in here," the girl gasped. "Please get me out … get me out! Get me *out!*"

He pulled the door open with his hands until the chain caught, and then he slid the blade of the pick against the space where the handle met the door.

He pushed the heavy bar in, then pulled it back and slammed it home. The handle gave. He hit it again and again. Each time he swung harder than the last, each hit opened the gap. He didn't have the strength he once had.

He didn't know how long he stood there slamming the pick, and he didn't know that the girl had stopped screaming and crying, or that the angry cries that filled the hallway were his own until the pick crashed through and the chain clattered to the gym floor.

The girl burst through the opening and grabbed hold of him. She pressed her face against his chest and she held herself there. He leaned the pick against the wall and wiped his wet cheeks with the back of a hand. He put his arms around her and then dropped them.

"Please. Please get me out of here," she begged.

In the darkness of the gym he could see them, hundreds of desiccated corpses, the bodies of the entire village.

ON ANNA AND JOHN'S first night in the village, they broke their house in, a personal ritual they did in all the new places they lived. They made love in each room. In their new accommodations, a little red aluminum-sided house behind the school, they didn't have much breaking in to do. The bedroom barely fit a twin bed, and the kitchen and living area took up the rest of the twenty-by-twenty house. The toilet, a white five-gallon bucket complete with an almond-coloured toilet seat, sat in a closet-sized bathroom with an unplumbed vanity and sink. Anna loved that someone, perhaps the teachers who lived there the year prior, had written in black marker on the side of the bucket THE JOHN. A plastic gallon chocolate ice cream bucket sat beneath the sink's drainpipe.

They tried a few positions in all the rooms, except for what Anna had coined the poop closet, and after some prodding, he even persuaded her to slip out into the plywood-enclosed foyer that covered the entryway.

As they stood there, her hand firmly holding the door closed, to keep anyone from seeing them, and with him standing behind her, they moved against each other, slowly, the cool, damp fall air raising their arms with gooseflesh.

"I feel like we're going to rock this little house off its blocks," she said.

He chuckled. "That would be kind of embarrassing."

He imagined the whole house falling off the treated timbers that held it up off the soggy tundra, listing to one side like a sinking ship, the spongy earth slowly swallowing them before they could escape.

"What will be embarrassing is if we get caught like this," she said.

"What's the name of this position, arctic entry?"

"Funny. Are you done already?" She was joking when she said this, but to add emphasis, gave a slight Kegel squeeze that sent him over the edge. He groaned and leaned in to her, holding her close.

"Just don't expect me to do this out here in the winter," she said.

They slipped back inside. She pulled a robe on and he just slid under the covers, naked.

"This is where I wish we had running water," she said, dabbing between her legs with some tissue. "Remind me again why the school is the only place with plumbing in the whole village when this state has tens of billions of dollars in oil revenue?"

NEITHER OF THEM had much energy to walk those first few days on the frozen river. His legs were out of shape and starved. The girl was in the same condition, if not worse. She walked thirty or forty feet behind him, a distance he chose to keep out of earshot of her questions.

When he finally stopped to rest, she caught up and sat down on the toboggan and ate a handful of snow. "When we get to wherever we're going, then what?" she asked.

"Then what? What do you mean, then what?"

"When we get away from here and if the rest of the world's not sick. Then what's next? Where will you go?" she asked.

"I don't know. I don't waste my time thinking about it," he said. "No use worrying myself about it until it happens."

She took another scoop of snow and seemed to look back at their tracks, a long line of dark holes in the white drifts that stretched into the distant sky.

"Well, I worry," she said. "I don't know anyone outside. I've got no place to go."

He took up the rope of the toboggan. "Well," he said, "worrying isn't going to get you there. Sit there, I'll pull you awhile." He began pulling her, wishing he could leave her worrying behind him.

An hour later they crossed the ski tracks. He dropped to his knees and hunched low, swinging the rifle from across his back. He didn't need to study the tracks. He knew what sort of tracks one person travelling alone on skis left.

"What is it?" the girl whispered. He knew she sensed his fear. Perhaps she could hear his lungs tighten and his heart accelerate.

"Tracks. A skier."

"Skier? People don't ski here," she said.

"I know."

From the angle of the round holes the ski poles had poked into the crust, the distance between the holes, and the slight outward turn of the tracks, he could tell the skier was making good time. Moving. Fast.

"Which way is he going? Toward Kuigpak?" she asked.

"No."

"Good," she said. "Let's get going. I don't like to know someone has skis."

His eyes followed the two long, dark cuts in the snow, like twin frozen snakes stretching for as far as he could see to where the wide river turned east and out of sight.

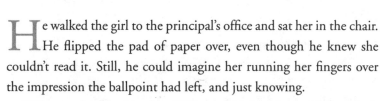

# 12

He walked the girl to the principal's office and sat her in the chair. He flipped the pad of paper over, even though he knew she couldn't read it. Still, he could imagine her running her fingers over the impression the ballpoint had left, and just knowing.

"Why are they dead in there? Why would they do that?" she asked.

"I don't know. Just sit here. Okay? I'm going to go check the kitchen."

"Don't leave me, John. Don't, please?"

"I have to. I'll be right back," he said, standing just outside the office. He'd turned and looked back at her. She had her legs pulled up with her arms wrapped around them. She kept wiping her nose against one sleeve and then the other. She hadn't stopped shaking and her eyes were closed tight, as if she struggled to keep them closed against some horrible vision. He went back in and wrapped her parka around her.

"You can lock the door if you want," he said.

"I'm not worried about anything that door will stop. We shouldn't have gone in there. Don't go back in there. Please …"

He let her words trail him down the hall. At the gym doors he took out the pistol and the flashlight. He pushed the black plastic switch on the flashlight forward and the beam cut the darkness of the gym. He stepped forward, sweeping the walls with the light first.

Handmade banners, written with sidewalk chalk on white and goldenrod butcher paper, still clung to the walls.

Go Bethel Warriors! Get 'Em Tundra Foxes! Fight Falcons Fight! Beat 'Em Shaman! Three Cheers for the Aniak Half Breeds!

The bleachers on one side of the gym had been pulled out. He passed the light once over them, wooden planks covered with the dead, as if they waited for the final game. Some bodies were hunched over. Some lying out flat. Others holding on to each other. He tried to look past their faces, but he couldn't. The face of one woman caught his eye, her skin drum tight, almost freeze-dried from a combination of the cold, dry gym, perhaps the heat of summer, and decay. He swept the light toward his path to the kitchen. Bodies covered the floor all the way across the gym to the open kitchen door. He shone the light through the open serving window. He thought he could make out a shelf still full of the silvery USDA gallon cans. He had to steady himself. He blinked hard and tried to focus.

Before he took a step he pointed the flashlight at his feet. A child, a boy, no more than three or four, stared up at him. The brown eyes dried, but still open, innocent. The look on the child's face not one of terror or starvation, or any of the horrors surrounding him—just some sort of contentment. He stepped gently over the boy, and then stopped and looked back at him. Holding the light on him. His skin pulled back tight against his face, his mouth slightly open with his teeth peeking out. His black hair seemed to grow from the rigid skin on his skull as he watched.

"What are you trying to tell me?" John whispered.

He took another glance around the gym and saw that the lunch tables, the tables that his school also had, were down, and several large garbage cans sat full of the disposable cardboard lunch trays.

"You didn't starve," he said to the boy.

He leaned down and looked closely at the boy's nose. The skin had tightened and shrivelled, but the boy's nostrils were clear.

"Not sick, either."

He aimed the light back toward the kitchen. He'd leave the mystery for someone else to unravel. If the kitchen had some food they could use he might be able to just let the kid and his eyes go. The fifty-odd feet across the gym could have been ten miles. The space seemed too far to travel, the walls too close, the bodies too near. He avoided allowing the light to stop moving, to hesitate for a second on any of the faces, but the arms and legs seemed to cover every couple of feet of gym floor. He had to step, twist, and step again to avoid crunching through a limb. He blinked hard again and bit at his lip. He wasn't moving fast enough. The ceiling seemed to be pressing down, the walls pressing in.

Halfway across he realized he was gasping, almost hyperventilating. He didn't know if it was from overexertion, the hunger, or something else, maybe something inside him trying to deny that the bodies scared him. He stopped and tried to slow his breaths. He blinked hard again and tried to shake the sensation that the bodies were surrounding him and coming toward him.

On one slow inhale he allowed himself to smell the air. Before, the warmer air outside had been rushing into the cool gym, but the air had equalized and was still. Perhaps until this moment his brain had known better than to test the atmosphere, to allow itself to calculate or quantify the stench of hundreds of human bodies confined to a single basketball court—but in that fraction of a second he smelled it; he smelled them. His empty stomach lurched. He sprang forward, four quick steps with the light searching for bare gym floor, to the door of the kitchen.

He dove inside, found the deep aluminum washing sinks and vomited. The first heave brought up little more than a handful of reddish bile, the second a little more, the third something that looked like blood. He slid down to the floor, shaking, his back against the sink, his pistol in one hand, the flashlight in the other, still on and shining across the kitchen floor.

ON THEIR FIRST FULL DAY in the village Anna and John decided to go for a walk. They hadn't reached the bottom step of their new house before the first kid, wearing red basketball shorts, no shirt, and rubber boots, skidded to a stop on his green BMX bike and greeted them.

"My name's Yago," the boy said. "Whatch yer names?"

"I'm Anna. This is John."

"Where you guys going?"

"We thought we'd go for a walk," she said, waving her arm at the black cloud of mosquitoes that had descended on them.

"Why?" the boy asked.

"We want to see the village, maybe go down to the river."

"I'll go, too. Okay?"

"Sure," Anna said.

John bent down and pressed his hand into the tundra moss. The stuff fascinated him. Up close he could see countless species of intricate sponge-like plants all connected to each other: lichens and moss and grass, roots, berries, mushrooms, flowers of all colours, all in the space of his hand. He pressed his fingers into the cool wet sponge and held it there for a moment. The ground felt alive.

They started down one of the boardwalks that connected all the village buildings with each other, like long, narrow wooden veins. Yago pushed his bike in front of them. John studied the two-by-eight wooden planks and then noticed the small black rubber threads still sticking to the sides of the boy's tires.

"Got yourself a new bike, huh?" he asked.

"No. It's not mine. My brother's. Mine's so cheap. It has a flat tire. Maybe I'll get a new one when dividends come."

The boy stopped and pointed to a house. "That's where I live," he said. "My bike's under the house. There comes my cousin Roxy."

A young girl was speeding down the boardwalk toward them. She rode a boy's BMX, wore a black baseball cap backward, and from the looks of it, was all tomboy. A second before she would have run into them, she skidded the bike sideways, blocking the boardwalk.

"Hey, Yago," she said. "Where you guys going?"

"I'm showing the new teachers around," he replied proudly.

The girl reached into the back pocket of her jeans and removed a can of chewing tobacco. She opened it and offered some to them. Yago took a pinch of the dark grains and slipped it behind his lower lip. The girl did the same.

"Aren't you guys a little young for that?" Anna asked.

"See those kids playing over at the playground, those little ones?" Yago said, pointing beside the school. "Those second-graders even already chew Copen. Everyone chews. Everyone."

The girl got off her bike and began walking it beside Yago.

"You know it's bad for you, right?" Anna asked.

The girl spat. "So. Seems like everything's bad for you. Stop the pop. No candy. No chips. No snuff. No, no, no—never anyone tells us what's good. Native food is only thing good for me to eat, my mom says. And that's so boring, always eating fish and ducks and things. You guys husbands and wifes?"

"That's Anvil's store there," Yago said, pointing to a building that looked like the rest of the village houses. A boxy one-storey plywood house, with ATVs and snow machines in various stages of disrepair parked outside.

"Yeah, we're married," Anna replied.

"What do they sell in there?" John asked.

"You know, store things," Yago said. "Pop, chips, gum, frozen pizzas."

"They got movies to rent there, too," Roxy said.

"Movies?" Anna chuckled.

Yago said, "My brother said they got dirty naked kind of movies in the back behind the curtain, too."

Yago looked at the girl and the two laughed. The girl covered her mouth with her hand, as if to keep the laughter contained.

The two kids reached the end of the boardwalk, at the edge of the ten-foot-high riverbank. From a distance, it looked to John as if the wooden walkway just went right off the edge of the bank, and standing at the edge he could tell why. The bank was eroding and had taken a portion of the walkway with it.

The girl shot a dark ball of saliva over the embankment and into the swirling rusted-brown water below. "How long you guys going to live here? Will you leave at springtime?"

Anna smacked a mosquito against the soft skin of her neck. "We just got here! Who knows," she said. "How can you not have a shirt on, Yago? Why aren't the bugs eating you like they are me?"

"'Cuz he stinks!" the girl said with a laugh. Yago slugged her in the arm.

"So dumb you are, Roxy."

John looked down over the bank as a large wall of dirt upstream calved and splashed into the water. "Wow," he said, "the water is really eating the bank up."

"See that house down there?" Yago pointed to a rusting Quonset hut hanging over the edge of the bank. Wood, sheet metal, and weathered pink insulation dangled down the bank and dipped into the water. "That was my uncle's house. Last summer, after they made him leave the village, most of it fell in the river."

"We might have to move the whole village, like those villages on the coast. They have to move. Even the graveyards," the girl said. "So scary, ah? To have to dig up those bodies? I bet they'll be haunted."

"Why are they moving villages?" Anna asked, pulling up the hood of her green fleece sweatshirt to keep the bugs off.

"The Earth is melting away," Yago said.

"So stupid you are, Yago! The Earth's not melting. The ice is melting and the water's swallowing up the land." She jerked her thumb at Yago. "He's only in third grade."

"My reading level's higher than yours," Yago said.

"My math level's higher than yours, dummy."

John looked downriver. He slipped his arm around his wife and watched a large flock of slender-bodied birds rise off the river and turn in a wide circle toward the grey eastern sky.

"Cranes," Yago said. "Wish I had my 20-gauge."

"You don't got no 20-gauge," the girl teased.

"Shut up. I can use my brother's."

Another large block of dirt crashed into the water downstream. The dirt disappeared beneath the surface, leaving only a ring of small ripples that shifted and vanished in the current.

Yago turned his bike around, unamused. "Seems like one of these days my dad will be able to park his boat right in front of my house if the world keeps falling into the river." He started riding off and yelled back to the girl, "Then your house will float out to China! The school, too!"


THE GIRL AND JOHN awoke to the tarp flapping and smacking against their heads. He grabbed the edge of the tarp and pulled it down over them and held it tight against the frozen tundra with his forearm. Above them the early light of morning lit the blue plastic that popped and snapped with each gust.

The chill in the air the night before was gone. The warm winds worried him, but he welcomed the change from the previous days of sub-zero temperatures and constant cold. He peeked out from beneath the plastic sheeting and could see nothing but white. There was no distinguishing the sky from the ground.

"Sounds like a blizzard," the girl said, lifting her hand out from her sleeping bag and holding the tarp off her face. She pulled her other hand free and began feeling around her bag. "My grass. Oh, no! Do you see it?"

John sighed and sat up. The tarp snapped open and a rush of wet snow and wind whipped against her face and against the back of his neck. She squinted and bolted upright and began feeling frantically around her.

"Don't let it blow away! Please, John." He spotted the bundle ten feet from them, poking out from a drift. Another gust hit and the bundle threatened to go flying across the open tundra.

"Grab the tarp and my bag!" he yelled as the next gust blasted them with a sheet of snow. He jumped out from the warmth of his sleeping bag and took two long strides. The snow and ice cut at his bare soles. He snatched up the grass just as another gust hit, and dove back under the tarp.

"Did you get it?" she asked.

"Yes. Of course," he said, stuffing his numb, wet feet back down into the depths of the bag. "Next time you can get it yourself," he said, slipping the grass bundle into her hands.

She lifted the bundle and held it to her nose and inhaled. "Thanks, John. Sorry," she said. "I didn't think it would storm like this."

He said nothing and reached into his backpack and put a gallon can of tomato paste on the inside edge of the tarp to hold it down. He waited for a moment to see if the can could keep the edge from flying up with the next blast of wind. It held, but to be sure he set the entire pack on the windward edge and pulled the tarp over the backpack at their heads. With the sled at their feet, he made a small blue human burrito.

John turned over on his back and stared up at the blue plastic, inches from his face. The tarp shook and crinkled with each wind burst.

After a while she asked, "Are you mad at me?"

"No."

"Thank you," she said.

"For what?"

"For saving it. For saving me."

"Well, if I didn't save your little handiwork you'd just keep asking me more questions now, wouldn't you?"

She giggled. "Probably," she said, taking the bundle out again and resting her cheek against it. She fell silent and he thought she'd fallen back to sleep when she asked, "We're not travelling today, are we?"

"No."

"What day do you think it is?" the girl asked.

He wanted to tell her how many days it was from the day he made his promise to Anna, but that would mean nothing to her, so instead he simply said, "I don't know."

And he didn't.

The tarp popped and snapped with another gust that seemed to last for several minutes.

"Do you think we can have some breakfast to celebrate?"

"Celebrate what? Another storm?"

"Maybe it's my birthday today. I'm twenty. If not today, one of these days. My birthday is December seventeenth. Sometimes in December we get warm winds like this. Big blizzards that never want to end. Then after my birthday, January comes. You know what the Yup'ik word for January means?"

"No."

"The bad month. It's not the bad month yet. Still a while away. That's how I know. But it's coming. I can feel it. Cold. Dark. Not long after my birthday. Can we have something to eat?"

"Sure," he said. "I'll open a can of peaches for your birthday."

"You don't need to. We should save what we have. We'll celebrate some other day." She reached toward him and touched his shoulder and softly patted her hand up to his cheek. Her warm fingers moved across the thin beard on his jawline and over his nose, lips, and chin. "How old are you, John?" she said, taking her hand away and holding it against her own lips and under her nose.

He rolled on his side and stared at her. His muscles ached. His back felt rigid and tired from pulling and walking. His feet were tired, still wet, but warm. "Thirty-one going on eighty," he said, adding, "I'm old."

"Well, except for that fur on your face, you don't feel that old," she said.

The wind ruffled the tarp, as if to punctuate the girl's statement. The gales were picking up momentum. The snow crystals tinkling against the plastic were strangely soothing, but he worried the storm would blanket them entirely, and as she said, "never want to end," he wondered if that wouldn't be so bad.

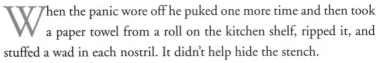

# 13

When the panic wore off he puked one more time and then took a paper towel from a roll on the kitchen shelf, ripped it, and stuffed a wad in each nostril. It didn't help hide the stench.

With one glance in the storeroom, the smell no longer mattered. The shelves were stocked, untouched. Gallon cans of USDA peanut butter, pears, corn, peas, green beans, fruit cocktail, and orange juice.

He opened a few cupboards and found cans of whole chickens and ham. There were boxes of Sailor Boy Pilot crackers, dry cereal, and chocolate chips. He tore into a restaurant-sized bag of chocolate chips and stuffed a handful into his watering mouth. He didn't chew them. He knew his stomach wouldn't handle the sudden flush of sugar. Instead he just stood there for a moment and rolled the chips around his mouth.

"John?"

The echo startled him—for a second the voice sounded like Anna's. He aimed the flashlight across the gym and peered at the thin outline of the girl standing in the doorway. Between them, a twisted maze of bodies.

"I'm over here. Just stay put."

"What's taking you so long?" she asked just loud enough for him to hear.

"We're saved. It's incredible. There's food here. Lots of food. I just need to figure out how we get enough out. Go back to the office and wait for me. I won't be much longer."

"I want to wait here."

"Fine."

He turned back to the kitchen and stopped at the freezer door. He didn't need to look inside, but he found himself pulling the handle and swinging the door wide. Cases of beef patties, chicken, frozen corn dogs, and frozen vegetables lined the walls of the cooler. From the soggy-looking boxes he guessed everything had thawed over the summer and then cooled, so he knew the meat was probably spoiled.

He stepped out of the cooler and saw the solution to getting out enough food quickly. A handcart loaded with green plastic dishwashing crates stood behind the door of the kitchen. With the flashlight lying on the counter he could see enough to work. He pulled the handcart over to the shelves and quickly began loading the crates with all the food the cart would hold. He loaded it to the top and wheeled it to the kitchen door. He grabbed the flashlight and aimed it across the gym toward the girl. She sat in the doorway, with her legs pulled up to her and her hands covering her nose.

He took a deep breath through his mouth and bit at the edge of his lip. He had almost forgotten the wad of chocolate tucked in his cheek. His teeth crushed the melted chips and he swallowed the sugary remains. He left the food behind and started across the gym, pushing arms and legs away. He needed a path, just enough room to get the food through. The bodies felt light. Stiff, but light. He expected more substance to them. The dead should weigh more, he thought. They felt more like shells or exoskeletons than bodies, and he pushed them away with his feet. He was about halfway when he heard the sound come from the girl, something just short of a gasp. He flashed the light on her as she dropped her hands from her face and her head whipped toward the entrance of the school.

"He's here! The hunter is here!" she whispered across the gym.

He reached for the pistol in his waistband, but it wasn't there.

He flashed the light toward the sides of the door where the girl stood.

"Take three steps into the gym and then walk along the wall to your left. Sit down there against the wall. Do it now. Go. Don't get up until I tell you. Go!"

He didn't wait to see if the girl had listened. He sprinted to the kitchen, pulled the food back from the doorway, and dove inside. He whipped the light around the room, searching for the pistol, and then remembered getting sick and sitting on the floor by the sink. He grabbed the pistol off the floor and slipped back to the kitchen door, clicking the flashlight off as he did. He stopped at the entry to the kitchen and tried to let his eyes adjust as a figure appeared in the gym doorway.

THEIR CLASSROOMS were high-tech. Every student had a laptop, and each of Anna's second- through fourth-graders shared a desktop computer. He had big plans for the LCD projector—his lectures would be funny and educational for the history and the English class. He wasn't so sure about the science, though. He didn't know much about teaching science at all. The idea of teaching in an area he wasn't interested in and couldn't even feign passion for scared him.

"Maybe you can just study things around here," Anna suggested. "You know, for biology stuff dissect some fish and ducks or whatever. See if someone will bring in a moose heart or something."

"A moose heart? Where do you come up with this stuff?"

"I'm a generalist. I teach second grade," she said, and laughed.

"Guess I'm going to have to learn to be more like you," he joked. "Christ, nine through twelfth grade, everything but math? They might as well make me teach math, too."

"It's going to be fun! Now get to making this classroom comfortable and inviting for your new students."

"This is strange to be in my own classroom, you know. I think I'd rather move around, like a college professor. That way I'm not responsible for making the place all comfy and inviting and stuff."

"You're being a real Johnny downer. What's this about?" she asked. She sat down on his desk and scratched at a mosquito bite on her temple. She'd been leaving her hair back in a ponytail since they arrived in the village, and he suddenly wondered who would cut their hair while they lived there. Would they have to wait until they flew out at Christmas, and could they even afford to fly out over the holiday?

"Come on. Are you worried about your new students? They're going to love you, John. Who doesn't love John Morgan? They have to love at least a quarter of you."

"Funny. What if that first day doesn't go well? Don't you worry about that? We're stuck here. If I have some punk-ass kid and his dad is school board president—how do I deal with that? I've never taught in a small school before. Don't you see? The school is the centre of the community. Its heart. Everything good and bad starts here or ends here. If I screw up, or someone turns the village against us? Then I'm the bad guy until further notice. No amount of blood quantum can fix that. It's just scary, that's all."

She laughed and reached over to him. She took his hand and began pushing back his cuticles with her fingernail. "The kids are going to love you, Johnny. You care—they are going to see that from the first moment. From the sounds of it, they've had a lot of odd and shitty teachers. I think they're going to appreciate your gentle heart."

"My gentle heart. Ha. That's a little presumptuous. You're the gentle heart. I'm the one with the wolf-jaw snap."

"I can't win! Sorry for trying *and* hoping." She got up and stormed to the door. "Screw you, mister!" She stopped and turned back and laughed. "How was that? Was I convincing?"

"Not at all convincing," he said. "You need to turn a few desks over on the way."

"I'm going back to my room to make some dinosaur mobiles to hang from the ceiling—you should make a few, too," she joked.

"Yeah, dinosaurs, I'll get right on that."

She paused at the door, her eyes stopped on movement outside the windows across from her. She pointed. "Look."

He stood up and watched as a father and son walked down the boardwalk between the village houses. The father carried a shotgun over one shoulder, and his other hand carried a handful of ducks by the neck. The boy's back was covered in white, his hands clutching a long white neck at his chest, an Alaskan version of Leda and the Swan.

"What's the boy carrying?" Anna asked.

"A bird. Swan, I think. Maybe a trumpeter swan."

"That's sad," she said.

"Sad? No way," he replied. "I bet they're delicious."

THAT MORNING the two of them left the village, with the girl riding in the sled to save her energy. Twice he glanced over his shoulder to check on her, and each time her head was turned back toward the village.

They hadn't made it more than a mile or so along the river's edge before she answered the question he'd never voiced.

"If there's someone left, someone like us," she said, "I think they'll know."

He stopped and rested for a moment. The sun had just started to lift above the long stretch of flat horizon, a grey cold sun that gave no heat or comfort.

"Know what?" he asked.

"They'll know we're not like the others."

"Sick?"

"No. The other people, the outcasts. They'll know we're not like the outcasts."

"How? How could they know that?"

Using his glove, he brushed some small clumps of ice collecting on his beard. The small thermometer clipped to his zipper read fifteen below. It felt colder. He clenched his toes in his boots. He couldn't feel the little toes, and once feeling in the big toes left they would have to stop and try to get a fire going.

"How are your feet doing?" he asked.

"I can smell them," she said.

"Your feet?" he asked.

"No. So dumb, John. The outcasts. I can smell them. But anyone else, anyone who spots us, even if they don't know I can't see with my eyes—they'll know. They'll see you helping me and they'll know we're not like them. They will know we're not *tenguituli*, wild people, and they'll know we're not outcasts. Those outcast people don't help no one but themselves."

He started pulling again. After a while he stopped and asked her, "What if we were both outcasts? Wouldn't we still travel together?"

She ran her mitten across the top of the snow and tasted it. He took off his glove and held his palms against his cheeks to warm them.

He tightened the rope about his waist and pressed forward, trying to ignore the hunger burning in his stomach and the cold fire scorching the tips of his toes.

"If we were, you would have killed me, to have the food you saved for yourself. Maybe eat me with salt and pepper. I jokes, John. I'm no good for one of those people. Besides, we're not like them, are we."

She said it like a statement. Not a question.

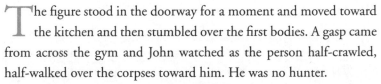

## 14

The figure stood in the doorway for a moment and moved toward the kitchen and then stumbled over the first bodies. A gasp came from across the gym and John watched as the person half-crawled, half-walked over the corpses toward him. He was no hunter.

John stepped back a little, waited for the right moment, and flipped on the flashlight, shining the beam straight into the man's eyes. The man jumped to his feet and shielded his face.

"That's far enough."

The man, wearing a tattered fleece jacket and Sorel Packs, shuffled another step forward and pushed a woman's leg out of the way.

He shone the light across the gym. A glint of steel by the door caught his eye. He shone the light at it and spotted two portable generators he hadn't seen before.

"Start clearing the path to the door and I won't shoot you."

"That food's going to make you sick. You can't take it. I came to tell you to leave it. Going to make you both real sick."

John shone the light on his pistol for a moment, for effect, and said, "Turn around slowly and start clearing me a path. I'm going to be right behind you. Try anything and you're dead. I should have already shot you."

The man turned slowly and started pushing bodies out of the way. John tilted the handcart back with one hand while holding the pistol and flashlight against the top box with the other. He started rolling through the path of bodies. The flashlight and the pistol pointed at the man's back.

The man began kicking the corpses out of the way with his boots. The sounds of his boots hitting them and the rough skin scratching against the floor made John's stomach turn again. He swallowed hard and steadied his breathing.

"They're going to get you," the man said.

"Are there more people out there?"

"Not out there. In here."

John flashed his light around the gym, suddenly paranoid.

"Who?"

"These people," he said. "You're stealing from the dead. That food is theirs. This is their grave now and you're stealing from them. We don't take from the dead."

The man stopped pushing the bodies away and turned toward John. With the light shining into his dark brown eyes the man stared at him, unflinching.

"You shouldn't have disturbed them," he said.

"Why did *you* come in here, then?"

"I'm not the one stealing from them."

"Yeah, but I'm not the one kicking their corpses. Come on, we're almost there. Keep moving."

"Out there, he'll get you."

"Who?"

He looked over his shoulder and grinned. "You know who."

"Keep moving."

Just before they reached the door he told the man to stop. He didn't want to walk out into an ambush. He needed a moment to think. If a group of them were waiting in the hall, he and the girl would be easy prey. If he shot the man now, he wouldn't be keeping his word. He didn't want the girl seeing him lie like that. He didn't know where the girl had hidden—he didn't want to call her out yet.

He wheeled the handcart within three feet of the man. "Okay, once we get to the door I want you to stop. Then you're going to turn around and wheel this cart in front of you. Don't test me."

Near the door he told the man to stop again. The man turned and took the cart and wheeled it out into the hallway, with John right behind him. John stopped at the door and looked down the hall in both directions. Nothing. The man set the handcart down and turned to him.

He was rail thin. Mid-thirties. A thin LA Lakers shirt with holes hung from his knobby shoulders beneath the fleece jacket. The man's black hair, shoulder length and stringy, almost mangy, hung in clumps from his head.

"You going to blast me now?"

"Not if I don't have to. Who's waiting out there for us?" John asked.

"No one. There's no one. Let me take a case of those chickens. Please. I'm so hungry. Come on, man. I helped you. One can. Just give me one can, dude. One."

"What about them?" John said, gesturing to the bodies in the gym. "I thought you were afraid of them."

"Too late for me now, too, I guess."

"I'm leaving here with this food. When I'm gone, you can go back in and take all you want."

John felt a hand on his back. It almost made him drop the pistol.

"Sorry, I couldn't stay in there no more," the girl said, her voice barely audible.

"It's okay," he said.

He watched as a smile spread across the man's face.

"I know you," he said to the girl.

Her face shifted. She took a deep breath and stepped back to the side of the door.

"I *know* you," the man said again, and in the dim light of the hallway, John could see the raised burns on his neck.

AFTER THE FIRST DAY OF SCHOOL, in their little one-bedroom shack of a house, Anna cried. She curled up on the couch, which was made from two wrestling mats stacked on top of each other with a heavy flannel sheet covering them, and cried.

"What the hell are we doing here?" she asked between sobs. "Who are we fooling? Why did you let me talk us into this? It's my fault, isn't it? I wanted this so much for you, I should have known this would be too much for *me* to handle, shouldn't I?"

The questions were building to a level of hysteria he hadn't seen since the day before their wedding, when her mother insisted she hire a real florist and not leave the flowers to her hippie friends. He knelt down beside her and tried to soothe her. He knew better than to set foot into one of her spring-loaded questions.

"They hated me," she said. "They looked at me, and stared at me like I'm some sort of hellish freak alien, and they hated me, John. *Hated* me."

"I'm sure they didn't hate you, Anna. They're second-graders. They don't even know hate yet."

"Thanks. That's so reassuring. Now I'm teaching them to hate! They weren't excited or motivated or interested. They just sat there and stared at me and didn't do or say anything. They wouldn't answer my questions or do what I asked them. They just sat there. Some of them covered their faces! They couldn't even bear to look at me!"

"I'm sure there's an adjustment period, you know? You're new here—new to their world—that's a big thing to remember."

"And I'm white. *White.*"

"And white. So what? You're dealing with kids. This whole school thing is as foreign to them as their culture is to you."

She looked up at him, her face awash in tears. "And you're the expert now? Is it just because you had a great first day? Or did your Native roots suddenly kick in?"

"I'm going to pretend you didn't say that," he said. He got up and went back to the stove and stirred the pot of chili. He tasted it, and added another dash of Mexican chili powder, more pepper, and two pinches of dried garlic, anything to make the tin-can taste disappear.

He tried his best to just answer the question. "It wasn't great. I mean, after the first two minutes I threw the whole first day of lesson plans out the door. We spent the day getting to know each other. It took me about thirty seconds after the first bell to see that they weren't ready to jump right into school mode."

"So what did you do?"

"We talked. Scratch that—I talked, at least initially. They asked questions, and more questions, and all I did was answer them one right after the other."

"Like what?" she asked.

"Where are you from? Do you hunt? Where have you been? Do you play basketball? Did I play college hoops? Why didn't I play in the NBA? Where are you from? Again. When did you get married? Why did I marry you?"

"They asked about me? They asked why you married me? Even your students don't like me?"

"Relax, Anna. They asked about everything. Then, when they couldn't come up with any more questions, I started asking questions. And that's what we did for the day. We just talked and got to know each other. Sometimes we just sat there and didn't say anything."

She stood up and let her hair down. She tasted the chili and poured herself a cup of hot water from the kettle on the stove and began to dip a green-tea bag.

"What sort of questions did you ask?"

"I started simple. Nicknames, favourite subjects, favourite sports. Then I asked about things they learned over the years in school, past teachers, and what they wanted to do in the future—but that's the one thing that stumped them a bit, or something they couldn't really answer."

"No one expects high school kids to know what their future holds," Anna said.

"Yeah, but not just that. The question really took them back. I mean—I tried to reword the question. You know, what will they being doing in ten years, and that drew even less of a response. Michael, that tall, skinny, talkative kid? He said they don't think about the future like that. It's against their culture, he said."

"To talk about the future?"

"Yeah, I guess. I don't know. Maybe I misunderstood him, or they just didn't quite get my question. This chili is as ready as anything from a can will be."

He began filling two blue plastic cereal bowls with the meatless chili. She took her bowl, sat down, and pushed her spoon around the bowl.

"You'll do fine, hon," he said. "Just give them some time. I would guess that with those young ones, they'll be a bit shy at first and then you'll have to beat them off you with a stick."

"Yeah, well, if tomorrow doesn't go any better, I might get a stick, and then you might be teaching here alone." She pushed her bowl away and he pushed it back to her.

"Eat. You'll need your strength to swing the stick tomorrow."

THE GIRL AND JOHN awoke to a rare clear, crisp day that reflected against the snow a blinding white and forced him to squint until his forehead burned like an ice cream headache. A strong wind pushed at their backs, and he was happy to not have to worry about frost-bite on their faces. Travelling went smoothly enough that his mind wandered back to thoughts of Anna and their first night together. He forgot the blind girl walking beside him, and the toboggan with their gear, a few cans of food, and her grass bundle. For those few moments he was in an anchored rowboat, rocking with the waves, in the middle of a lake, naked from the waist down, with Anna on top of him. Above them, the stars of a Wyoming night sky pulsed.

The memory slipped away when the girl asked if they could stop for water, but that night, when the two of them made camp beneath the stars, exhausted, the memory came back, and he escaped to the boat again. She rocked with the waves, dropping down onto him, letting her long brown hair fall over him, covering her eyes, and when she lifted her lips to him, her withered face twisted with pain, and she coughed and lurched toward him.

"John? John? You're nightmaring again," the girl said, gripping his shoulders.

"Sorry. Sorry."

"It's okay," she said. "Anna … That was your wife?"

He nodded, then remembered she couldn't see his head move. The girl smiled and returned to her work with the grass.

"It's okay. You must have been dreaming of her," she said, and put the end of one grass stalk into her mouth.

He tried to close his eyes, but as soon as he did, Anna's face would reappear, the horrible image hanging in the sky above him. He tried to see through it, to the stars, but it wouldn't go away.

"What did she look like?" the girl asked.

He couldn't answer her. She waited for a while, and then asked another question. He knew she changed the subject for him.

"It's clear tonight. Can you see the northern lights? We say those are spirits playing in the sky. I heard elders say they will even come get you if you whistle at them. So don't whistle. Are they there?"

He stared out at the black above them, speckled with faint stars, but no wisps of aurora.

"Nope. Just the stars."

"Are there any satellites? I remember seeing those blinking lights travelling across the sky. My brothers said that's where we got our TV shows. I wonder if we still had electricity if we could get TV still. You think there's still TV anywhere?"

He scanned the sky. He hadn't thought about satellites. Were they still transmitting? Could they tell him anything he didn't already know? If he spotted one, what did that mean?

He closed his eyes. She was gone.

"I don't see any," he said, "but that doesn't mean they aren't there."

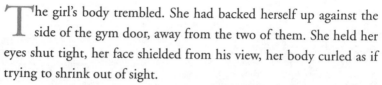

# 15

The girl's body trembled. She had backed herself up against the side of the gym door, away from the two of them. She held her eyes shut tight, her face shielded from his view, her body curled as if trying to shrink out of sight.

"I know her," the man with the burns on his neck said. "I can't believe the little blind one is still alive."

"Shut up," John said to the man, and then turned to the girl. "What's wrong?" he asked. Her nostrils flared and her white eyes narrowed, as if she could see the man standing in front of her.

"Little Bug," the man said. "She's one of my kid sister's girls. Lying little bitch made some bullshit story up and got me kicked out of our village."

John pointed the gun at him. He eased him back a few steps against the other side of the wall.

"That's enough," John said, pressing the pistol into the man's chest.

"She's my relative. Take the food and go. I'll take care of her. We're family."

"I don't think so. Step back."

John knelt down beside her. Tears wet the sides of her cheeks, and the muscles in her jaw trembled. "Is he who he says?" he asked.

She nodded.

"He's your uncle?"

She nodded again.

One of her hands had found the ice pick, which he'd left against the door frame. She scraped with her thumbnail at the cold steel.

"What do you want me to do?"

She took a deep breath, then let it out in stuttered white bursts that steamed from her nostrils. She took another and it came out smoother.

"John," she whispered. He leaned in close to her. "Let me talk to him."

He stood up and motioned to the man with the barrel of the pistol. "She wants to say something to you." He crossed the hallway as the man approached the girl. John watched, but he was also thinking about the food stacked in front of him. His stomach burned. Nothing sounded as good as a big spoonful of peanut butter. Chicken sounded better, but he knew it would be a while before he could dig into a chicken leg without getting sick.

"Little Bug, I never thought I'd see you again," the man said, and as he said this she stood, swinging the ice pick like a baseball bat. The side of the heavy steel bar smashed against the side of the man's head, sending him to the floor. Before either of them could react, she jumped on top of him, thrusting the bar sideways against his throat, pinning him. He gasped for air and tried to push her off. His starved muscles could do little against her rage.

John started to step in, but once he saw the girl had the upper hand he stood by with the pistol pointed at the floor, his finger beside the trigger.

The girl's breath came from her mouth in frosty bursts. The man quit struggling.

"You going to kill me?" he gasped. "You blind little bitch? Try check if you can."

"Why would God let someone like you live and so many suffer? Why?" she cried.

She pressed the bar harder against his throat. Blood seeped through the black hair at his temple.

"Why did all those good people in there have to die and you live?"
The man looked up at John. "Please," he gasped, "she's crazy."

"I wish that water had burned your eyes ... Tell him how you got
your burns."

"Please," he begged again, "I can't breathe."

"Tell him what you did to me!" She lifted one knee and pressed her
kneecap against the bar. The man started to choke and convulse.

A DOZEN STUDENTS all at different ability levels filled the desks of his
classroom. This was his challenge. It didn't take either of them long to
realize that the village kids had already known more teachers in their
life than most graduate students. Just a quick glance at the file cabinets
with different folders from different years, he could see the turnover in
teachers from year to year was incredible. There had been one constant
in their academic lives—inconstancy.

For all he knew, he and Anna might not be there the next year
either, so he decided to quietly stuff the district curriculum guide-
lines in his desk and find a way to show his students how to teach
themselves.

On the day he started the new approach, he sat for a while at his
desk, with a smile, just looking them over. They would peer up at him
and then glance away, shyly. They were a patient group. Five boys and
seven girls. They sat at their desks, some of them with light jackets
on, all of them wearing T-shirts, jeans, and Nike or Adidas basketball
shoes or knee-high black rubber boots.

Alex, the kid with the Bulls cap, John pegged as his biggest challenge
in maintaining any sort of respect with his students, tried to hide the
pinch of snuff in his lip as he asked, "Why you always smiling at us,
John?"

He wouldn't tell Alex to spit out the snuff and go to the principal's
office. He knew there were more important battles to win.

"Why am I smiling?" He stood up and walked to the whiteboard.

"You guys have told me that you don't think any of what you have learned in school is important, that it doesn't have anything to do with you. Right?"

"Well it don't," Alex chuckled. "You see any Eskimos using geometry shooting ducks?"

The class laughed.

"Well, what about history? Why might history be important to you?" John asked.

Sharon, a skinny girl with glasses and hair always tightly braided, raised her hand. He called on her, knowing she would have a well thought out answer. From day one she had established herself as the brain of the class.

"If we can learn from our history, we can make better decisions and we can understand the world better," she said, covering her mouth shyly when she finished.

"Right, Sharon. Great start," he said. "But why might history be important to you, as Yup'ik students—Yup'ik people?"

"It's not," Alex said. "They want us to learn names and dates of old white and black people who are dead. I've got better things to do, man."

"Exactly. Exactly, Alex. Yes! What if I tell you that none of what you've learned so far really matters?"

He looked at each of them. A few of them, including Sharon, seemed a bit befuddled. Alex sat back, pleased with himself. For the first time, John thought he might have a shot at reaching him, maybe all of them.

"Let's start with the first dude you learned about in history. Who was it? One hint. He sailed the ocean blue ..."

Jack, a quiet, sullen death metal fan, flipped his long hair and finished the rhyme. "In 1492, Columbus sailed the ocean blue."

The rest of the class looked at Jack, surprised.

"It's like a song lyric, dog. I don't forget lyrics. Ever."

"Yes. Columbus. Nice work, Jack."

Alex sighed. "Oh man, Columbus sucks. He found the Lower Forty-eight, big deal."

"Right again, Alex. But you're not right about what he found. You're right that Columbus sucked. He—well, let's just say he wasn't the kindest, most friendly explorer. Maybe we could say that what he was a part of is more horrible than you could ever even imagine. What if I told you that this first hero you learned about in history wasn't who you have been taught he was at all? What if I told you that most of what you have learned and will be expected to learn"—he paused and held up their history book—"was a bunch of BS?"

"That would be pretty cool," Alex said. "It would be like *The Matrix*. A conspiracy, man, the whole world school teaches us about is one big fat lie."

IT TOOK THE GIRL AND JOHN four days of steady travel to reach the first village. He figured they made about three miles a day, maybe less. He half expected to find someone alive, someone who could take care of her or maybe tell them not to bother going upriver. Instead, little remained but the charred skeletons of the dead and their houses. He sat at the river's edge watching the village for an hour before he decided it was safe enough for them to approach.

No smoke and no houses that looked livable told him all he needed to know. There probably wasn't much of a reason to even waste the energy and walk through what remained, but if they could scrounge up a few pieces of wood they might be able to put together a fire for the night.

"Why is this village completely burned and ours wasn't?" the girl asked.

"I don't know," he said as he took one last long look at the village, checking for any signs of movement.

"Do you think someone burned it to kill the disease?"

"I don't know if that would matter. Could have just been a fire too, in all the chaos. It's hard to say what happened as people got sick. People do crazy things when they're scared."

"When my family got sick, I tried to help as much as I could. Even my grandma said she remembered hearing about the sicknesses back in the old days. She said not many lived and times were really hard back then. She said it would be just like that. Just like the Great Death. She was right, I guess. I don't know why they called it great. Death's not very great to me."

He pulled the sled and she walked slowly beside him. He kept the rifle at the ready as they entered what was left of the village.

"I think I smell burnt bodies," she said. "I hope they weren't alive."

He turned away from one house, the walls and roof scorched, two half-burnt, half-decayed corpses stretched out on the bare floor joists, the plywood floor covering burned around the bodies, their jaws open, some teeth exposed.

"Will it be like this in every village?"

"I don't know."

"What does it look like?" she asked. "My sister Molly lived here with her husband and four of my nieces and nephews. Their house was three down on this side."

She pointed toward a house with pilings that had burned, the house tipped on its side, a mound of twisted black sticks.

"There's not much left here. Not much at all. Sorry."

"Maybe she was in town. They were going to move to Bethel to get jobs. I hope they moved early. Maybe she's safe. I hope the kids are safe."

He picked up a few pieces of half-burnt wood and decided they'd camp away from the village. He couldn't smell the bodies as she could, but it didn't matter. They didn't need to sleep near a crematorium.

"I think we'll move a little more upriver, see if we can't camp somewhere with shelter—in case it gets windy. Sound good to you?"

"Yeah," she said. She turned and listened for a moment and he lifted the rifle.

"What is it?" he whispered.

"I heard something, and it feels like someone's watching us."

He spun slowly, trying to catch the slightest movement in the burnt houses around them. His eyes searched for tracks in the snow. Nothing.

An odd sound echoed through the suddenly still air, the sound of a single drop of water, magnified, almost comical-sounding. He turned and saw it—sitting on the flagpole outside what had been the village post office—a giant raven, coal black, staring down at them.

The bird made another water-drop sound and then squawked at the two of them and flew off.

"It's just a raven," he whispered, "trying to scare us."

"Maybe he's trying to tell us something. Yup'iks used to believe ravens were special a long time ago. Maybe they created the world, and the animals, and people. We never shoot them. Never eat them."

"Or maybe he's telling us he created this whole awful mess and that we should get moving."

"Which way did he fly?"

"The direction we're headed."

"Can you still see him?"

"Yeah," he said, and blinked the frost off his eyelids.

"Watch him," she said. "Tell me what he does."

"He's flying away."

"Keep watching."

He focused his eyes as the bird flew upriver, almost out of sight. Just before it slipped from view he saw something, something he'd never seen before. The bird rolled, mid-air, almost like a fighter jet, turning upside down, free-falling, just for a second, then back to his normal position before he dropped beneath the horizon.

"Anything?"

"He's gone. It looked like he dipped his wings or something, but he was so far away I couldn't tell."

"I hope that's what he was doing. I hope. I hope. My dad said that hunters watch the raven and if he flies upside down he's dumping luck off his back. Maybe he dumped some luck on our trail."

He helped her sit down in the sled. He set the firewood on her lap, and they headed in the direction the raven flew, toward where the raven's luck fell.

# PART II

# The
# Monster
## in the
# Lake

*A strange crocodile-like animal, known as pal-rai-yuk, is
painted on the sides of umiaks and on the inside of wooden
dishes by natives along the lower Yukon and Kuskokwim
rivers ... According to the traditions of the people of this
district the climate in ancient times was much warmer than
at present and the winters were shorter. In those days the
mythic animals referred to were abundant in the swampy
country between the two rivers.*

—AS RECORDED BY EDWARD NELSON, 1899

# 16

He wouldn't have had the strength to unload the sled after loading the food and pulling it from the school, but he wasn't about to leave it outside the old woman's house for the night. The old woman and the girl helped him at the top of the stairs. They took the boxes and stacked them inside the arctic entry. The woman wouldn't let him bring the cases of food into the house, and she refused his offer to go get more for her.

"I'll leave a couple of cans of chicken and some peanut butter," he said, knowing that she wouldn't refuse him if the gesture came more as a statement or command than a question. She said nothing, and he knew her hunger would consume the superstition.

He removed a single canned chicken and a gallon can of pears. He took one of her big soup pots, opened the can of frozen chicken, and dumped it in. He poured some water into the pot from a brown plastic pitcher and put the can of pears directly on top of the stove and flipped it over every few minutes. When the can felt warm enough he opened the pears, dumped the pears in a bowl, and poured the sugary juice into a couple plastic cups. He handed one to the girl and offered the other to the old woman. She refused. He set hers aside and poured himself a cup. He sipped it slowly, savouring the sweetness, the cold syrup sticking to his dry mouth.

The old woman broke some tundra tea needles off a twig and set them in a pot on the stove. "*Qia-qanaarituten?*" she asked the girl. The girl just sipped from her cup of pear juice. "Why the girl not talking?" she asked him.

He shrugged. "Let her tell you," he said, stirring the pot of pears and the chicken.

After a long silence the woman asked him, her voice barely audible, "How did they die in there?"

"I don't know," he said. "Maybe poison. They looked like they just fell asleep."

The old woman stirred her tea and looked down at the cup of juice he'd set aside for her. "They heard the sickness was in the village and made an announcement on the VHF radio," she began. "Everyone go to the school for a meeting, even the children. They said everyone had to go because the sickness was coming. Everyone would be safe at the school. I went and hid in the steam bath. I didn't think they would say bring childrens to an important meeting. When I seen the village police coming house to house, I just hid. When the sickness came long time ago, the missionaries made us put signs up, a black X outside a house, and no one could leave or go into a house with a sick sign posted on the door. I thought that was what they would do here. Back then it was so bad. So many people would die. I remember a line of bodies all the way to the graves. Not enough people left to bury them properly. So scary back then. Worse than this time, but maybe only since I'm old and I seen a lot of bad things."

Her tea started to boil. She tipped the pan and filled her mug. She gripped the mug with both hands and blew on the steam rising off it. She took a sip. They sat silently for a long time. He stirred the chicken. The good thing about the canned chickens was they were already cooked. All they needed was for the meat to thaw and get warm enough. He felt like Pavlov's dog, his mouth no longer dry. The chicken smell coming from the pot was almost overwhelming. He knew their stomachs weren't ready for chicken, but the broth would be divine. It didn't take long before he decided that he would eat the meat, too. The hunger was too strong.

He poured the girl the last of the thawed pear syrup. "Here," he said, "have more juice." She took it without saying anything, drank it, and moved off to the bedding in the corner of the house.

"All night," the old woman said, "the village was so quiet that night they all went to the school. I stayed in the steam bath. I heard some drumming for a while. Like they were having Eskimo dance. Then singing, mostly church songs. I wanted to go to them so bad. I wanted to see what those sounds were. I fell asleep. Then late, I woke up because I heard dogs barking and snow machines, and then motors. Then in the morning—nothing. They never came out from that place."

"The generators," he said. "There were two generators in the gym. The doors were locked from the inside. Keeping someone out, or making sure no one changed their mind. They probably ran the generators, and died from carbon monoxide poisoning."

"I should have been there with them. I should have stood up to those who were afraid of the sickness. Some of them would have lived. The children could have lived. Look at me. Look at you. Even I'm old, I'm still alive. I should have stopped them. How could they just let them all die like that? We survived other diseases. We don't need to die like that, killing ourselves. Yup'iks were once warriors, you know? We fought to survive. We fought to protect the village. We didn't just give up."

"I saw what happened in some of the other villages," he said, removing the pot from the stove, "what happened in ours. And Nunamuit. Maybe what happened in there wasn't so bad. They would have just fallen asleep. No coughing. No fighting. No starving." He began cutting apart the chicken with his grandfather's old knife.

"Yup'ik people don't steal from the dead," the old woman said.

"I didn't steal this from them."

"You shouldn't eat it," the old woman said.

"That's what I said about your duck soup."

"It's okay," the girl said, sitting up. "*Assirtuq.* We can eat it. I told him we could take the food. It's okay with them. I know it is. Maybe they left that food there for us. Maybe they protected it for us. So we can live. So we can fight back."

"They used to say if we took things from the dead they would come back and haunt us," the old woman said. "People had respect for the dead. You used to even see guns and valuable things at the cemetery and no one would touch them."

The girl felt her way back to her spot near the stove. He held a bowl out to her and she took it. She inhaled deeply from the bowl, reached in with her fingers and removed a leg. The meat was lukewarm. She took a bite and chewed without looking up.

"How do you know this food is okay?" the old woman asked.

"Some things I just know," the girl said. "Like I knew someone good would be here for us. Like I knew you would be here."

They ate in silence until the girl set her bowl down and turned to him. She seemed to stare at him with her white eyes until he set his own bowl down, finished chewing a mouthful of chicken, and asked, "What is it? Why are you looking at me like that?"

"My little cousin Winnie, did you see her there? She had long, really long hair, almost to here." The girl brought her hand to her waist.

John picked up his bowl and took another sip of the broth. His stomach churned and gurgled. He didn't know if he could keep it down.

"Or Kall'aq, my other cousin? Really short, but tough. He had a big scar on his cheek, here," she said.

"No," John said. There were so many bodies.

"Or the twins. Gina and Paula. They're two or three," she said.

"I don't know. How could I know?"

"I don't know. I'm starting to think I just didn't feel like the kids were there in the gym," she said.

"IT'S LIKE ALCATRAZ," he said to Anna as they walked down the board-walk toward the school in the grey light of the morning. The cold, damp air hung in his nostrils, reminding him of his grandfather's root cellar. A musty smell, with a hint of winter and death, he thought.

He had given serious consideration to stealing a boat and fleeing the village, permanently. His students were great, but it was the confinement of the place that was getting to him. Not like the outside world, where he thought the blitzkrieg of media and consumerism might crush him. This was different. Those old worries were gone. Time had stopped. None of the old worries that created his anxiety were important any more. Anna had played a big part in saving him from those old days of a constantly knotted stomach and general unease with life. But now the inability to leave, to just pick up and go somewhere other than the school or their little shack and get away was beginning to haunt him. His days and nights were spent confined within a fifty-yard radius. He needed out.

"I don't know what to tell you. We're stuck here. At least until Christmas break," she said.

"You mean Slaviq? One day at Christmas is hardly a break."

"Yeah, but airfare will be cheaper in January anyway—no one else will be celebrating Russian Orthodox Christmas. Two weeks is two weeks. We could go to Hawaii or something. Maybe you're getting cabin fever."

"No shit."

"Maybe we should get one of those lights for when winter hits. You know, the kind they use for depression, for seasonal affective disorder," she said.

"I don't have depression. I just need to go somewhere other than this. You can't even go for a walk here, for Christ sakes!"

His boot hit a patch of frost, and his foot slipped out from under him. He pitched off the edge of the boardwalk, his legs landing in the half-frozen muck as his hip slammed against the edge of the planks.

"Damn!"

He sat up and brushed off his pants.

"Ouch, that looked like it hurt," she said, trying not to laugh.

"Go ahead, it's funny. Laugh it up. Winter hasn't even hit and I'm already going nuts here and you're not taking me seriously. I moved to Alaska to be outside and get into the wilderness. We're surrounded by water and trapped here. Trapped. So yeah, laugh at this too. Laugh at it all."

He started to get up and she pushed him back down with a gentle shove. "Lighten up, tough guy," she said. "I'll find you a friend who can take you out for a boat ride or something."

"Don't talk to me like I'm one of your little pants-pissing snotty-nosed students," he said. "And I don't need your help finding friends."

She extended a hand to help him up. When he didn't take it, she pushed him again, only this time a little harder.

"I didn't mean it that way, John. Get over yourself! You think I'm not tired of having nowhere other than my classroom to escape to? Listening to you sigh and mope and burp and fart your way around our little house?"

"Are you done insulting me?"

"No. I'm just getting started, mister."

He scrambled to his feet and marched, more carefully this time, toward the school, leaving her behind, for the first time ever.

NOT LONG AFTER SUNSET, the girl asked what Anna looked like, and he hadn't been able to tell her. Not because he wouldn't, but because he couldn't. All he could see or remember was the sickness that had consumed her beauty.

"Did she have dark hair or light hair?"

He packed the snow for their bed by stomping around on the tarp and then kneeling in the empty sled. He pushed the snow on the edges to form a small wall, in case the wind picked up, and then started to unload the sleeping bags from the pack.

"Did she have blue eyes?"

"Will you help me here? We need to get camp set up before it's too dark."

"It's always dark for me, John. I'm not trying to make you mad."

"It's just that I'm tired. I could use some help," he said.

She knelt down and felt for the backpack. She pulled the sleeping bag out and stretched it over the tarp. After the last blizzard he'd learned to fold the tarp with half of it beneath them and the other half wrapped around them to shield them from the unremitting winds. She took her grass bundle and placed it within arm's reach.

He waited until she crawled into her bag before scanning the horizon one last time. They were easy targets out in the open and with a tarp covering them, constantly rustling; they would never hear an enemy's boots crunching in the snow.

He secured the covering and removed his boots. He held his hands on his toes and tried to warm them. The girl was already feeling the strands of grass, the way she always did to find her starting point. He watched her until her fingers stopped and she sat up on her elbow with her body turned toward him.

"Some of my memories of what people look like are gone," she said. "Now, for most of them, I only remember what they sounded like, or how they smelled. I hope your memories of her aren't bad ones."

"They aren't," he said, stretching out on his back and pulling the top of the sleeping bag up over his shoulders.

He didn't want to remember Anna like that. So pale, so wasted, so far beyond the vibrant, healthy woman she had been. Her cheeks sunken, the skin stretched across her cheekbones, her lips dried, cracked, bleeding. Her eyes vacant, drying, helpless, with the life all but gone.

Even when he tried to imagine her before the sickness, he would see that face. The sick face. The face that begged for help, for him to do something. Those eyes that might have even questioned why it wasn't him. Why he wasn't sick, too. Why he couldn't do anything to help her.

The image of those final days stained his most cherished memories of her. She didn't wear a veil at their wedding. That was too old-fashioned for her, but if she had, in his dreams he would have lifted the thin white fabric to find the ghost who had been his wife.

"Describe her to me," the girl said as she began weaving and braiding her strands of grass.

She was beautiful, he wanted to say.

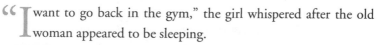

## 17

"I want to go back in the gym," the girl whispered after the old woman appeared to be sleeping.

"We have as much food as we can carry," he said.

She propped herself up on her elbow, facing him. "No. I want to see if they are there."

"Who?"

"My cousins."

"They are there. Everyone was in there. Now get some rest." He rolled over on his back, closed his eyes, and tried to sleep. In the darkness of his closed lids he saw the beam from the flashlight moving over the dead in the gymnasium and what he didn't see made him sit up with a lurch. On his hands and knees, he clawed his way to the door and heaved. The chewed chicken pieces and broth splattered against the plywood floor of the entry. His dinner wasted. He stayed on his knees, gasping at the cold air rushing past him into the house.

"What's wrong?" the girl asked, standing over him. She ran a hand over the top of his matted hair. "What is it?" she asked.

"I told you stealing that food make you sick," the old woman said from across the room. "The spirits gonna haunt you until you take it back."

"It's not the food," he gasped as he fought another heave.

He could see the notebook sitting on the desk in the office. The three words, *For the children*, scrawled in black ink. "The kids," he said to the girl. "You were right. I think I saw only one boy, maybe a couple of others. The rest were adults."

"Shoulda been mostly kids in there," the old woman said, sitting up. "You sure you seen only a few little ones?"

John crawled back to his bag. He was shivering and instantly hungry again. The bile burned at his throat, and when he spoke again his voice was raspy.

"Mostly adults."

"Are the kids anywhere else in the school?" the girl asked.

"No," John said.

"Maybe they still alive somewhere," the old woman said, adding, "Even if they run away and become *qimakalleq*, you two gotta go find them."

HIS STUDENTS WERE on to Columbus and they weren't happy. He'd pulled an old Howard Zinn essay from a website, one that used excerpts from Columbus's own journals, and had them read it. The assignment was to read the essay and then write Columbus a letter expressing their feelings. They read the essay together, and when they reached the end, he had them each turn their laptops on and quickly write the letter.

"Five minutes, as fast as you can. Don't worry about grammar or spelling or anything. Just get your gut reaction down. Give America's dead old hero a piece of your mind."

He took a sip of lukewarm coffee from his mug and watched them hunch over their keyboards. Even Alex, who had started the morning with attitude and a touch of anger he hadn't seen before, was hunting for letters on his keyboard with two middle fingers extended as if he was giving the bird to the world.

"Time's up," he said. "Now quickly scan through what you wrote and pick a sentence or two you wouldn't mind sharing with us. Someone want to start us off? Sharon? Thanks for volunteering."

Sharon held her long braid of black hair against her cheek and cleared her throat. "'What kind of hero makes mothers so scared they kill their babies to protect them from people like you?'"

"Ouch. Yes. Columbus will have trouble answering that one. Who else? Juliana?"

He was surprised to see the girl volunteer. She was a junior, cute, and painfully shy. She had said less than a hundred words to him since school started, and she hadn't turned in a single assignment.

She held her hands over her mouth, looked down at her computer screen, and after what felt like several minutes of silence read in a hushed voice, "'Dear Columbus, in all my years of school I remember only one name in history. That name belonged to you. I thought you were a brave hero, but the first words you wrote in your journal about those Native peoples? You thought they would make good slaves! Is this why you have your own holiday? Does our country celebrate you because you taught *kass'aqs* how to treat us Natives? Are you a hero in history because you showed the world we didn't matter? The Native people should have taken their children and run when they saw you coming.'"

The girl stopped reading and held her hands over her mouth, tight, as if she couldn't believe what she had just read. Alex began clapping his hands and the other students followed his lead.

"That's good stuff," Alex said. "Mine sounds stupid compared to that."

"Beautifully done, Juliana. Thanks. Anyone else?"

Jack raised his hand. "I don't want to read, but what Ju-Ju wrote made a question in my mind."

"What's that?"

"If our history books lie about Columbus and kids are taught he's so great and did all these great things, what else do we need to learn about? What about here? What kind of stuff happened here when outsiders came to the Delta? I don't even know, man."

The class responded to Jack's comments with nods and a general raising of their eyebrows.

He took another long sip of the lukewarm coffee, just to let the question linger for a moment. He'd hoped the Zinn piece would stir their minds, but he didn't expect them to turn the question upon their own history of contact.

"Well, what do you know?" he asked them. "What do you know about your own history?"

They stared back at him for only a second or two and then began to lower their eyes.

"Do you mean our culture?" Sharon asked.

"Yes and no. I mean, what have you guys learned about your own history? How long have your people been here on the tundra? What was life like before gus-sucks and when they arrived? What happened when they came, or since then?"

They shrugged.

"Why you care about this stuff?" Jack asked. "This just a trick to get us to like school?"

"Good question, Jack. That's critical thinking, my man. Question everything. Even question why someone like me is trying to teach you something. The truth? Well, I want to learn about this stuff too," John said.

"Why do you care?" Alex asked.

"I guess because my grandmother was Alaska Native," John said.

"Cool," Sharon said, and her classmates nodded approval. "Was she Yup'ik?"

John shrugged. "I don't know. My grandfather never told me," he said. "Pretty sad, eh?"

Alex removed his baseball cap and set it on the edge of his desk. "I guess no one ever taught us that stuff about our ancestors neither, John," Alex said. "That's what's pretty sad. It's like they don't want us to know the history of our own people."

JOHN AND THE GIRL awoke to a light rain. The temperature felt as though it had risen twenty degrees overnight. The sky had lightened, but he worried the rain would continue and the ice would weaken and they would be unable to travel any farther. He started a small fire with some driftwood and stretched his back. The warm air felt good, but odd, almost springlike. The air didn't sting at his nose and his bare hands weren't aching from constantly being cold.

The girl pulled back her sleeping bag and let a few drops of rain drip into her mouth from a hole in the tarp.

"A warm-up," she said. "Chinook. That's an Indian word, I think. I don't know our word for it. I don't know if we have a word for this kind of warm in winter."

"I hope it doesn't last. We'll be in trouble."

"Could last forever," she said.

"What do you mean?"

The day before they had come across a fox with a fresh snowshoe hare kill, and he'd shot a round from his pistol in the air and scared the fox off. The girl called it the raven's gift. She said that was the luck the raven gave them. He cut a small piece of the half-frozen meat from a back leg and roasted it over the fire. As the meat cooked, he wondered if it was the same fox he'd seen in the village.

"I heard the elders say that a long time ago it was warm here and that it could get warm again. King salmon would even spawn in winter when there was no ice," she said.

"That's impossible—the elders couldn't know of a time like that. That would be tens of thousands of years ago. There's no evidence in recorded history of a warm time like that."

"So," she said, pulling out a newly braided section of grass and sticking it in her bundle. She crawled out from her bag and pulled on her jacket. She began stuffing the sleeping bag into the backpack. "Sometimes," she said, "I think about how the rest of the world lives like the world is theirs. But when the world says that's enough and when they get sick, and things aren't working, like TV and computers, who is going to tell the story of your people? What could you tell your kids about you *kass'aq* people and how your people lived?"

He took a small bite of the charred leg. The outside was black, but the meat just below was still deep red, raw, and cold. "Who said I'm gus-suck? And who cares? I won't be having kids," he said.

"Even so, what could you tell them about how your people lived?"

"Nothing," he said. "I could tell them nothing about my people."

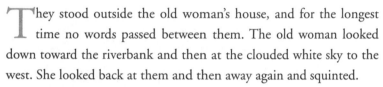

# 18

They stood outside the old woman's house, and for the longest time no words passed between them. The old woman looked down toward the riverbank and then at the clouded white sky to the west. She looked back at them and then away again and squinted.

The girl kicked the snow crust around her black boots. He could tell she didn't want to leave the old woman and that something else was bothering her.

"Another big storm coming soon," the old woman said. "The bad month is coming, too. Maybe cold weather starts tomorrow night. If you travel like I told you, then you'll be by Bethel when it storms. I don't think you should go in that town. I told you that. I think the hunter came from that ways. He'll be going back. Watch for him. Maybe wait for night and see if there's any lights. Even before all this dying, on clear nights we could see the lights from Bethel and other villages in the sky. Not any more. The sky is always dark at night over that way now."

She pointed toward the northeastern sky, and then said, "But if I seen lights in Bethel now, I think I would be scared."

"Where are my cousins?" the girl asked, and then repeated something in Yup'ik in the same tone.

The old woman shrugged. "I don't know," she said. "If they are *qimagalri*, then they are out there somewhere. You know more than me about where they can hide. Maybe by the mountains, but I'm just an old woman."

"Come with us," said the girl. "We need you to find them. We need to protect them from the hunter. If he finds out they are alive, he will kill them all."

"There's nothing for me up that river," the old woman said. "Now go, I want to get back to my fire."

The old woman turned and slowly hefted herself up the wooden steps. She stopped at the top and turned back to them. "Trust her eyes," she told him. "She sees more than me and you ever will."

JOHN POPPED HIS HEAD into her classroom and watched as Anna helped one young girl pull her rubber boots on. The other students had already left for the day. She'd told him about this girl a few days ago. Something was happening at home, and every day the chubby little second-grader was reluctant to leave the classroom. Anna lifted up the girl and sat her on her desk. Tears streamed down the girl's cheeks.

"Why don't you want to go home?" Anna asked.

The girl tucked her chin down into her thin pink jacket, avoiding all eye contact with her teacher.

"It's okay," Anna said, "you can tell me."

The girl whispered something, but John couldn't hear her.

"Who is drinking at your house?" Anna asked. "Is there somewhere else you can go? Maybe I can walk you to your grandma's house? Okay?"

The girl looked up and spotted John. Her face flushed and she lunged toward Anna and buried her face in Anna's arms.

Anna held the girl and told him to get home, school was over for the day and he had work to do.

"What work?" he asked.

"You need to put some food on our table. Go home and get your rain gear on. You're going hunting with Carl. I'm going to go for a little walk with Nina here."

He started down the hall toward his room. She'd concocted some sort of plan, and just the thought of getting out was enough for him to forget their little squabble earlier that morning about whether they should spend the fifteen hundred bucks it would cost to leave during the holiday break, still three months away.

He pulled his jacket on and kicked off his loafers and began pulling on his green rubber boots, then returned to her classroom. She stood in the doorway, holding the little girl's hand.

"My guns aren't even here yet. Plus, I don't have a shotgun."

"You're going with Carl. He said you could use his gun until yours get here."

"What are we going hunting for?"

"Birds, he said. I told him you'd meet him down at his boat around four."

As he passed her in the hallway he stopped and kissed her. He patted the little girl on the head. "I'm sorry for today," he said. "I just ... cabin fever, like you said."

"You just need some fresh air."

He kissed her again. "Thanks, thanks for always saving me," he whispered into her ear. "Isn't she the best teacher in the world?" he asked. Nina looked up at him and smiled. She nodded and wrapped her arms around Anna's leg.

"No swans," she said. "I don't think I can eat swan just yet."

THE MORNING AFTER John spotted the fox with the hare hanging from its mouth, he cooked a single leg over a small driftwood fire. They had made camp in the willows along the river and he thought they should stay and rest for a day before moving on. He wanted to think the broth from the night before had given him a little boost of energy, because when he woke up, he felt stronger. One more night of rest and a little more protein and he felt they could push on and reach the next village.

The girl walked down to the riverbank and returned with an armload of driftwood. For a blind girl, she had an ability to walk over uneven terrain that impressed him. Initially he didn't think she would make it very far with him, but she was slowly proving herself.

"That smells so yummy," she said.

"It's almost ready."

"Upriver, I don't know how far, we might see some moose or caribou. You could shoot one and we would have more than we could eat. We could follow the herd and have enough food forever. We would never go hungry again. That's if you're a good enough shot." She paused and then added, "I jokes."

She dropped the wood near the fire and warmed her hands.

"If it gets really cold," she said, "we're going to need a shelter, not just this tarp. You know, if your feet get cold you can put grass in your boots like I got. You need some?"

He shook his head. "Do you think it's going to get colder? This is cold enough," he said.

"I don't know when, but it will get cold. Real cold."

"I'll figure something out when it does," he said.

"I know."

He took a bite of the hare leg, and then took his knife and cut off half for her. The dark red meat, charred black on the outside and deep red on the inside, tasted wild and rich. His body screamed to him to cook up the rest and devour it all.

She ate silently, and when she finished he asked if she wanted the leg bone. She did. He watched as she chewed the end off with her teeth and then sucked at the marrow. She turned the bone around, bit through the other end, and handed it to back him.

"Here," she said, "this will give you more energy."

He took the bone and followed her example. The marrow tasted like he'd bitten his own tongue, bloody and raw.

"Do you think the rest of the world is having to do this?"

"Eating hare?" he said, trying to joke, not wanting to contemplate a real answer.

"I mean survive like us. What's the rest of the world doing right now? Don't you wonder that? Are they starving too, or are we the only ones who've been forgotten?"

He handed the bone back to her and placed a few more sticks on the fire. He didn't have an answer for her. He rarely did. Instead, he just let the silence hang over them like the smoke that rose from the embers and drifted through the willows along the riverbank like a parade of spirits.

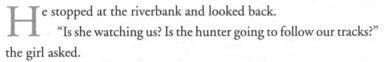

# 19

He stopped at the riverbank and looked back.

"Is she watching us? Is the hunter going to follow our tracks?" the girl asked.

"I don't know," he said.

And he didn't. Instead, his thoughts were on the school, the food in the school, and the missing kids. The sled was loaded with all he could pull. Any more would be wasting his energy. The two of them had food now and that was all that mattered. That and moving on up the river. They had already stayed too long. The cold was coming. He could feel it in the wind. He wondered if he shouldn't go back and burn it before someone else, the hunter, discovered the gym full of bodies and put the pieces together.

He slung the rifle over his shoulder and pulled the rope tight around his waist. He'd retrieved the ice pick from the school, and one quick glance inside the gym confirmed it—there were only a handful of kids. Four or five. There should have been at least thirty or forty. He hoped they had escaped the sickness, the outcasts, and the hunter, if there really was such a person. Ski tracks and an old woman's ramblings were all he had to go on. He couldn't let a mystery man continue to haunt him.

He tapped the point of the pick into a frozen chunk of dirt at the top of the riverbank.

"Let's get moving," he said.

"Will you talk while we're travelling today? I just want to listen to you talk. Talk about anything," she said.

"We've got a ways to go today. Shouldn't be wasting time talking about nothing. She said we've got about ten miles to Bethel."

"Why we going to the town? Will we look for them there?"

"I want to see it. Maybe at night, from a distance, like she suggested. And no more talk about the kids. What makes you think they are alive any more than the kids in the other villages?"

"Because she knows something," she said, pointing back toward the old woman's house. "I think she knows. She keeps saying they might be *qimakalleq*, I think that means runaway and becoming wild or something. She knows they are alive, too. I don't know why you don't open your goddamn eyes. She knows."

They dropped down the riverbank slowly until they got to the ice. He let the sled slide down in front of him, holding on to it to keep it from flipping over. Once they reached the river ice, he slammed the pick down. The steel bar gave a dull thunk, and a grapefruit-sized chunk of ice erupted from the surface. The ice was much thicker than when they had arrived. Not four or five feet thick, as it would get in a couple of months, but at least safer for them to walk on, half a foot thick, maybe more.

He led the way, pulling the sled with their supplies and food.

"I'm sorry I was mad. Will you tell me about where you came from today? I want to know about how you grew up. Please. Just talk today. Talk for me. Will you?"

He widened his stride and set a course down the edge of the river toward a large bend where he planned to cross to the other side to get out of the icy breeze, which was beginning to pick up, drying his eyes and nipping the end of his nose.

Off to the west, across the tundra, he could see the wind lifting ghostly wisps of snow. He didn't want to be walking with a gale cutting through them all day. It would be best to walk beneath the riverbank so that the cold wind would sail right over the top of them for at least a few miles until the river made another oxbow and headed straight into the line of fire.

"I just need something else to think of, that's all. Something other than my jerk uncle back there. Other than the scary man on skis. Other than my cousins, who I know need me. That's why. Please?"

The girl picked up her pace and trotted to be at his side. The river in front of them spread out flat and smooth, and the girl walked with confidence, as if she knew this, as if she could see out in front of them, the broad expanse of nothing spreading before them into the horizon in a fine white line.

"If you don't talk, I'm going to think about him. I'm going to think about what he did to me before I burned him, and I'm going to keep wondering if I should have pushed harder. Crushed his throat until he was dead like the others, dead like he should be. And I would be no better than him. That's all. And I'm going to think about the hunter and how he's going to come after us when he finds our trail. And then he's going to go after the kids and then there will be no Yup'ik people left in the world."

They walked for a while in silence.

"You could tell me about when you were little and I could just listen. I don't want to keep thinking what my uncle could still do to some other little girl he finds, or what the hunter could do to the old woman back there all by herself."

He adjusted the rifle strap digging into his shoulder and stopped to check the sled. He remembered the pack of cinnamon gum he'd found in the school office and tried not to think of the haunting note sitting on the desk as he opened a piece, took a small bite, and gave her the rest. The wind burned his fingers and he quickly stuffed them back into his gloves. He thought of the chocolate chips at the school and regretted not taking them. His childhood and his grandfather's wild stories about Alaska seemed so distant it couldn't even matter. He thought of the chocolate chips again.

"I used to stack firewood all around the porch of my grandpa's house. He'd pay me in candy or gum," he said.

"Tell me what his house was like," she said.

"It was a log house in the woods. Small, one room and a loft, with a woodstove for heating and cooking. I slept in the loft when I stayed with him, and he would keep the fire going constantly. It would get so hot up there in the loft I'd sweat right through the old wool blankets and down sleeping bag. He always had a big cast-iron Dutch oven sitting on the top with a chunk of deer or elk roasting with some onions and potatoes. He'd cook it until the meat just fell off the bone. That meat would cook until it was so tender and juicy. And he would sit by the stove on a thick larch stump and hum old country songs and sharpen his hunting knife and tell me that he never should have left the north. Then he'd get up and dig in his ratty old leather hunting pack and pull out a Hershey bar and tell me to go split and stack more wood if I wanted the chocolate."

"You're making me hungry," she said. "Please, tell me more. Did he tell you stories?"

"Not really, but he used to joke, 'I'll trade you back to the Eskimos for an old Winchester rifle and some chocolate,'" he said, and as he said it, he could hear his grandfather's raspy old voice, but it felt like some past life he'd only imagined.

"YOU CAN USE that 20-gauge," Carl said, pointing to the shotgun leaning against the bow of the skiff. "You ride up front and shoot."

The tide had dropped the river several feet, leaving the bow high and dry. The two of them pushed the aluminum boat down into the water. He glanced at the baseball cap, light jacket, and jeans his new hunting companion wore and wondered if he wasn't overdressed with his camouflage Gore-Tex rain pants, rain parka, hat and gloves.

"Your wife said you were going crazy being stuck in the village. She told me you liked to hunt. Surprised me that you never went hunting with me yet," Carl said.

Carl climbed over the edge of the bow, past the two bench seats, and leaned over the motor. He flipped the latch and the prop dropped into the water. He squeezed the black rubber ball on the hose and primed the fuel line.

John stood by the bow, still not in the boat, waiting for Carl to start the motor. "Didn't know how hunting worked around here," he said. "I didn't want to impose."

Carl chuckled. "You don't impose. You just go hunting," he said.

Carl gave a quick pull and the motor sputtered. He pulled the small choke out, pushed it in, and gave John a nod. John pushed the boat out and jumped in. He grabbed the shotgun and sat on the second bench. He faced the bow and rested the weapon across his legs. The weight of the gun felt good there. Carl eased the boat forward into the current. He tapped John's shoulder and pointed to a box of shotgun shells lying in a plastic grocery sack behind his seat.

John opened the box and took out a handful of shells. He stuffed them into the oversized pocket of his rain jacket, broke the barrel, and slid one shell into the chamber. The single-shot gun had the look of a relic. The long barrel was rusted, the bluing of the metal long gone, the trigger guard cracked. The sight on the end was simply a small shiny silver bump. He snapped the gun back and rested it again on his lap.

The boat picked up speed, raising the bow up out of the water until they were on step and speeding along the edge of the steep cut of the riverbank.

"See the high bank here?" Carl hollered over the motor. "This is where the deep water is. Shallow over on that side. If you're ever going to travel here, you'll have to learn how we navigate the water."

John nodded and asked, "How can you ever know where you're going with all these lakes and rivers everywhere?"

THE RAVEN'S GIFT 141

"I guess you learn or get lost and die," he said with a grin as he turned the tiller and cut the boat sharply across to the other side of the river. "There's a big sandbar right there," he said. "It goes all the way down there. You have to cross here. If you hit the sand right under the water, you're stuck, big time. You know which direction we're headed?"

John shook his head. "No idea! Just going around that big bend has me all turned around, these rivers are so twisted."

Carl pointed behind them. "That way, straight across the tundra, is Bethel. That way, down this river, you can get to the Kuskokwim River. This way, if you went far enough, you could get to the Yukon."

"You can get to the Yukon River from here?"

Carl raised his eyebrows. He had two white splotches, one on his cheek and another on his neck. They didn't look like scars or burns, more like skin with no pigment.

"It's a long ways, across some big lakes and a few beaver dams, but you can make it," he said. "It's not on any maps, but we go that way for moose hunting. Probably not this year because gas is too much."

"How bad is it?"

"Eight fifty something."

"A gallon?"

Carl raised his eyebrows. "Makes hunting almost too much. Any more expensive and we're going to be in real trouble." He let off the throttle. "Get ready," he said and he pointed to the horizon.

He cut the motor and whispered, "Maybe you're good luck, John. Cranes."

A giant black checkmark circled high in the air above them. The flock of slender, dark birds dropped toward them like thin black crosses and then turned again and descended out of sight several hundred yards away.

"They're on the river around the next bend," Carl said, starting the motor. "We'll go fast around the corner and you can shoot. Get ready."

"Are they legal? Cranes?"

"Only thing Fish and Game and the scientist guys care about lately is blood samples to check for bird flu. We shoot what we need to eat. Tonight, hopefully, it's crane."

He gunned the boat forward and John slipped his hand into his pocket and took out two shells and held them in his left hand between his index and middle finger like two cigars so that he could get off a couple of quick shots and impress his new hunting partner. He tried not to think of what Anna would say about shooting cranes. You might as well have shot an albatross, he imagined her saying in disgust.

JOHN AND THE GIRL ate the last of the hare, and he'd kept the bones, just in case they would need to break them open and boil them for the marrow. They tucked the tarp in a grove of willows so that the fire couldn't be seen from the river. All he wanted to do was curl up in his sleeping bag beside the fire and sleep. That night, for some reason, he wanted to sleep almost worse than he wanted something of substance to eat. Just a night with solid, restful sleep. No nightmares. No waking up and straining his ears for approaching footsteps.

The girl crawled into her sleeping bag between his bag and the fire. He knew she somehow felt safer there. Safe between the warmth of the fire and his gun. She set the bundle of grass beside her. Touched it once, and then put her hands inside her bag to warm.

"Why do you think I lived?" she asked.

He thought for a while, even though he had no answer. Her survival made little sense. He didn't want to tell her that she wouldn't have survived much longer if he hadn't found her, but he didn't know that either. The girl was tough enough to do whatever she put her mind to. She'd already proved as much. But why had she lived? Why had either of them lived?

"What are you weaving?" he asked.

She ignored him and asked her question again.

He couldn't find the words to answer. He almost wanted to ask her if she thought this was really living, if they really had survived, but he didn't.

"Why do you think you survived?" he asked.

"Sometimes," she said, "I think I'm just here to help you get to where you think you need to go. Maybe even I wish that's why I'm here. When we're walking and not talking I think about what's left in my life and it's just all empty. I feel empty, you know? Hollow like a drum. My heart's a drum, a tundra drum that pounds and there's no one to listen, no one to dance. I have no one. Nothing. I can't even see all that I've lost. I've lost everything. My family. All my cousins. The village. If I'm here to help you get somewhere, then there's at least a reason for this."

"I hope there's a better reason for you being here than to just help me. I doubt that's reason enough," he said.

"I do help you, don't I? I'm not totally useless to you, am I?" she asked.

He pulled his arm out from his sleeping bag and ran his hand down the back of her head. Her face was turned away from him, but he knew she was crying from the way she held her breath to hide her sobs.

"I don't think I would have been brave enough to leave, if I hadn't found you."

He was nearly asleep when she asked him one last question that left him searching his memory until she was fast asleep.

"Was I pretty when you saw me before? John, do you remember ever seeing me before, at Christmas, the Slaviq starring celebration at Carl's house?"

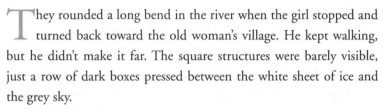

# 20

They rounded a long bend in the river when the girl stopped and turned back toward the old woman's village. He kept walking, but he didn't make it far. The square structures were barely visible, just a row of dark boxes pressed between the white sheet of ice and the grey sky.

"What is it you're trying to see? Quit worrying about someone who we don't even know is out there."

"It's not too late to go back," she said.

"We're not taking her with us."

"We'll need her. She knows things we don't know."

He nodded, but said nothing.

He started walking again, but when he didn't hear her footsteps behind him he glanced back over his shoulder and stopped. She had already started in the other direction, and somehow she was heading straight for the village, and at a pretty fast pace. The thought of leaving her, them, made sense enough. There was plenty of food in the school. Maybe even enough for them to make the spring. Without the girl he could travel quickly and efficiently.

She didn't falter in her progress. He had no doubt she could make it back to the village on her own. She didn't need him. Or at least that was what her display of independence told him—but he knew better. An old woman and a blind girl were not going to improve his chances, and their odds of making it weren't that great either. Travelling alone would afford one other luxury. He wouldn't be responsible for anyone any longer, and he wouldn't have to deal with the girl constantly hounding him to go find her cousins.

He thought about calling out to her, to give her one last chance, but decided against it. She was far enough away. She wouldn't hear him if he tried. He spun back around, pulled the rope tight, and continued on, his back to the village and the blind girl.

He bit at his lower lip as he marched on through the snow. Using his left mitten he brushed the freezing tears from the corners of his eyes and tried to convince himself he would be better off without the girl, and that the tears were from the cold winds and not her decision. He pushed the memories of first finding her and her voice from his thoughts and tried to replace it all with images of Anna, of his students, of anything but her. Then the ice pick caught a hard ridge of snow and he suddenly remembered the heavy steel there in his right hand.

One glance at the pick was enough. In his mind he saw the girl swinging it, smashing into the man in the gym and then nearly crushing his throat. She still had fight in her, and despite everything, she would continue to fight. Her uncle was still there hiding in the village somewhere. Maybe he watched them leave. He might even be watching her return.

And then there was the old woman's hunter. If he was a hunter, he would find the old woman and the girl, and then, if they were still alive as the girl insisted, he would find the children.

John made a small arc to avoid having to jerk the sled around and started back toward the village. His strides were long and brisk, the wind at his back. He could catch her before she reached the riverbank.

HE SAT ON THE cold green linoleum floor of their house, clicking away at the keyboard of a school laptop. He was commenting on Alex's online journal. The kid had zero understanding of grammar or writing conventions, but his writing had a unique voice. The kid's bitterness cloaked a sense of despair and hopelessness.

"Listen to this," he said, reading to Anna. She stood at the stove heating oil for their nightly popcorn snack. "'Most nights I sleep on a foam pad, if I'm lucky enough to sleep. The TV stays on all day and all night. There is always someone watching movies or shows. I'll put the pad down, on our plywood floor, somewhere I can still see the screen. I don't see little houses like mine on those shows, and I never once seen someone sleeping on foam mats in houses with no water, only one or two bedrooms. Thirteen maybe fourteen people. Babies crying. My sister and her boyfriend humping, like no one knows what they are doing under those blankets. I don't never see real life like that on the TV. That world is supposed to be the real world. I hear teachers say that. "Back in the real world," they say. I've never seen their real world, just TV. I probably never will live to see it. Don't really want to. I don't think I would fit in there, it would be like trying to find space to sleep for me here, me and my sleeping pad and nowhere quiet. It's funny that the outsiders who come here call that the real world, and they don't even know what Yup'ik really means.'"

"What does Yup'ik mean?"

John shrugged. "Guess he's right."

"Is that Alex again?" she asked. "Man, that kid. You wish you could … I don't know, help him out somehow. You're probably the first teacher ever to give him a chance. Think what he could do."

"Think what any of them could do," he said, closing the laptop and stretching out on the floor. At the floor level he could almost feel the wind from outside, cutting straight through the walls. The cold air felt refreshing against his face, the back of his head pressed against the cool floor, his eyes on the square tiles of the ceiling. "They have had shitty teachers and zero challenge from day one. How can anyone expect them to even feel good about themselves, let alone maybe go to college or a tech school?"

The corn started to pop. She shook the kettle.

"Maybe that's the point. For the culture to survive, they'll have to stay here. Education at once seems like the answer and the problem. Go to school and lose your way of life, or don't and live your way of life. If they go away to college, what's going to bring them back? There aren't jobs. There's no economy."

"They could teach, for one. There has to be some sort of sustainable economy that could be created here. There's always telecommuting. Anyone can work from anywhere. Even here. Plus, I'm not buying the culture thing because three-quarters of my students tell me that all they do is go to open gym, watch movies, play video games, and hang out. Only a couple of them hunt. The girls help with raising the little ones, but that's it. That's why I hope I can keep them fired up about this project stuff. I just hope it doesn't get me into trouble with the district office."

She turned off the burner, slipped on the oven mitt, and dumped the popcorn into a large stainless steel mixing bowl. "I hardly think the district is going to care if you're inspiring your students to study their own cultural history."

"Well, I'm not exactly getting them ready for the standardized tests," he said.

She held a piece of popcorn above him. "I don't mean to change the subject," she said. He opened his mouth and stuck out his tongue. "But ..."

"But what," he asked, opening wide.

"I'm out of birth control," she said, dropping a large white kernel into his mouth.

HE NUDGED THE GIRL from her sleep and stretched his legs and looked down at them. His black snow pants looked more like a rodeo clown outfit; his legs, butt, and midsection had lost so much muscle mass that the pants felt and looked ridiculously huge. The whole scenario felt off that morning.

"Can I sleep a little longer?" she asked.

"Yeah. A little. I want to get moving soon."

"I can get up now."

"Sleep. I'll wake you."

He stood and walked a few yards and relieved himself. The light rain the night before had crusted the very top layer of snow. Walking in the crunchy surface would take extra energy.

He watched the horizon for any signs of movement. Life seemed to be in short supply lately.

By the end of the day he hoped to be on the main river, and that the ice of the Kuskokwim would be sound for travel. They couldn't walk across the lumpy tundra in the snow, or fight the tangled willows and alders that clogged the banks.

There were a couple of villages between them and Bethel. They would find food or survivors at one of those three, he wanted to hope, but on this morning, the hope just wasn't there.

"John," the girl whispered, just loud enough for him to hear her. He saw her sitting up in her sleeping bag, the blue tarp covering most of her. He followed her finger and saw what she was pointing at.

He crouched and slowly crept to her as she felt around beneath the tarp and came up with the rifle.

"Thanks," he whispered. "Cover your ears."

He quietly put a round in the chamber and crept forward. His breathing picked up, and he tried to steady himself and the barrel to get a clean shot. He wished he had kept the girl's rusty .22. With his gun, such a big calibre, he had only one chance.

The ptarmigan clucked and pecked at the black lumps of tundra protruding through the snow. There were half a dozen of the bright white birds, but that did nothing for his odds. One shot and they would be gone. He knelt with one knee in the snow and the other up as a rest for the rifle. He first placed the red bead of the sight on the head of the lead bird. Its wide, round black eyes on the white head seemed like the perfect target. Then he hesitated and lowered his aim toward the midsection and waited for the right moment.

A head shot, to preserve as much meat as possible, was risky, and missing meant no food. A solid body shot meant fresh meat, gunshot or not. He held steady. Then he thought about the trajectory of the bullet, and how he might wait until the birds lined up, and then shoot.

He waited. At one point he had two, then three, almost in a line. He paused for a fourth. He rested his finger against the icy metal of the trigger, waiting. Waiting.

Just as he started to squeeze a round off, the lead bird lifted its head, and they started running, their little legs scurrying, their heads leaning forward. He followed them with the gunsight. They picked up speed and lifted off into the air before he could get a shot.

"No! No!" he screamed at the birds as they set their wings and glided to safety several hundred yards away. An impossible distance with no cover or chance to sneak up on them.

He slumped to the ground, clutching the rifle to his chest.

"I'm sorry," he whispered to the girl, remembering something she once told him about thoughts and the animals you hunted being able to hear those thoughts. "I'm sorry," he said again, and the weight of his mistake began to press him into the frozen moss and snow beneath.

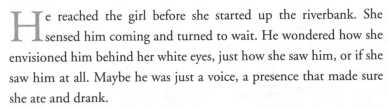

# 21

He reached the girl before she started up the riverbank. She sensed him coming and turned to wait. He wondered how she envisioned him behind her white eyes, just how she saw him, or if she saw him at all. Maybe he was just a voice, a presence that made sure she ate and drank.

"I knew you'd bring my grass back to me," she said.

"I just came back for more canned peaches," he said.

"You lie!"

"Wait here," he said, climbing up the bank as he pulled his rifle off his shoulder. The strange sense of déjà vu grew as he peeked the rifle over the edge of the bank and scanned the village for movement. A black rubber boot stepped on the end of his barrel.

He pulled back on the stock and swung the barrel skyward, just as the old woman's laugh cracked the cold silence.

"How you live this long being so dumb?" she asked.

He took a breath and tried to ease his pounding heart.

"Jesus, woman. I could have shot you."

"I would have shot you first," she said, and she lifted into the air an old 20-gauge pockmarked with rust, the cracked and weathered wood stock wrapped in black electrician's tape.

"This was my husband's. Got a half box of shells left, too."

She pointed to a blue-grey plastic fifty-gallon garbage can lid, upside down, with a blanket tied to it. A rope extended to her waist.

"I got the foods you gave me in here, most of it, my knife, and a caribou hide."

He helped her down the bank to the river ice and the girl. They hugged, as if they hadn't seen each other in years. The old woman put her bare hands on the girl's face.

"You knew we would come back for you?" the girl asked.

"No. But when you left I thought I could hear their voices."

"Scary," the girl said.

"Not those ones in there," the old woman said, pointing first to the school and then up the river. "The kids."

CARL, THE SCHOOL'S CUSTODIAN and maintenance man, quickly became his new best friend in the village. They would have coffee in the morning, while the kids shuffled into the gym half-awake to stand in line for plastic bowls of government-issue cereal or thin, dry pancakes or instant scrambled eggs. The two of them would eat together at lunch most days, sitting with the students on the folding cafeteria tables in the gym, and then have another cup of coffee afterwards, watching the students clean up and put the tables away before the kids began their pickup basketball games until the next class started. They would talk about hunting, fishing, and the classic days of professional basketball with Larry Bird and Doctor J.

After school, he would hurry to their house, grab his rain gear, and do his best not to run down the boardwalk to the house Carl lived in with a wife, six kids, mother, and grandmother. Once at the house he would climb the steps and take a deep breath before going through the arctic entry, where Carl had an old white drop-in freezer on one side loaded with birds and frozen fish, and coats and boots and other outdoor gear hung on the opposite side.

In the middle, in the path that led to the next door, which opened into the main living area of the small three-bedroom house, were various obstacles to avoid—all of them foul smelling. A full honey bucket might be waiting to be dumped, or a pile of geese ready to be plucked, or a black garbage sack bulging with fish or bird guts. Always something new, and always something odorous awaited his arrival.

Once inside, he would exhale quietly and say his hellos to the usual crowd of people gathered around the television. Carl or his wife would say, "*Kuuvviara.* Have coffee." And he would. He would pour himself a cup of lukewarm coffee from the pot sitting on the stove, and then pull out a metal folding chair and wait to see if Carl felt like hunting.

While he waited his eyes would roam the items covering the wood-panelled walls, the paper elementary school certificates and awards, the gold-framed paintings of the Virgin Mary, Russian saints, and several pro basketball posters. Most of the time he would watch Carl's wife, Carrie, or his mother prepare the evening meal. Usually, one of the women would sit on the floor, *uluaq* in hand, cutting a bird or a fish. Once, it was a beaver Carl had shot the night before.

The last evening they took the boat out together, Carl stood in the kitchen, gazing out the window that faced the river. He slid a hand beneath his shirt, a thin white cotton tee with STOP PEBBLE written in large red letters. "Probably not much reason to go out tonight," he said, "but if you want to, we can."

He turned and smiled at John.

"I wouldn't mind."

"Me neither," Carl said. "River could freeze up any time. Maybe when we get back you could help me pull the motor on the boat. Get it ready for winter."

"No problem. That's the least I can do."

Carrie looked up from the stainless mixing bowl in her lap, while her hand continued stirring the mixture of lard, sugar, and berries. "I'm making your favourite kind, John. Salmonberry *akutaq*," she said. "Carl, we're almost out of water, too. You'll have to haul some when you get back. Have John help you if he wants my famous Eskimo ice cream."

"Yours is the best a-goo-tuck I've had," John said, attempting to say the word as well as he could. He looked at the plastic garbage barrel that they used for their drinking water, a green can sitting beside the stove with a round plywood cover. "Do you think you'll ever get running water in the houses?" he asked.

Carl finished his coffee and set the mug in the sink, a traditional white sink, except there was no faucet, just three holes where the fixture should have been. "Not in my lifetime," he said. "If we had oil wells here, or if there were more *kass'aqs*, maybe then. Some company is putting a gold mine up the Kuskokwim. Maybe if they take a couple billion dollars of gold out they will think about helping us get running water, but I doubt it. No one in the Lower Forty-eights cares that we shit in buckets and have to haul our water. Nobody cares if they deploy three-quarters of our best men and women to the desert. No one cares if our kids have tuberculosis. Sorry, enough complaining. You ready to go?"

John nodded. He finished his coffee and put the cup in the sink. "Thank you," he said to Carrie. She smiled and raised her eyebrows.

"We say *quyana*," she said.

"I know. I'm working on learning some words," he replied.

As they packed their rain gear and guns in the boat, John asked about the mine. He hadn't heard about any gold mines nearby.

"It's not that close," Carl said. "Maybe two hundred miles up the Kuskokwim from here. Lots of old mines in the Kilbuck Mountains. There's the old Nyac ghost town, a mine where the school district used to have a summer camp. Real nice up there. The kids love it. Maybe if they ever have it again, you and me can work there. There's some active gold mines around there, too, but they're pretty small. Mostly old family operations. This Donlin mine is going to be way bigger. They say it could really cause some problems for our fishing on the Kuskokwim."

"Mining isn't known for ever saving any fish," John said.

"People round here need work so bad, though. I don't see anyone stopping that mine. Climate change is killing all our salmon. Commercial fishing is all but dead here on the Kuskokwim. Not doing well on the Yukon either. Not like Bristol Bay. They still got good fishing there. Now the Pebble mine could be a fight. Fishermen and environmentalists and Natives and politicians and a giant mining company. Might get dirty."

"What's going on in Bristol Bay?" John asked.

"You never heard of Pebble?"

John shook his head.

"Just a little pebble. They say it's going to be one of the largest open-pit mines in the world. Five hundred billion dollars' worth of gold at the headwaters of the world's last great wild salmon run. How do you like that? Five hundred billion, with a *b*. How can people like us, with nothing, have a voice against money like that?"

They stopped on the boardwalk, just above Carl's boat. The tide was down again and they would have to climb down the bank and push the boat several feet to get it floating.

"Five hundred billion? You sure?"

Carl raised his brows again and said, "Those Natives there over the ridge, I think some people will help them try to fight the mine, but only because of the salmon industry. Not here, not on the Y-K river deltas, man. Who cares much about what happens around here, to us? They never did. Never will. We're the invisible people. But sometimes, maybe I think that's okay, you know. Real people can't live off oil and gold forever. Yup'iks used to know how to live without these things. Maybe if all of this goes to shit, maybe some of us could still survive like we used to."

John stepped aside as a young boy raced past them on a bike, a yellow five-gallon bucket in one hand. A group of sled dogs stood up from the dirt mounds they were staked to and started yelping and howling. The sound echoed across the village. Feeding time.

JOHN AND THE GIRL had been trudging through the knee-deep powder for hours. He stopped and looked back and thought he could still see their camp from the night before, a small bank of snow just at the bare horizon like a miniature white haystack. He doubted they had travelled over a mile, and sunset was just another hour away.

"Did my story about the Big Mouth Baby scare you last night?" she asked.

"You didn't really tell me any story. Just said some baby with a big mouth was out there, and no. It didn't scare me," he said as he gave the sled a sharp tug to get it moving again.

"I thought maybe what I said gave you bad dreams, because last night you asked me if the baby was coming. Do you remember that?"

He stopped walking and turned to her. "No. I don't. And let's quit wasting our breath talking for a while, okay? Can you do that? I don't want to hear about some toddler with wolf teeth or about the outcasts or what your grandpa taught you about living off the land. Okay? We haven't made it anywhere today. Nowhere, you get it? We won't survive if we can't make it more than a mile or two a day. At this rate it would take us ten years to get anywhere."

"It's not a toddler, it's a baby," she said.

He yanked hard on the sled, but as if in response to his anger, it didn't budge. He groaned and pulled again and started forward. He glanced back over his shoulder and she was still standing where they had stopped.

"Come on!" he yelled. He didn't want to stop again. The sled was moving and for the time being he had forward momentum. If they could just make it another half mile or so before dark.

He looked back again and she was gone.

He stopped and turned, and then felt a tap on his shoulder. He spun around, half expecting to see someone holding her, a shiny blade to her throat, or a pistol to her head.

"Why are you stopping again?" she asked.

He swallowed and licked at his cracked lips. "I wanted to make sure no one was following us," he said. "Help me pull this. I'm tired of pulling."

He helped her take hold of the rope and together they began towing the toboggan. The girl was strangely quiet for too long, and after a while he began to feel guilty. He was about to say he was sorry when she said, "My grandpa first told me about the Big Mouth Baby when I was just a little girl, and maybe tonight, if you're not so crabby, I'll tell you the story."

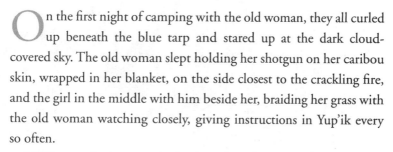

## 22

On the first night of camping with the old woman, they all curled up beneath the blue tarp and stared up at the dark cloud-covered sky. The old woman slept holding her shotgun on her caribou skin, wrapped in her blanket, on the side closest to the crackling fire, and the girl in the middle with him beside her, braiding her grass with the old woman watching closely, giving instructions in Yup'ik every so often.

"Will you tell us a story, in *kass'atun*, so John can understand?" the girl asked.

"It's fine. I don't need a bedtime story," he said.

For a long while the old woman said nothing. Then she clicked her tongue, sighed, and began a story. "*Ak'a tamaani*, a long time ago, there was a shaman called Big Belly."

"Big Belly—Big Mouth Baby—I'm seeing a pattern here," John joked.

"Shh," the girl whispered. "We don't interrupt stories, John."

"Sorry."

The old woman continued. "He wasn't always called Big Belly. I forgot what they call him before his belly got so giant, but he was a good shaman. He would travel under the ice and bring good luck to the hunters. The hunters wanted luck, so they cut a hole in the ice, but the shaman used his magic and could tell there was already another evil shaman travelling under the water, so he said he would wait for that shaman to go back to his village. But the men didn't listen and they forced him to go down under the ice. Just like he thought, he ran into the evil shaman flying beneath the ocean, and when one shaman met another they would use their magical powers and fight. When they encountered each other, they had a huge battle. The other shaman was evil and more powerful and he broke the good shaman's back. When the fight was over the good shaman went home, but he was swollen from the seawater and his back was broken with a giant hump like a brown bear. Using his arms, he pulled himself into the village. He asked one of the strong young men to hit him in the back with a club. The young man clubbed him four times until his back was straightened. His back was fixed but he started to *miryaq*, throw up, salt water all over the man's house. Everything smelled like the ocean. Even though he was real sick, and vomited all that water, his belly stayed big and bloated like a frog stomach until he died. He never went under the ice again, and from then on they called him Big Belly."

"Cool. I've only ever heard scary stories about shaman," the girl said.

"Shamans were important back then. We had good shamans and bad shamans. The shamans were our priests, our doctors, our counsellors. The people would go to them when they were sick, if they wanted a baby, or if they needed luck hunting. This was before we knew about hospitals and Jesus and heaven. Back then those shamans could travel to places and talk to animals, giants, and even the little people. Bad shamans would put spells on enemy villages and make people sick or crazy, but good shamans could heal the sick and change the weather and bring animals during times of starvation. Back in those days of the shaman, Yup'iks could become animals and animals could become Yup'iks. There was just a thin skin, like the surface of the water or young river ice, that separated the worlds."

"Maybe the hunter is a bad shaman," the girl said.

The old woman sighed. "I don't think he got any powers," she said.

"Did you ever see a shaman?" the girl asked.

"No. They were gone already, I think. Or they were afraid of the missionaries and didn't let people know they had the magic. My grandmother used to tell me about a shaman she knew. One of the last medicine men she saw. He had only one arm and he carried a spirit wand. She said that wand had a carved ivory head with sharp teeth and eyes that were always watching you. I used to have bad dreams about that little stick with a head on it, even I never seen that shaman or his cane."

"What other kinds of magic did the shamans have?" the girl asked.

He was glad to have the old woman there to answer the girl's nightly routine of endless questions. The chatter filled the void of silence and kept him from having to think about anything other than what the old woman was talking about, even if most of what she said made little sense.

"They used bird feathers like wings and would soar up into the sky like ravens and see the world below. They could fly to the moon in times of hunger, where there were many animals, and bring one back to refill the earth. They could pull a wolf skin over their head and become a wolf. Others would go beneath the ice and go where the seal spirits were and ask them to return to feed the people. In hard times we always relied on the shaman. They even say some of them could go into the future and come back and tell about what they seen there. I heard of one shaman who told the village to burn his body and then the next day he came back cold and wet, but alive. I remember stories of one shaman who went down under the ice and when he returned he had eyes like snow, a white-eye shaman, with beautiful snow-coloured eyes like you."

"Like me?" the girl asked. "He was blind?"

"No one is blind," the old woman said.

The fire popped in the silence as the girl imagined the possibility. She turned away from him and coughed into her sleeping bag.

"If I was a shaman, what could I do?" she asked.

"Maybe if you had those kind of shaman magic the world wouldn't be this way. You could transform us all into whatever we needed to be. Maybe you turn this guy into a bird so he can fly wherever he thinks he needs to go. Me? I want you to turn me into an old bear. Always warm. Always fat," the old woman said, and laughed.

"If I had those powers I would ... I don't know what I would do," the girl said.

"Time for rest, girl," the old woman said.

The two stopped talking for several minutes. The old woman's breathing slowed and he could tell she was about to fall asleep. From the tone of their voices when they spoke, and their easy, relaxed breathing, the two were on some sort of happy campout. He was cold, but comfortable, maybe too comfortable just listening to them and not thinking about anything else.

"Were they born as shaman or did they have to learn how to use the magic?" she asked.

"*Naam,*" said the old woman, one of the few Yup'ik words he'd learned from his students, which simply meant I don't know.

"If I was a shaman, I would fly above the tundra and find my cousins," the girl said.

AN HOUR BEFORE CLASS one morning, Alex came in, sat down at a desk, removed his cap, and put his head in his hands. His long black hair fell, covering both his hands and his face.

"What's wrong, Alex?"

John moved to the desk beside the boy.

"You okay?" he asked.

The boy said nothing, and John could see his legs trembling under the desk. John sat for a while, silent, giving the boy time.

After a while John just started to talk, mostly because the silence was making him uncomfortable.

"The other night I went hunting with Carl. He was telling me about the gold mines that might be developed up the Kuskokwim River and the big one near Bristol Bay. He says those mines could really hurt the river and the culture. He doesn't think anyone will care about the effect this will have on people in the villages downstream. I was thinking that students like you could make a difference. If you wrote, like you do in your online journal, so the rest of the world could hear your voice, well, that could really make a difference. There's no voice from this part of the world. I've been impressed as hell with your work, Alex. I just wanted you to know that."

"I don't even know why I'm talking to you," the boy whispered. "Didn't sleep last night. Couldn't."

John had been waiting for a chance to talk to the boy alone, to make a serious connection, and he could feel it coming.

"My cousin in Kuigpak died," he said with almost no emotion.

The boy kept his head down, but John could see tears dripping onto the shiny grey surface of the desk. He reached a hand out and patted the boy's back.

"I'm sorry."

"He hanged himself in the *maqi*. He put on his basketball uniform and tied an anchor line around his neck inside the steam bath. My older brother lives in Kuigpak. He found him."

John got up and got some Kleenex from his desk. He set a handful on the desk. "Here," he said.

"He emailed me, two days ago. Never said shit about wanting to die. Just said I could have his old autographed Kobe Bryant poster next time I went over. I just thought he didn't like Kobe no more."

Alex wiped his face and turned to John. His eyes were bloodshot, angry.

"You know how many funerals of people who did this I been to in my life?" he asked.

John shook his head.

"Too many. One time I tried to add them all up. I stopped at thirty-two and lost count. And you know what? We'll all go there, to Kuigpak, the whole village will go. I'll miss a week of your classes, and no one will say it's wrong. Not one person will stand up at his funeral and say he shouldn't have done that. No one will say we need to stop killing ourselves here. No one will. Not one single person. And then someone else will do it. We're like the Arawak people after Columbus came to their island, man. We're killing ourselves to avoid this shit life."

"Why do you think that is?" John asked.

"It's our culture not to talk about it, they say. We don't talk about the dead. We don't say bad things about the dead. You don't say anything about them. But I don't think the Yup'ik people lived here for thousands of years by killing themselves."

"Maybe you should write about his loss, then. Write how you feel and share this burden."

Alex stood up and wadded up the tissue into a tight ball. "Write? Write about what? What good will that do? Maybe some *kass'aq* like you is going to fly in here with a new program and save us from ourselves?"

He put his cap on, flipped the desk over, and stomped toward the door.

"No," John said softly, "you'll need to save yourself first and then help save the others."

"Save this!" he said, stopping at the doorway and holding up his middle finger.

He leaned his forehead against the door jamb and took a deep breath. "Sorry, John. I'm just hurting inside, you know? I'm going to go to his funeral and then I don't know what. I need a break from all this, this place. Maybe go to Anchorage or Bethel for a while. Maybe stay in Kuigpak with my bro. Help him out. He's a wreck. Worse than my cousin was."

"You're not dropping out, are you?"

"No, I'll come back. You'll see me again. You've been a pretty cool teacher, John. I learned more from you than in my whole high school days put together. Sad thing is, what I learned is that I don't know nothing about my culture and that I can't trust yours, theirs I mean, but still, that's more than I've ever learned. I guess that's something. See you, man."

The boy gave a half-wave and disappeared down the school hallway.

"THE BIG MOUTH BABY is a monster everyone knows about," the girl said as she tucked her grass weaving away and pulled her sleeping bag up to her chin. "I'm surprised you never heard about it. Maybe one of the scariest of our stories."

"I'm not really into hearing a bedtime story," he said, "especially not a scary one." He wiped at the frozen balls of snot beneath his nose with the back of his hand. His knees hurt and his toes ached from hunching over the small pile of kindle. He'd spent too much time and energy trying to get the thin green willows to ignite, and now the only burning was happening at the tips of his fingers.

"A woman really wanted to have a baby," she began.

John resigned himself to listening, figuring that at least if she was telling stories, she couldn't ask more questions.

"She went to the shaman and said, 'We have been trying to have a baby, with no luck.' The shaman told the woman, 'You will have a baby, but you must promise me that you will feed and care for this baby no matter what happens. No matter how the child looks or acts, you must love it and show it to everyone.' The woman agreed. The shaman danced and said some spells over her. She went home and soon was pregnant."

John interrupted her. "And then let me guess. The baby was born with a giant-ass mouth. I think I get the rest."

The girl ignored him. "This was in the old times when a woman gave birth by herself or only with the help of her mother. This woman was in the back of the sod house, and the people didn't have walls then, in those underground houses, only grass mats that they used for beds and for privacy. She made her mother leave and gave birth behind one of the grass walls. She didn't let anyone see the baby, and she just tucked it away in the back of the house, in a dark little corner, and covered it with caribou hides and grass mats so no one would see it.

"The baby would cry and cry and the mother would tell her daughter that she shouldn't be ashamed of it and she needed to breast-feed it and show the child to everyone like the shaman said. But the daughter refused. The daughter would go to the back of the house to feed the baby, and never showed it to anyone. The mother finally peeked between the grass strands in the wall and could see the baby. It had a mouth that covered most of its face, stretching from ear to ear. And the teeth. The baby had rows of long, sharp white teeth.

"The mother reminded her daughter not to be ashamed of the baby, but she still refused. She kept the child in the back of the dark house, always covered. One night the mother heard a strange crackling noise coming from the back of the house. She lit the seal-oil lamp and peeked through a crack in the wall and could see it. The baby could already crawl, and he sat on top of his mother. He'd been breast-feeding and eaten his way into her chest. Blood covered his face, and the crackling she heard was the crunching of her daughter's ribs.

"The mother quickly put on her parka and ran to the men's house. She told them the Big Mouth Baby had eaten her daughter and would come for them next if they didn't escape," the girl said. Her voice dropped to a whisper, as if she'd scared herself with her own story. "The people quickly and quietly ran away from the village and never returned."

"That's it?" he asked, with a chuckle. "That's your scariest story?"

"Well, there's more, but that's the scary part," she said.

"What's scary about that?" he asked.

She wiggled her sleeping bag closer to him and pulled the top closed until she was speaking through a small, mouth-sized hole.

"The Big Mouth Baby is still out there," she whispered, "still crawling around in the brush along the river, looking for people to eat."

## 23

He crawled back into the snow cave and closed up the entry hole with the old woman's garbage can lid. On his hands and knees he crept to his sleeping bag, which the girl had pulled out for him. He thought the girl and the old woman were asleep, tired from the day's journey, but they weren't. They waited until he settled in.

"What does it look like?" the girl asked then. "Did you see anyone?"

"I couldn't see much," he said. "Still a ground blizzard. The wind is letting up some, though. I could see plenty of buildings still standing. I could see the air tower, some houses. The big fuel tanks look different—burned up, I think."

"You seen any lights?" the old woman asked.

He didn't answer. He couldn't answer. He didn't know what he saw. The town didn't exactly look inviting. And he couldn't say for sure if he'd seen anything at all.

"This is bad. No one's alive in Bethel either?" the girl asked in a whisper, as if she couldn't believe or didn't want to believe.

He pulled his bag up around his shoulders and then took off his wool hat and stuck his pistol in it near his head, where he could grab it quickly if he needed to.

"There's people there," the old woman said after a long silence. "Too many for them to all die. But some of them might be not the good kind, too. Bethel scared me even before this bad thing happened. Never much liked going there. I don't know why you wants to go to

Bethel. We should keep going upriver. We should just go right past that place. Nothing for us downriver, and nothing there, not in that town. Nothing."

"What do you think, John?" the girl asked as the old woman tried to muffle another cough.

"I think if she knows something, she should tell us."

"I know they aren't there," the old woman said.

"But you don't know *where* they are, either. Right?" He sighed and turned away from them.

"You know," the old woman said to the girl.

"I don't. No. I don't," the girl said.

"You do," said the woman. "If they are still alive, you can find them."

He dug a small handful of snow out from the wall of their dark little cave and put it into his mouth. They should have chipped and melted some ice or chopped a hole in the river. He was thirsty and his lower lip had started to bleed from the hunk of chapped skin he'd bitten off.

"I think I'm going to see if there's anyone there who can help us," John said. "See if anyone that knows what's going on. I'm not going to pass up the biggest town in hundreds of miles. If someone is alive there, they should be able to tell us something. I want to know what happened."

"When I was a young girl like you," the old woman said, "I remember in the spring, before breakup, we would take our dog teams and go across the tundra to the mountains. All around we saw caribou, snowshoe hares, and porcupines. The men hunted and trapped, and us kids, we had so much fun. Lots of trees up near the mountains, and so many good firewoods. We always had a big warm fire with meat roasting on alder sticks, and we could sit at our camp and listen to the winds whispering through them branches. Then, when the long days came and the ice went out, the men would build boats and load up the dogs and kids and everyone and float down to the tundra just in time to start king salmon fishing."

"What did you see?" the girl asked John, as if ignoring the old woman's story.

"I told you what I saw. Nothing."

The old woman continued her story. "Big lakes up in those mountains too. Real big. Deep lakes with giant trout. They say one lake, Heart Lake, had a *palraiyuk*. Long, skinny monster, like one of those kinds that Crocodile man wrestled on TV. Yup'iks used to draw that creature on our kayaks. Real big long, narrow mouth with lotsa teeths, and little pokies sticking out all down its back to its tail. But there was a story about someone who killed the last big monster up there. The man's wife was getting water and that creature jumped up out of the water and snapped its mouth down on her and slid back into the water with her. The man tried to shoot it, but his arrows just bounced off its armour. So he went and killed a caribou and used it like bait. When *palraiyuk* came back to eat the caribou he took his last arrow and shot it in the heart. He cut the monster open and saved his wife. My grandpa used to say they would climb through the backbone hole of the skeleton on the beach of that last monster the hero killed. But some people say those lakes might still have *palraiyuk*."

"Scary," the girl said.

"Lots of scary stuff out there. Sometimes there is only a real thin layer separating our world and the spirit world," the woman said. "When I was maybe your age there was a young boy, Gabe Fox. You heard stories about him?"

The girl nodded, and said, "We always talked about him when we were out camping. Tell John."

"He was real. A real boy. He was orphan, living at that place we call Children's Home. That was up the Kwethluk River where they keeped orphans from the last epidemic. Gabe Fox didn't like that place, maybe the priests treat him bad or maybe he was in trouble, so he ran away. He *qimakalleq*, run away and become nervous and scare easy like a fox. People seen him all the time, but he either hiding in the wilds or he not wanna get catched."

"What makes you think the kids did like Gabe Fox and *qimak-alleq*?" the girl asked.

"Because they wasn't in the gym," the old woman said. "They run away to somewhere. Somewhere safe. But we need to find them before they *cillam quella*."

"I don't know that word," the girl said.

"Maybe it means before they are made cold by the universe," the old woman said. "*Cillam quella.*"

He turned his back to them and sucked the moisture from the handful of snow until all that remained in his mouth was a small ball of ice.

CARL AND HIS WIFE, Carrie, sat across the dinner table. They were their first dinner guests, in a village where sharing food and meals was nothing new, but formal dinners, complete with tablecloth, napkins, and the spoon-fork-knife set-up were unheard of.

"So fancy," Carrie said, pointing to the display of silverware. "You guys always eat like this?"

"No, just for special guests."

"I should have dressed up! I could have worn my town shoes!" Carrie said.

They laughed. John caught a glance between Carl and Carrie and suddenly felt very uncomfortable for them. Anna had overdone the table setting. The low lights. The candles. The separate serving dishes. It was overboard. Too much of a show for their guests.

Carl tried to make small talk. "Got a letter from my brother in Kuwait. Hundred and twenty degrees there, he said. He said he dreams of snow and ice. He knows pretty soon the river will freeze up and you and me can start hunting ptarmigan. Maybe I'll show you how to trap marten and otters."

"That would be nice. I'd like that. Hundred and twenty. Ouch. Is he doing okay there?"

Carl shrugged. "Best he can be for an Eskimo in the oven."

"Sorry we don't have sour cream," Anna said, setting a plate of baked potatoes on the table. John shot her a look, but she was too absorbed in delivery of the dinner to catch his telepathic messages. Had their kitchen been in a separate room from their dinner table he might have had a chance to whisper in her ear to quit with the fanfare, but he couldn't, and he felt the damage was already done. He'd worked so hard to fit in with Carl, to just be a hunting partner and not an outsider, and dinner seemed like a good way to let Anna in on the fun.

Now, as Anna opened a sixty-four-ounce can of grape juice and poured it into wine glasses, he could only hope to ever be invited out hunting again.

As Anna poured the juice she said, "I sure wish we had a little white wine to go with the chicken, but since the village is dry, this grape juice will have to do."

Carl and Carrie laughed. John eased up a bit.

"You could sit that juice next to the furnace with some yeast and make homebrew," Carrie joked. "That's what some people do around here. Too bad bootleggers don't sell wine. Otherwise Carl could get a bottle from his no-good brother in Bethel."

"You have a brother in the National Guard and a brother who bootlegs?"

"Anna!"

Carrie turned to John. "It's okay. His brother there is a bum. Doesn't work and only sells weed and vodka. Poisons his own people for sixty dollars a bottle."

Carl shrugged. "He'll get caught someday."

Anna dished out the chicken and then passed her homemade gravy across to Carrie. John realized Carl and Carrie were waiting, hesitating almost to serve themselves, so he dug in, leading the way. He took a spoonful of green beans and lumped them on his plate. He forked two large chunks of chicken beside the beans, stuck a potato with a fork, dropped it beside the chicken, and then smashed through the skin and made a decent trough for the gravy.

Soon they were all eating and chatting, the tension overcome with food and friendship. John squeezed Anna's leg beneath the table and then lifted his wine glass full of grape juice in a toast.

"To our new friends. And to good duck hunting in the spring. Cheers."

Their glasses clinked and they each took a sip.

"Next time," Carrie said, "I'll have you guys over for seal soup."

HE STAYED IN HIS SLEEPING BAG well past sunrise. He thought the girl would think he was just sleeping, resting from the long day of walking. He wasn't. Dawn came and went. The sun never broke through the clouds, leaving the sky above them a sullen white that blended with the horizon.

He had his back turned to her, to their snowed-in tracks. The man on skis could have followed them, and readied to attack, and he wouldn't have seen it coming. Instead, he just remained frozen, on his side, and stared blankly at the white expanse in front of him, an endless emptiness that stretched out and almost seemed to curve with the earth, no trees, no brush, nothing but white upon white.

She was quiet for the longest time; perhaps she didn't want to wake him, or she was scared something was wrong. The wind had died with the sunrise. The entire world fell silent, dead.

"It's hard for you to breathe today," she said. He could hear her working the grasses, braiding, twisting, her mouth opening and wetting them.

He said nothing. He had nothing to say.

"I can tell by how you take a breath and then hold it, for too long. I used to do that lots. Not just because I couldn't see, but from other things. Other things in my life that made it hard, you know. Hard to want to take one more breath. I know how it feels."

She put her hand on his shoulder. He couldn't feel any warmth from it through the sleeping bag, but he could feel the weight of it, where she left it resting on his arm, and then she patted him gently, as if he were a sick puppy.

"There's going to be days like this when we don't want to live no more. I had plenty of days like that, so many days in that house by myself, you know. So many nights, when everyone was sick, all that sickness and dying. Crying at night. Screams. Then quiet. Just black nothingness. And those smells. I didn't want to live with that quiet and those smells. I wanted to know why I was being punished again. I never did anything wrong and God was punishing me by letting me live."

She took her hand away, maybe to brush at her tears, but he couldn't be sure.

"I thought about walking out on the tundra or into the river. The .22 wasn't powerful enough, you know, for that. And I couldn't get my legs to take me outside. I was too scared of what might be outside. Sometimes I worried that I would go out there and I would see again. I would see everything that had been ruined."

For a long while she fell silent. He closed his eyes and tried to imagine her world for a moment. Perpetual darkness, a world of only sounds and smells—but then she had something else, that sense of hers, some ethereal understanding of the world around her. He wondered if this was common to blind people, or just the girl, and the strange circumstances that allowed her to still be there, alive.

"I wanted to die, but I was too scared. I didn't want to die alone. Now I know at least I'm not going to die alone, and I'm not scared. We find reasons to want to live."

He took a deep breath and let it out. The cloud of warm vapour from his lungs hung in the air around his face and slowly disappeared. He unzipped his bag and sat up.

"Let's get moving," he said. "Can't mope around all day and feel sorry for ourselves, can we?"

She smiled and began packing her grass weaving bundle and her sleeping bag. He scanned the horizon in all directions to make sure they were alone and then stood up and stretched. He watched her bundle the sleeping bags and the grass inside the tarp and place them on the toboggan.

"You're not going to die," he said to her, and they started off across the snowy tundra, travelling east toward the river.

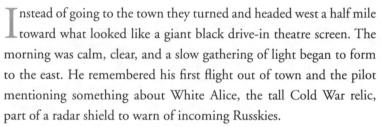

# 24

Instead of going to the town they turned and headed west a half mile toward what looked like a giant black drive-in theatre screen. The morning was calm, clear, and a slow gathering of light began to form to the east. He remembered his first flight out of town and the pilot mentioning something about White Alice, the tall Cold War relic, part of a radar shield to warn of incoming Russkies.

The storm during the night had created new drifts, and the girl and old woman struggled until they reached the crest of a small hill, where the wind had blown the surface clear, leaving hard-packed frozen tundra. The old woman kept watching behind them, searching continually, he suspected, for the hunter. They made better time, and before long, the giant black shield loomed over them.

"What are you going to do?" the girl asked when they reached the base of the tower.

"I'm going up. See if I can spot anything," he said.

He handed his rifle to the old woman, went inside, and grabbed the first rung on the ladder that led to the top, some seventy feet above them in the darkness. He began to climb. His arms and legs barely seemed to have the strength to lift him, but slowly he managed to pull himself up.

At the top, he hoisted himself up and over the edge. He rested for a moment, on his stomach, as he tried to catch his breath.

"You okay?"

He leaned over the edge and held his finger to his lips, and remembered she couldn't see this. "Quiet!" he said. They were a mile from town, but he didn't want to take any risks.

He crawled on his hands and knees to the far edge and scanned the horizon. An orange haze began to appear in the distance with the rising sun. From the top of the tower he could see the town, the wide, sweeping river, and the rolling mountains in the distance. Before surveying the town he looked back at their tracks and followed them toward their last camp beneath the bluff. If someone was following them, he didn't see any movement.

The town looked as lifeless as the white wasteland surrounding it. The single red light he had seen the night before, perched high on a radio tower, was still lit, but that was the only sign of life. No smoke. No movement. No sounds.

Parts of Bethel bore the familiar snow-covered blackness of ruin, just on a much larger scale. The monstrous white fuel tanks that once bordered the river at the centre of town were gone, replaced with twisted, blackened metal craters. The half-charred ruins of the town stretched out before him like a commune for the undead. The vision of a burnt and frozen town reminded him of a Robert Frost poem, something about the world ending in either ice or fire. Bethel appeared to have died twice.

ONE SATURDAY MORNING Anna and John awoke to snow. A soft, light blanket covered the ground overnight, and the worn and dirty village appeared renewed, refreshed, and the two of them could feel a strange sort of excitement bristling through the community. Men dragged their snow machines out from beneath their houses or removed the tarps that covered them. Young boys tried to stockpile snowballs as more snow began to fall.

John sat on his steps watching what he thought was probably the last outside basketball game of the season. Four boys played in their

T-shirts and rubber boots on the wooden play deck. The chill in the air bit at his ears, but apparently had no effect on the boys, or their game.

Anna came out and sat on the steps beside him, wearing the same as he did, her new winter boots, wool hat, and Gore-Tex parka. She was ready for the change in seasons. They both were. Frozen lakes, rivers, and tundra meant they could get out for walks somewhere other than laps around the school gym or through the hallways or down the icy boardwalks.

"How soon until the river freezes?" Anna asked.

"Carl said it will all be frozen by next week. Safe to walk on in another couple of weeks, maybe, and then safe for snow-machine travel by the end of the month. If it stays cold."

"If?" she said, picking at a frozen chunk of mud on the bottom step.

"He said it warms up often now, sometimes twice a winter, and makes the ice rotten—treacherous. Climate change, worse here in the Subarctic."

John stood and stretched. He'd been playing open gym with the men the last few weeks, trying to get back into shape, and had pulled something in his back going up for a rebound.

"You think we should order some cross-country skis or something?"

"What did Carl say?" she joked.

"What's that mean?"

"Nothing. He's just your answer to everything now. I thought you would have asked him."

"He said once in a while every few years a teacher will try skiing. No one else skis."

"So you did ask him?" she asked with a laugh.

"It seems like something we could do to get out and get some air, you know? That or buy a snow machine. Which we can't afford."

"Think they can ship skis out here?"

"If they can ship out snow machines and four-wheelers I think they can ship out some skis."

"Are they expensive?"

"Who cares? If they let us get out and see some country, they'll be worth it. Skis would make all the difference trying to get around."

She pointed to the flat landscape. "I can see all the country I'm going to see from here. Maybe next year we get them. We should save our money for now."

One of the boys undercut another going up for a shot. The shooter's legs came out from beneath him and he crashed to the hard wood deck and cried out in pain.

"Ouch. That hurt," John said.

"It looks like he might have busted up his arm. Think we should check on him? What do they do if someone gets hurt like that?"

"Carl said … Just kidding. They send a medevac flight out from the Bethel hospital. I'm going to go see if he's okay."

"What if they can't fly and can't travel by river?" Anna asked, holding her hand out to catch some of the snowflakes. "What happens then?"

"They shoot 'em, I guess. That or wait."

THE GIRL ASKED HIM how it felt to shoot one of them. She didn't ask him if he had. Just how it felt. "Did you feel bad?" she asked.

That morning the air burned cold deep inside his lungs. The breeze cut through his clothing and felt like lit cigarettes pressed against his cheeks and face. Even his teeth were cold. He pretended that he couldn't hear her behind him in the sled over the sound of the ice and snow scratching beneath the plastic toboggan.

"I don't think I would feel bad," she said. "I was sure I would have to kill them, but they never found me. You shouldn't feel bad. They would have killed you and ate you. I know it. Especially since you're *kass'aq*. They would take your guns and your stuff and think nothing of it since *kass'aqs* started this sickness."

"What if I told you I'm not gus-suck?" he asked.

"Are you black?" she asked.

"No," he said.

"Indian?"

The weight of the girl and the gear in the sled became too great. He stopped, took a breath, and tried to pull again. He couldn't move her. The snow conditions were changing, creating resistance against the bottom of the toboggan. Or he had run out of juice.

"My cousin once asked me if I would kill someone to have my eyes back. I said I couldn't, but now I think I could. If they were bad, I could do it. Why would some people choose to stay and help and those others leave? How come people are so different? Do you think it takes something like this to show people's true side? Like you can see their soul?"

He turned and looked down at her, sitting in the sled, with his pack resting on her legs, the rifle across her lap. "I'll give you a hundred dollars if you don't ask another question all day," he said.

"What would I do with a hundred dollars?"

"That's another question."

"I'm just killing time."

"You're killing me. You might as well be one of them and kill me."

"You don't have to be mean."

"Mean? Mean would have been to leave you."

"That's what I'm talking about. How many people would have chosen to help me? That wasn't a question. Not many, that's how many. I don't think many people would have helped me. I don't know why you are different, but you are, John. That's why I don't think you should feel guilty."

"Why would it matter if I'm a gus-suck? Or black? Indian? Or Eskimo? And who said I feel guilty?" he asked.

"That doesn't matter. Your skin colour. Not to me. And I'm not talking about feeling guilty for killing outcasts, John. I mean sorry for still being alive. If you're like me, then you feel bad, too. Maybe that's why I cry at night sometimes. I think that is why you have those dreams. The guilt is for getting to live. Isn't it?"

John replied, "When I was a kid my grandpa told me that in the wilderness people died of shame and guilt. I'm not going to die out here of shame *or* guilt."

"I wish I could pretend I didn't feel bad, too," she said.

"Pretend? What do you want me to say? Yes, it haunts me. Every breath I take hurts. Every time I blink and I'm still alive, I ask why. Why me? Why this place? Every sunrise seems unfair and wrong. And every night is purgatory revisited. Is that what you wanted me to say?" he asked. "Is it?"

The girl lowered her face to the rifle sitting in her lap. "Well?" he asked again. "Is that what you wanted to hear?"

"No," she said softly. "That doesn't sound like guilt at all."

"No? What does it sound like, then?" he asked, a flash of anger warming his face.

She looked up at him. Her white eyes staring at him—through him. "Selfish," she said, her voice sad, but full of defiance, "you sound selfish."

He reeled around and began pulling, the cold surrounding him, pressing against his skin, chilling his muscles, slowing him, grinding him into the ice beneath his frozen feet.

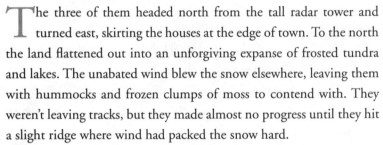

# 25

The three of them headed north from the tall radar tower and turned east, skirting the houses at the edge of town. To the north the land flattened out into an unforgiving expanse of frosted tundra and lakes. The unabated wind blew the snow elsewhere, leaving them with hummocks and frozen clumps of moss to contend with. They weren't leaving tracks, but they made almost no progress until they hit a slight ridge where wind had packed the snow hard.

The old woman had said little since they left the snow cave. He didn't know if she was worried, or just mad at him. She protested his decision to explore what was left of the town, but since the tower and his mention of the light, he noticed her pace had quickened. She held the 20-gauge out in front of her as if a ptarmigan might fly up in front of them, or worse.

"Where we going to sleep tonight?" the girl asked.

The old woman pointed toward the darkening sky behind them. "We're going to need somewhere protected," she said. "Maybe it's going to get real windy, and bad cold. Least the snow will cover our tracks."

"How do you know that?" he asked.

"It's still now. See those high, thin clouds over there? Wind is coming." She stopped walking and turned to him. "What do you expect to find?" she asked.

He shrugged and looked out over the town. He hoped no one

was watching the horizon because he wasn't doing a very good job of keeping below the skyline.

"We can keep going straight across here," she said. "The river comes back around and past town. We can shortcut. We'll camp in the brush by the tall bluffs, and then we won't have to go into that bum town."

"Maybe you two should go. I'll check out town, and then come find you."

"No," the girl said. "I don't want you to leave us."

He pulled the rope to the sled tight. "Look," he said to them both, "I need to know what the deal with the light is, maybe see if I can find some snowshoes, skis, or a sled. Anything to make travel easier. If it's bad in town, we'll get out. We'll head that way and meet at the bluffs. Okay? Maybe we can find something out about the kids *here*."

"If it's bad, next time you'll listen to what I have to say," the old woman said.

THE DOOR TO THE FIRST BLACKHAWK opened and a man in a Santa Claus suit shouted and waved to the villagers gathered at the edge of the mechanical blizzard settling around the two choppers. The door on the other aircraft slid open and two Anchorage-based news camera crews poured out, followed by unarmed National Guard troops carrying cases of Florida oranges, presents, and of all things, ice cream.

"I love it when Santa brings us fresh fruit," Carl said with a smile.

"They do this every year?" Anna asked. She stood beside John, her arms folded around Nina, her new constant companion.

Carl nodded. "But I wish this year he was flying with reindeer. I could use some fresh meat."

"Don't say that in front of Nina!" Anna shouted over the chopper's rotors.

"Think we'll be able to get out caribou hunting?" John asked.

"Maybe if we get more snow," Carl said. "Maybe if the herd comes on this side of the mountains this year."

"What's the deal with the news people?" Anna asked.

Carl scowled. "Showtime. Look at how we bring happiness to the cute little Natives."

Anna elbowed Carl and said, "What turned you into Mr. Scrooge!"

"Anna," John said, embarrassed at her jibe.

"You're right, Anna," Carl said. "I shouldn't get mad about those news people. It's just how they only show our kids to the rest of the state when they're getting handouts from Santa in a Blackhawk. I'll quit being Scrooge." Then he smiled, and added, "And then I'll gladly take a case of oranges from Santa!"

They watched as the children gathered around the portly, white-bearded man in the Santa suit. The braver older kids pawed at his soft red jacket, the long pointy hat hanging down the side of his face, and his white gloves. The younger, shyer kids giggled behind their mittens and trailed behind him toward the gym for an early Christmas celebration. The news crews followed, with one petite reporter trying to walk and report, talking into the camera lens and struggling against the wind to keep her long brown hair from covering her face.

Anna laughed. "I think Mr. Scrooge here should be the village spokesperson," she said.

"Me? No way," Carl said. "I'm too shy."

"Speaking of shy," Anna said, patting her little sidekick on the head. "Go on, Nina! Go see what Santa has for you." The little girl shook her head and buried her face in the side of Anna's snow pants.

Anna nudged Nina toward the group of kids. The girl clung to her leg, and Anna made exaggerated clown-like steps toward Santa with the little one in tow.

HE SPOTTED A MAN in the distance, staggering across the tundra with no apparent direction or destination. As soon as he saw the dark figure, he pushed the girl to the snow, pulled off his mitten, and rested his right index finger on the icy metal of the rifle's trigger. His eye focused on the round red bead of the sight at the end of the barrel. He held it half a foot above the approaching man's head to compensate for the distance.

The person stopped, and for a moment John worried they had been spotted.

"One of them?" she asked, her voice barely audible in the wind.

"Can't tell."

"What's he doing?"

"Stopped. Now he's turning in circles."

"Maybe he's lost?"

"Maybe."

He squinted to see if he could see the man's face. Something didn't seem right with the man.

"What's he wearing?"

"A black jacket. Leather. Basketball shoes. No hat. No gloves."

"Is his jacket zipped?"

The man turned around again, toward them, and he could see the jacket was open. The man waved at the air in front of him as if dismissing someone and began to stagger toward the endless white of snow-covered tundra and lakes.

"He's leaving."

"Which direction?"

"West."

"There's nothing that way. Not for a long ways."

"How did you know his jacket was unzipped?"

"He's freezing to death. Too far gone. He thinks he's getting warm."

They waited until the man was just a black spot on the flat white horizon before John stood and helped the girl to her feet.

"Why didn't you ask me to help him?" he asked.

"There's nothing we could do for him," she said. Her milky eyes seemed to scan the grey wall of clouds the man was headed toward. "When someone used to get lost on the tundra, if the searchers didn't find the body they would say he became *tenguituli*, wild. If a raven finds the person and removes part of his liver he becomes light and can't understand humans no more and becomes part of the wild nature. If you find a wild man you have to spit on him or take one finger and push him down into the ground to save him. That man's not wild, not yet."

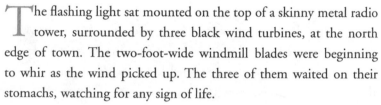

# 26

The flashing light sat mounted on the top of a skinny metal radio tower, surrounded by three black wind turbines, at the north edge of town. The two-foot-wide windmill blades were beginning to whir as the wind picked up. The three of them waited on their stomachs, watching for any sign of life.

Behind the turbines sat the blackened wood skeleton of a large rectangular house, and beside the house a forty-foot-round metal fuel tank. The painted tank looked something like a giant Coca-Cola can that had been cut in half and turned into a workshop or house of some kind.

"You two wait here for me. Can you shoot this?"

The old woman nodded.

"I'll trade you."

The old woman took the rifle and handed him her shotgun and four shells that she pulled from her parka pocket.

"If anyone other than me comes this way, start shooting. I'll signal if it's okay to follow."

As he got up, the old woman reached out and grabbed his hand. She didn't say anything, just squeezed his glove, gave it a firm shake, and dropped it.

He stood up and scrambled toward the tank, trying to stay as low to the ground as he could, but at the same time realizing he was one large easy target against a flat white backdrop.

He reached the first turbine pole and pressed himself against it. The pole vibrated with the hum of the blades turning above him. The houses stretched in a row toward the east, and most of them looked to be in the same condition as most of the village houses he had seen. Burned out. Windows broken. Lifeless.

A heavy black cable ran down the tower with the flashing light and into a metal tube that spanned the distance from where he was standing to the tank. There was a chance that the turbines simply powered the light and nothing else, but there was also a chance that someone was inside the tank.

After a quick check to make sure the barrel of the shotgun was clear of snow, he started toward the round container, the shotgun held waist high. His steps were slow, and he watched for the slightest movement. If someone was inside, now they surely knew he was coming. The tank and the turbines wouldn't have remained without some sort of struggle. He was sure of that.

He looked back quickly to check the old woman and the girl and was relieved that they were barely visible. Just two small, dark lumps two hundred yards out. As he turned back he caught sight of a bright red line cutting through the mist of ice and snow his boot had kicked up. A laser perimeter. He'd seen something similar on a television show about hunting man-eating tigers and the men who put themselves out as bait to hunt them. If people inside hadn't known he was coming, they did now.

A square slot in the side of the tank opened and a rifle barrel slid out. He thought about running, but doubted there was any use. He lowered the shotgun and raised his right hand in a half-hearted wave.

"Don't shoot. I'm not looking for trouble."

"And I'm supposed to ignore the two riflemen you have waiting for me out there?"

The voice from inside the tank sounded high and raspy.

Before he answered, he turned back and looked out toward them.

"I've got an old woman and a girl travelling with me. The old woman does have a rifle, and she'll use it, but like I said, we're not looking for trouble."

"A little late for trouble. What do you want?"

"Saw the light. Hoped you might be able to help us."

"Damn light. I oughta shoot it out. Look, I don't have any food to spare, if that's what you want."

"We don't need food. Just a safe place to stay tonight. And listen, I need to know—is it all gone? I mean the rest of the States. What the hell happened?"

"You don't need food?"

He shook his head. "We can make do with what we've got for now. Do you have news?"

"News? I'll tell you what. You shell out the food for dinner tonight, and you can stay here. I'll tell you what I know, but I don't think I have to warn you. I'll shoot you as soon as look at you any longer."

John nodded.

"Bring those two around the front. There's a metal cabinet there. Lock your weapons inside. You can keep the key. I'll open the doors when you've locked them away."

"Thank you."

He turned and waved and the old woman and the girl slowly got to their feet. He started out to meet them and help pull the sleds. The wind picked up and the turbines whined, and as he walked toward his two travel companions, he realized the windmills were the first sounds of civilization he'd heard in what felt like a lifetime.

JOHN DUCKED DOWN to crawl into the plywood steam bath. He felt as if he were entering a child's fort. The first small room, barely big enough for two men to undress while hunched over, was a dry room. There were two overturned buckets to sit on, two red towels Carrie had put inside for them, and another bucket of water with a hand-carved wooden ladle.

"First steam, eh," Carl said. "We undress in here, then go inside. If it's too hot, you come back out here to cool down. I'll try not to steam you out, first time."

He took a sip of water from the ladle and handed it to John. John held the wooden spoon to his lips and drank deeply. He realized he hadn't tasted cold water in a while. The school's well water tasted funny, so they had been adding a small amount of lime Gatorade mix to hide the iron. This water tasted clean and cool. Refreshing.

"Where's the water from?"

"River," Carl said as he pulled off his shirt and jeans. John followed suit, removing his coat and pulling off his shirt. He looked down at his pasty chest and felt a bit awkward. Carl stripped off his underwear, took another sip from the ladle, and pulled a knitted cap from a rusty nail on the wall.

"You might want to wear this to protect your head. Ears, too."

"Is it cold in there?" John joked.

"This isn't like one of your city-boy saunas. You'll need it. Don't want to burn your little white lobes."

John took the blue knit cap and pulled it over his head and ears. Carl opened the plywood door and ducked inside. John followed and quickly closed the door. Inside, the temperature felt humid and tropical. Warm and relaxing. John could handle this. Suddenly it made sense why people chose this method to get clean. A person could just sweat a little, rinse off, and be refreshed.

They sat on bare plywood, in an area the size of a kitchen table. Sitting on his butt, with his legs pulled up, his head nearly touched the ceiling.

"We sit like this," Carl said, tucking his head down and putting his legs beneath him. "I'll just put a couple of scoops on at first. Put your head down so you don't get burned."

In front of them, the floor recessed, and in the space sat a large black and rusted barrel stove covered with smooth, fist-sized blue and grey river stones. In front of the stove a square tin held steaming-hot water. Carl grabbed the wooden handle in the water and pulled it out; a tin can was nailed to the end. He stirred the water and then poured a full can over the rocks.

With a hiss the water instantly turned to steam and a wall of heat slammed against John, nearly causing him to cry out in pain. Carl stirred the water in the can again and poured another cupful over the rocks, slower this time. The heat intensified and John tucked his head between his legs and pulled his arms and elbows in close. The heat burned against his flesh. He held his breath to keep from breathing the wet, fiery air.

"One more?" Carl asked.

John grunted out an "Okay." This time he kept his head down, heard the hiss, and tensed his muscles to brace for the blast of burning heat. The air seared his skin and he felt as though he were inside a furnace.

"Hot enough?" Carl asked, joking.

"Yeah. Shit."

"You can go out there and cool off."

"Are you?"

"Not yet," Carl said. "Feels too good."

"Sure does," John said, lying. His skin was on fire.

"One more. Then we'll take a break and get water."

John tensed for the hiss and groaned as the hot air burned against his shoulders, buttocks, and knees.

"*Ak'a*," Carl said. "*Kiircepaa.* Hot, eh?"

The heat died down a little, and Carl waited for John to make a move. The heat was getting to his head, but he wanted to let Carl know he could take it. Or at least he could pretend to take it.

"You ready for water, or you want more?"

"Whatever," John said. "Cold water sounds perfect."

Carl waited. John pulled the door open and crawled out with the cloud of mist that erupted against the cold air in the entry. Carl followed and closed the door.

"Holy shit, that's hot," John said, looking at the red splotches appearing on his shoulders and arms. "I hope this goes away."

Carl smiled. "We'll do that a couple more times and then wash up."

"Wash up? Hey, I'm clean. I think I burned the dirt out that round," John said as he dipped the ladle and handed Carl the first drink. Carl drank half and poured the other half on his head. His black hair glistened and steamed in the cool air.

"This is how we stay clean with no baths or showers. Steam for a while and then wash up. Not bad, eh?"

"It's something, all right. Wow." He felt light-headed.

"That was nothing. You should steam with me and my brothers. Probably melt your skin right off the bone."

Carl cracked the door to the outside. The chilly night air rushed in, and John leaned back against the wall and sighed. The heat poured off his body and he felt relaxed, alive, rejuvenated, and tired all at the same time.

"Maybe next time your wife can meet you here when we're done. That's how most of our kids entered this world. Steam bath's the best way. Best way for romance. You guys can't have kids?"

"We're still kids ourselves. Not yet."

"Shoot. Here, most people your age got six or seven kids. You're way behind. Ready?"

"It's going to be hotter, isn't it?"

Carl smiled and headed inside.

HE HAD BEEN pulling the girl in the sled for hours when she asked about Anna again. When he didn't reply, she asked another question that made him even angrier.

"You said 'I promise, I promise' in your sleep last night. What did you promise her? Promises get people into trouble, you know?"

He was about to tell her to shut up, to never open her mouth again, when he spotted a thin snake of smoke rising from a plywood shack on the riverbank ahead of them, the roof of the smokehouse half covered by a green plastic tarp. He slowly sank to his knees and looked back to the girl on the sled.

"I smell the smoke," she said.

"Just a little ways upriver. Looks like a fish camp."

The girl closed her eyes, tilted her head back, and lifted her nose. She took a deep breath and her face shifted. She took another smell of the icy air and then shook her head.

"It's not good," she said. "The smoke. It's ... not a fire. They're smoking meat." Then she added, in a scared whisper, "Bad meat."

Fear replaced his anger. He surveyed their choices. They could turn around and waste energy they didn't have, or try to sneak past, below the fifteen-foot-high riverbank, just out of sight of the camp, and hope no one would see them. The problem with sneaking past was the tracks they would leave. One set of size-twelve boots pulling a heavy sled.

Either way, they would leave tracks, and either way he wouldn't sleep knowing those tracks would lead from that smokehouse straight through the snow and right to their next camp. He wondered if the skier had somehow doubled back and was waiting for them.

He sat in the snow for a long time without saying anything. The girl held the rifle across her lap and he took it from her, put a round in the chamber, and handed it back to her. He pulled her behind the round shield of roots from a limbless spruce tree that had washed down from far upriver during the spring flooding.

"I'm going to have to go up there," he said. "I want you to start counting to yourself slowly. When you get to two hundred, start screaming. Loud as you can. When you hear me shooting, quit screaming."

She nodded.

"You'll come back?"

"I'll come back. Anyone else comes near, start shooting. You'll know when it's me."

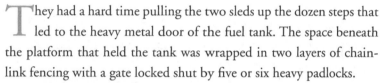

# 27

They had a hard time pulling the two sleds up the dozen steps that led to the heavy metal door of the fuel tank. The space beneath the platform that held the tank was wrapped in two layers of chain-link fencing with a gate locked shut by five or six heavy padlocks.

"Why he want you to put the guns in there?" the old woman asked as he closed the metal cabinet and began to lock it. He stopped, opened his jacket, and took out the Glock. He didn't feel comfortable leaving the pistol, but he wasn't about to betray the demands of the man inside the tank. For all he knew the guy would make them walk through a wind-powered metal detector.

"He wants to make sure we aren't going to rob him."

"Maybe he gonna rob us. Maybe take our food," she said.

"If he does that, the ghosts will haunt him. Right?" he said.

"You shouldn't joke with her like that," the girl said quietly.

John gave a light rap on the door. A square peephole opened and a light blue eye appeared. He looked away while the man behind the door evaluated them, and then several metallic clicks from the other side preceded an oiled and silent opening of the door, a thick, solid door that reminded him of a bank vault.

A lanky, bone-thin man stood behind the door. He held a light snow-camouflaged assault rifle in one hand and quickly waved them in with the other.

"In. In. Move it. Come on," he said.

"Our food?"

"Pull it in. It's not safe out there."

The man reached down to grab the rope to the old woman's sled and pulled it in. They followed. With the toboggan inside, the door swung shut and the man clamped two deadbolts and locked several baseball-sized padlocks. The man turned and looked at a four-by-four-inch security screen, never putting down the assault rifle. The screen flashed the images from at least three cameras mounted somewhere outside, each one covering a different side of the tank.

"You're alone?" he asked.

"Just the three of us," John said.

He looked at the girl. "Christ, she's blind?" he asked, then added, "From the sickness?"

"No. Before," the girl said.

"Blind. That makes for good winter travel, no? Here, you ladies sit down. With all that's happened, I've lost my manners."

He pulled out two metal folding chairs. The old woman and the girl sat.

"Let me get some tea brewing," he said, turning to a small hotplate with an old teakettle.

While he filled the kettle from a small silver spigot that drained into a deep sink, John looked around the small structure. The building was insulated with some sort of spray foam and then painted white. One small fluorescent bulb lit the space. Against one wall sat a double bed, beside that a desk with a computer and a small ceramic space heater. Against the other wall a woodstove, a plywood table, and a workbench, complete with ammunition-reloading equipment.

The man turned and gave them a thorough once-over, again. He was balding, with long, stringy red hair in the back and on the sides. The wisps of hair on his face and chin didn't constitute much of a beard, and his icy blue eyes were set behind a pair of flimsy wire-rimmed glasses.

"Name is Raymond. Folks used to call me Red."

He extended his hand toward John.

"John Morgan. This is—" he said, and stopped, stunned. After everything, he didn't even know the girl's name. He looked down at the floor.

"It's okay, friend, it's just a name," Red said, slapping John on the shoulder.

"I'm Rayna," the girl said. "This is Maggie."

"Where'd you guys travel from?" Red asked.

"Nunacuak," the girl said, "and she's from Kuigpak."

"You related to the Alexie family there?" Red asked.

The old woman nodded.

He pointed to a small photo of a wedding picture, a healthier Red standing beside a smiling Yup'ik girl. "My wife's mom was from Kuigpak," he said.

"I know her," the old woman said. "She's my husband's cousin."

"*Nulirqa tuqumauq,*" he said, the Yup'ik words coming with difficulty from his mouth. He shifted in his boots, and then turned away from them to tend to the tea.

He poured the tea into small blue plastic coffee mugs and passed them out.

"I thought I'd taken every precaution to keep us safe," he said.

He poured himself a cup and just held the cup for warmth. After a while he took a sip and said, "You want news."

John nodded, glanced at the girl and looked away.

The man took a sip of his tea and sighed. "Well," he said, "I don't suppose the answers I have will do any of us much good. Tell me that you've got some sort of real meat in your sleds there, and I'll tell you what I know."

"IT'S THE OFF-SEASON NOW. We can hit Mexico or Hawaii for cheap," he argued. "A little break would be nice. A little escape. I could use it. I should have ordered some skis. I'm starting to feel trapped again. Hell, I should have flown out of here on Santa's Blackhawk."

Anna and John headed upstream in the dark, where the river led to one lake after another. The wind had died down enough to make walking on the ice possible. A few days earlier they cut the nightly walk short because Anna was getting blown sideways and could hardly stand. The fresh coat of snow gave their boots some grip, and the relative calm made the sub-zero temperatures feel almost warm. The clear blue-black sky seemed within reach, and a waning pale moon lit the snow.

"Let's wait until summer. You can make it. Save our money and then take an extended break somewhere special," she said. "Ten days isn't enough. It's a day and a half to travel each way! Besides, didn't Carl say he would take you caribou hunting?"

"Not enough snow to travel where the herds are this year," he said. "Carl said they might just appear out of nowhere at any time, but probably not this year."

"Like Santa's magic reindeer! Look, we can celebrate Christmas with them and go starring. Carrie said it's so much fun."

"This is starring enough. Packing this entire village into one house? Singing and eating fish-head soup or moose stew for hours does not sound like fun to me," he said.

"Don't be a Grinch. Wow. Look at those stars. Turn your headlamp off. You don't even need it."

He snapped off his headlamp and let his eyes adjust. The snow crystals covering the lake ice sparkled in the moonlight.

"That feast we went to last week nearly killed me. You know I can't handle being crammed in like that, with so many people."

"Well, I'm going to try it. You're the one always talking about participating in village activities. Fighting your fears will be good for you, remember?"

"So we're staying?"

They stopped walking. She leaned in close to him and warmed her nose against his neck.

"I think we should," she said. "We'll cuddle up, read some good books. Go for some walks on clear nights like this. It'll be nice. Maybe Carl will let you borrow his snow machine and we can try to drive to Bethel or something. Get some Chinese food."

"We'll need more snow for that."

They continued walking. The moon hung just above the snowy tundra plain, and two long shadows walked beside them. He pulled back his parka sleeve. His watch read 6:30.

"I can't wait until the sun sticks around a bit longer," he said.

"I kind of like the long nights myself. It's romantic. Can you imagine that three or four hundred people will be coming here for Slaviq?"

"You're really excited about this whole Russian Christmas thing, aren't you?"

"What's there not to be excited about? A week of celebrating Christmas? Food? Singing? Come on, Ebenezer."

"I just can't visualize it," he said, reaching down to scoop up some snow. "Packing so many people into these little houses. I don't see how they can hold the weight. It just sounds crazy to me. Plus it's *Russian.* Don't you find that odd?"

"They were here first."

"Second. The Yup'ik people were here first, remember."

"Excuse moi."

"Now if this was some sort of traditional Yup'ik celebration, I'd be all about it."

"You don't have to be so anti-Christian all the time, you know. Maybe this celebration has some roots in their old ways of life. You don't know."

"Okay, I give in," he said. "Just promise me we don't have to host dinner for the whole community. We don't have enough food to pull something like that off. I don't know how anyone does."

She grabbed on to his arm. He flicked some of the snow he was carrying in her direction. He scooped up another handful and pressed it into her face and rubbed it playfully. She laughed and when he pulled his glove away, the snow remained on her cheeks and lips. He pulled her toward him and licked it off her salty cool skin.

"Mmm."

"Thanks a lot! Now my cheeks are going to freeze," she said. "Let's go home and you can make me dinner." They turned back and headed toward the village. Then Anna stopped. "It's so beautiful. I love how the moonlight makes it look like a desert of white diamonds that just lead to the edge of the earth. We're lucky to be here. Together, under this azure sky ... I can't think of anywhere else I'd rather be. We don't need to go anywhere else for the holiday, John."

"Is that what colour it is?"

She took a deep breath and turned to him. "You think anyone can see us this far out?" she asked, pressing her hips against his.

"Why?"

Anna kissed him and pulled him down, on top of her, to the snow-covered surface of the lake. She rolled over on him, her legs straddling his waist, and stuffed a handful of snow into his face. She pulled off her mitten and unzipped the front of his snow pants. Her icy hand slid beneath the waistband of his fleece pants.

"What's the occasion?" John asked as she kissed him again and he tugged at the zipper at the front of her parka with his gloves.

She unzipped the snow pants' sides and pulled off the Velcro enclosures and slipped the back of her pants down. She eased herself onto him and giggled and kissed him again. She sat up and he pressed his back into the frozen lake and he rested his head on the ice and snow and stared up into the night sky. She floated above him, warming him, loving him as only she could. As she rocked her hips on top of his the world seemed to split into three, Anna, her white diamonds surrounding them, and the blue-black sky above—and together the three felt endless, limitless.

WHEN THE GIRL STARTED SCREAMING, four men burst from the smokehouse carrying axes and knives. John stood behind the open door, his back pressed against the plywood wall, his pistol ready.

Her scream at first sounded too real, and he had to fight the urge to dive back down the riverbank. The shriek filled the still air, and for a moment the men stopped to locate the awful sound.

Through the crack between the door and the jamb he could see no one was left inside. Just a small flickering fire and the green light coming in through the tarp-covered roof.

He stepped from behind the door and fired two shots into the first man who turned at the motion behind him. The screams stopped and the other three men wheeled and he unloaded his clip into them.

Silence followed the ringing in his ears. He took his final clip from his parka pocket and jammed it home with the flat of his palm. As he turned to make sure the first man he shot was dead, something inside the smokehouse caught his attention. He kept an eye on the soot-coated bodies of the men, strewn on the riverbank in front of the smokehouse, as he walked forward, pushing closer, the shaking pistol out in front of his body, his finger clenching the trigger.

The room was bare, except for a pile of dishes and bedding. He half expected a pair of cross-country skis to be leaning outside, but there were no skis or poles. Smoke drifted out the door; the barrel stove had no chimney and instead emptied the smoke into the shack. His eyes rose with the smoke to the two slender logs that spanned the roof. Thin red strips of drying meat dangled from one of the logs. Hanging from the other log, tied with yellow anchor rope, two long, thin limbs. When he leaned in and squinted in the smoke, his eyes followed the limbs to their end. Two small brown hands swayed in the green smoke.

He spun away from the door and vomited what little was in his stomach. His morning meal—two bites of hare meat—the rest acid and blood from his stomach slowly devouring itself.

When he was finished, he rolled the men onto their backs. He wanted to remember their faces. He wanted to know what sort of men would become worse than animals.

Soot and grime covered their foreheads and cheeks. The first two men were Yup'ik, the third a white man, his mouth opened and in a half snarl, his teeth rotted to sharp points. When he rolled the fourth man over, the man closest to the riverbank, John cried out.

The dead man staring into the grey-clouded sky above them wore what had once been a white cotton T-shirt with red lettering. The lettering had faded, the words STOP PEBBLE barely legible among the blood and stains.

He knelt down and put his cold hand to the dead man's warm forehead. With all the soot and dirt, the starved, tight skin of his face, he couldn't tell if the man was Carl, but it didn't matter. In his heart it was his old friend, stretched out dead in the snow, and he understood a little more about what a man would do to survive.

# PART III

## The
# Raven's
### Gift

*"You will be very lonely by yourself," said Raven. "I will make you a companion." He then went to a spot some distance from where he had made many animals, and looking now and then at Man, made an image very much like him. Then he fastened a lot of fine water grass on the back of the head for hair ... waved his wings over it as before and a beautiful young woman arose and stood beside Man.*

—YUP'IK CREATION STORY, RECORDED BY EDWARD NELSON, 1899

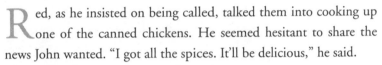

# 28

Red, as he insisted on being called, talked them into cooking up one of the canned chickens. He seemed hesitant to share the news John wanted. "I got all the spices. It'll be delicious," he said.

John didn't argue.

The bone-thin man opened up the top of the can, thawed the chicken, can and all, in a pot of water, and began preparing the meal. The girl and the old woman rested on the bed, and John sat quietly, just watching. It felt good to be somewhere safe and warm.

John pointed to the computer. "That work?"

"You mean is it connected to the world wide weird? No. If you need it to type a letter or something like that, it will work like a charm. With my batteries and the mills, and the solar panels I have on the roof of the old house, I've got plenty of juice. Everything but a hot shower. Totally off the grid."

He pulled out the chicken and dropped it on a cutting board. Then he dumped the juice from the can into a pot. John was glad to see this. He didn't want any part of the canned chicken going to waste.

Red glanced toward the bed. He leaned over to John and whispered, "You look like you could use a pick-me-up?" He opened a cupboard and pulled a nearly empty bottle of gin out from behind some pots. He poured a finger's worth into two small glasses and handed John one.

"To the last of the real people," he said, gesturing to the women on the bed.

They brought the glasses together with a soft clink and John took a small mouthful and just let it burn. The bitter taste of pine needles and juniper berries reminded him of the mountains and the old woman's tundra tea. Not his usual choice for a drink, but under the circumstances, he'd drink cooking wine.

He swallowed and held the glass to his nose and inhaled deeply.

"Thanks. I needed this," John said.

"I wish I could tell you there's more where that came from, but what you see here is the last of it. I should have learned how to make blueberry wine or something. Too late for that now, I guess."

He cut the chicken and then poured some rice and water into one pot, and in another dropped the meat in and dumped curry powder, dried lemongrass, and some other spices. "I won't make it too spicy," he said. "Yup'iks tend not to like stuff that's too hot. Lukewarm and bland is the standard fare. That or fermented. Which I suppose is spice all its own."

He covered the pot and turned a chair backward and straddled it. Then he stood up and turned the chair around and sat down in it. Then he stood up again, took the bottle back out, and poured the last of the gin.

"Your first question is where is the cavalry, right? Why didn't anyone come for us?"

John nodded. "Something like that," he said.

"First-year or second-year teacher in the Bush?"

"First. Going on a second, I guess."

Red nodded and took a sip. He stopped and watched the surveillance monitor.

"Let me warn you that I am a certified conspiracy nut, so take what you will from what I'm about to tell you. Won't say I saw this shitstorm coming, but as you can see with your own two eyes, I was as prepared as anyone could ever hope to be. Didn't expect the government to do anything to help me. Didn't want the government to help me. So naturally, I'm suspicious. I'm paranoid. I'm your standard survival nut. With that said, I got a sneaking suspicion the feds are responsible. And if they didn't create the sickness themselves, they sure didn't do anything to stop the slaughter." He took another sip and sat for a moment.

"Why would anyone want *this* to happen?" John asked, incredulous.

Red shook his head. "You're a teacher. Figure it out. Tuskegee syphilis experiments? Government-sponsored sterilization? The smallpox- and measles-infected blankets given to the Sioux? Sarin gas bomb testing in interior Alaska? Nuke detonations in the Aleutian chain? I could go on and on. This here? This could just be another big government romp in the Arctic sandbox."

John swirled his gin and took another sip. "I know enough history. And the proof is where, behind the grassy knoll?"

"Proof? My wife worked for the hospital. Heard from her, read some of her work materials, and did my own research. The Alaska bird flu plan was available to anyone with a mind to read it. There was one key line that I remember. Haven't been able to forget it, in fact. The plan had these assumptions about who would survive the flu. It said, 'Most people who have access to clean water, food, sanitation, fuel, and nursing and medical care while they are sick will survive.'"

"That wasn't even the case for most of the people out here *before* this all happened," John said. "There was a plan? They knew the flu would strike here? No. No way. Not possible. Why didn't anyone know about it? I was a teacher. I would have been told something. What to do. How to prepare. The school district would have informed us."

"Sure as shit there was a plan! Read it myself. Wish I had it for you to see now. You'd see the hole in it, plain as day. This isn't Monday-morning quarterbacking, either, John. The scientists only factored in the sickness. Apparently there was little to no consideration taken for the culture, the close living quarters, or the remote location. If they had ever hoped to actually stop the flu and help people here, they would have allotted a few more doses of Tamiflu. They would have initiated practice drills. The estimated infection rate was fifty percent, with only a three or four percent mortality rate, but that wasn't factoring lack of sanitation, heat, food sources, or adequate medical attention."

John felt light-headed. He stood up, sat down, quickly stood back up again. He steadied himself against the counter. He lifted the lid, set it aside, and watched the curry boil. He took a deep breath and returned to his chair.

Red stirred the pot, put the lid back on, and continued. "Or, you know, maybe that *was* all factored in, thus your answer to why no one came to save the day."

"So what *exactly* are you saying?" John asked.

"In case you didn't figure it out, if this disease is natural, southwestern Alaska is the perfect area for one hundred percent quarantine. That's *if* this was natural. If it wasn't, well that's another beast."

John set his glass down on the table and stood back up. He paced the small tank. He tried to not let thoughts of Anna's death mingle with his anger.

"First off," Red continued, "this is the biggest goddamn waterfowl refuge in the world, and the people rely on the birds for food. This wasn't a case of *if* the flu hit, it was *when*. And would H5N1 make the jump to people and mutate? Would it go pandemic on the tundra, spread across Alaska and northern Canada and then down to the States? But then that raises the question, What if they knew this would happen? Worse yet, what if some small group of rogue pharmaceutical scientists manufactured the sickness and brought the bug here themselves?"

"Honestly? I think you're completely full of shit. Delusional. Out of your gourd," John said. "Our government wouldn't knowingly let so many suffer, Red. Ever."

"No?" Red laughed. "Quarantining this area makes perfect sense, man. You kill two birds with one stone. You keep the pandemic from mainstream society and you find a simple solution to people draining taxpayer dollars. Those same people who sit on vast gold and petroleum reserves, I might add. Of course, what do I know? Could be the feds infected the region with this bug to create an anti-virus from the sole survivors like you and me. Or, it might just be the end."

"You're crazy," John said.

"Been called worse, my friend, been called a helluva lot worse."

John picked up his glass and took another sip while Red stirred the pot. The sweet aroma of curry and chicken filled the small room. Movement on the video screen caught Red's eye. He set the lid back on the pot and gestured for John to join him in front of the screen.

John rose, half expecting to see the old woman's hunter racing on his skis toward the tank.

"Damn," Red whispered. "Here comes company."

ANNA STOOD POUNDING against the door with her heavy mittens. He opened the door to find her bundled up in her down parka, with a grin that threatened to swallow her face. She insisted he visit a house for the Slaviq celebrations.

"At least one house," she said. "It's so fun. Festive. There's food and singing and this amazing feeling. They bring in this big star and spin it and sing. It's this incredible feeling of family and friends and community. I've never felt this before. You've got to try it. Just once. Plus, the next starring is at Carl's. He wants you there."

"One? You realize it's eleven thirty at night?" he asked.

"I know! It's like time doesn't matter, doesn't exist. That's part of what is so cool. It's the whole village. Come on."

He pulled on his boots, hat, and jacket. "I don't know if I can stomach her beaver stew right now," he said.

"Carl saved some of the oranges that Santa and the soldiers brought, and someone told me Carrie had muskoxen meat from her brother's family on the coast. That sounds interesting, doesn't it? Florida oranges and prehistoric meat! Hurry! If we get there early we won't have to stand in the porch."

They scurried down the steps and along the snow-covered board-walk toward Carl's house. The gusting wind at their backs seemed to push them, and John didn't look forward to trudging back with the blowing ice crystals cutting at his face. The blasts made a low, barely audible whistle as they walked between and around the houses. Ahead, he could see people filing into Carl's little home.

"If it gets to be too much, I'm out," he said as they reached the front steps.

The men shook hands and nodded and smiled as they entered. Many of the women hugged Anna, as if she hadn't spent the whole evening with them at another house. The place was packed with people standing against the walls, and some sitting on the floor. The chairs and couch and beds, every available place to sit in the house held a warm body.

John took a deep breath and tried to relax.

Carl waved him over.

"Hey! Glad you came, buddy. Let me find you a chair."

"It's okay, I can stand."

"No way, you're my guest of honour. Here." Carl spotted an empty yellow five-gallon bucket beneath the kitchen table. He pulled the bucket out, flipped it over, and slid it up to the table. "There you go! Sit with the elders."

John smiled in appreciation and looked around the table at the five old men.

"Hello. I'm John."

The men nodded and two of them introduced themselves. Then they pointed to the other men, introduced them, and explained that they didn't speak *kass'aq*. John turned his eyes to the spread of food on the table in front of him. Pots and large yellow and green plastic bowls covered the entire table and each of them was filled to the top with stew, soup, dried fish, cut-up oranges, and variations of *akutaq*. He glanced around at the elders, short, thin old men he'd never seen up close before.

Wrinkles covered their faces with dark lines and endless crevices, contour maps of history, weather, hunting. He wanted to tell them he wasn't just another outsider but that his grandmother had been Native, maybe even Yup'ik. He wanted to question them. Listen to them. Hear their stories. And apologize all at once. Instead, he sat there. Dumb.

More people filed in. And still more.

He worried Carl's small house would collapse. He thought he could almost feel the thin plywood floor and the joists protesting the weight. Anna sat in a corner, a snotty-nosed toddler sitting in her lap, sucking on an orange peel and running his hand down her cheek, as if testing the softness of her pale flesh. She caught John's glance and winked.

The singing began as another group filed in, and for a brief moment a pretty younger woman caught his attention. She looked straight at him and almost through him with whitish eyes. He glanced away, not wanting to stare, and then back and she was gone in the crowd. A man entered carrying a star on a wooden spinner covered with shiny red Christmas garland. The contraption looked like an oversized pinwheel, complete with sparkles and a stick to hold it up.

Someone led a prayer to bless and keep the troops overseas safe, and then a man began to spin the star and everyone started to sing.

The song, a Yup'ik version of "Silent Night," caught him off guard. He looked over to Anna again, and she was singing too. Smiling and singing. He took a deep breath and tried to relax a little. Tried to feel the spirit of the season. An atmosphere of joy and excitement was building in Carl's diminutive house, and he could feel it. It was that or claustrophobia about to kick in with the warm crush of bodies.

For once he just went with it and tried as best he could to join in the song.

FOR ONCE HE UNDERSTOOD the girl's sensitivity to smell. They made camp beneath the riverbank a quarter mile from the fish camp where he'd shot the men, but the horrible smoke was still there, lingering. He rubbed snow in his nostrils and wondered if the girl could smell it on him. In his clothes. On his breath. In his mind.

When he shut his eyes he was again behind the smokehouse door and one man emerged, then another, and another. And he shot them all. The girl's screams echoed in his ears and mixed with the gunshots.

He hadn't said anything about what he saw in the smokehouse or how many men he'd killed. He knew the girl was formulating her nightly questions, and when the first one came he breathed a sigh of relief.

"How old were you when you first, you know? Did it?" the girl asked.

He understood she was doing this for him, asking inane questions and then answering them in her own way.

She rolled over and spoke to the back of his head, the campfire at her own back. He couldn't tell if she was still playing with her grass weaving. The wind changed direction, blowing their campfire smoke toward them. He coughed and wiped at the smell of burnt flesh somehow in his nose again.

"I don't count the first time," she said. "I don't want to talk about or even think about that. Later on, you know. I almost tried it. Seems like everyone I knew had humped before. They would go out at night right before the village curfew and do it in empty steam baths, in those covered porches, or even under the school. Sometimes if everyone was at open gym or bingo games, the boys would try make me go to their house. I thought maybe if I let someone be with me they would maybe want to be my boyfriend. My cousin told me I would find someone to love me that way. I was too scared, though. I didn't want to be blind and pregnant and alone, you know?"

He sat up and stared out into the dark back toward the fish camp. He imagined the men he'd left in the snow slowly coming back to life. A finger or two moving at first. Eyelids fluttering. Maybe he hadn't killed them after all.

"So," she continued, "if you don't count what my uncle did, I'm still one, I guess. A virgin. Probably going to die that way now, too. Never got to love someone."

The men's eyes were open. Lips moving.

He sank back into his sleeping bag and turned over on his back. Above them, the sky swirled dark with clouds. She was trying so hard to help him leave the smokehouse behind.

"You've got a long life ahead of you. There will be love for you someday," he said.

The first of the men sat upright. Then the next.

"Was your wife? You know, when you married her?" she asked.

"Sex and love, the two are different. Don't equate the two. No more. Please. No more questions. I can't deal with them right now. I know you're trying … just not tonight," he said.

"Sorry," she said.

"Sorry for snapping. Let's sleep, okay?"

"Will you ever again?" she asked.

He turned away from her and took a small handful of snow, balled it up, and put in on his dry tongue.

The men back at the fish camp crawled to their feet.

Someone had relit the fire inside the smokehouse.

"Will you?" she asked.

They stumbled down the bank.

Axes and knives in hand.

"I was fifteen," he said, "in a small little dome tent in a backyard

in the summer. Her parents were at church. It was nothing special. I
don't even remember her name."

"I want it to be special," she said.

"It will be," he said, as he fought a vision of the four hungry corpses
lurching through the dark toward their camp.

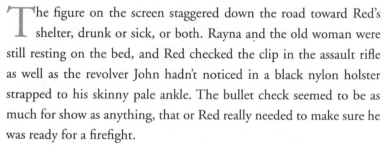

# 29

The figure on the screen staggered down the road toward Red's shelter, drunk or sick, or both. Rayna and the old woman were still resting on the bed, and Red checked the clip in the assault rifle as well as the revolver John hadn't noticed in a black nylon holster strapped to his skinny pale ankle. The bullet check seemed to be as much for show as anything, that or Red really needed to make sure he was ready for a firefight.

"Should just shoot the poor bastard to put him out of his misery," Red said.

"Is he drunk?" John asked.

"I doubt it. My bet is that the only booze left within a thousand or so miles is right there in our glasses. He's either delirious from hunger, or the bug. Or all three."

"What'll we do?"

"Nothing. There are people who have survived by any means necessary. The living dead, that's what I've called 'em. I avoid them and if they give me any shit, I put them down. I would hope someone would do the same for me."

John nodded. "The girl calls them outcasts," he whispered. "A group of them we encountered were cannibals."

"Like I said, any means necessary."

John nodded his head in the direction of the sleeping girl. "She claims she can smell them," he whispered.

"You know as well as I that you can see it in a person's eyes. The eyes change when you kill a man, and they change again when your reasons for killing ain't right."

John leaned in closer to the screen. The person stopped, turned in circles, and then faced their direction.

"Does this camera zoom in?" John asked.

Red flipped a switch on the small control panel beside the screen and brought the image in closer. "It doesn't zoom," he said, "but it can pull the picture in digitally. How's that?"

John put a hand over the top of the screen to block the reflection from the fluorescent above. He brought his face close to the screen. "Shit," he said under his breath.

"You know him?" Red asked.

John nodded and swore to himself again and said, "I think he's one of my students."

The figure appeared skittish, less than human, almost feral. His movements were sharp and jerky. Was this one of them? One of the girl's wild people? He glanced at her sleeping on the bed, and he knew he couldn't stand there in the warmth and safety of Red's shelter. He knew if he woke her she would beg John to do something magical, save him, perhaps spit on the boy or take one finger and gently push him down into the frozen tundra.

John pulled his parka on and from his pocket removed the key to the cabinet outside. "I'm going to have to get my pistol out," John said, walking toward the door. He stopped and pointed the key at Red and then the girl. "If something happens to me, take care of the girl."

THE WEEK AFTER Anna and John's Slaviq celebrations, the remnant of a monstrous Japanese typhoon crawled its way north, into the Bering Sea, and slammed into the Aleutian Islands first and then the Yukon and Kuskokwim deltas with hurricane force, bringing record winds and snowfall.

They struggled through the three- and four-foot-high drifts to get to school only to find out that the District Office had called off classes, anticipating the blizzard would worsen.

John turned on the coffee pot in the main office and while it percolated, sat at the secretary's desk and listened to the radio, KYUK, a Bethel station, the only radio station in the area. Dave, the balding principal, poked his head into the office and waved.

"I'm heading home for a while. See what this storm does. I'm going to keep those main doors open, in case someone didn't get the message over the VHF."

"Looks like we're the only ones who didn't get the message," John joked.

"I was about to stop by your house. I don't know why they don't have a phone hooked up at your place yet. Teachers are usually the only ones without the VHF radios. Anyway—you mind sending anyone who comes in back home? Walk any of the little ones, for liability."

John nodded.

"This storm sounds like it could last a while," Dave said. "Nothing like a good Bering Sea blow. Nothing. This thing might shut down air travel for several days. Well, enjoy the extra day of holiday. We don't usually cancel school unless the chill factor is below seventy-five. Not many snow days, so make the best of it."

"Yeah."

Dave slipped out, and John heard the familiar intro music for the KYUK morning news. He reached over and turned the radio up. The young female reporter spoke with far too much gusto for a Monday morning.

"Top stories we are covering for today: The school district battens down the hatches for what might be a record blizzard, the father of the K300 Sled Dog Race has decided to run the Iditarod one last time, and the Yukon-Kuskokwim Health Corporation struggles with a flu outbreak in Hooper Bay. But first, national news."

John turned the volume button down until the red power light clicked off the radio. He filled two plastic cups with coffee and headed to Anna's classroom. She had a radio in there, and he wanted her to hear news of their extended vacation from the radio and not him.

THE DAY BEFORE John and the girl would reach the old woman's village, she told him another of her favourite memories from when she could see. They had stopped to rest and melt some snow for drinking when she began telling her story. As she spoke, he took out the pot and broke a handful of twigs from a spruce tree wedged between the riverbank and the ice. The tree had a small yellow rope tied around it, something he'd learned about from Carl. The rope meant someone had claimed the driftwood, but the hundred or so miles the large spruce had floated and the yellow rope meant little now.

The dry wood caught easily and he had a nice little fire crackling in minutes. He filled the pot with snow and began melting it. They would walk another couple of miles and he knew they hadn't taken in enough liquid the night before, plus some water would quell the burn inside their stomachs.

"We used to make fires like this in August when we went picking berries. My dad would start the fire, then my grandma would keep it going. He would go catch some silvers and then bring them back, maybe just one or two, and Grandma would cut them up and cook them right on the fire. I can just taste that silver salmon now. I miss fish. I wonder if we could maybe catch a pike or whitefish?"

"I don't have any fishing line and no way to chip through the ice," he said.

"Maybe we can find some. Yup'iks used to make fish traps, too. They made them from willow. Round traps that look like those space capsules, except hollow and made with bent willow trees. Fish swim in the hole in the middle and they can't get out. You could make a fish trap."

"I don't think I could. I've seen pictures. Don't think I have what it takes to make one."

"Darn. I could eat fish right now."

"Me too," he said.

She sat down near the fire and removed her mittens. She held her hands out, palms facing her, letting the flames warm the backs of her hands. He noticed the thin band of ivory on her right ring finger.

"Another thing I really remember, one of my favourite times, is getting down close to the tundra, with my face almost in it and just staring at all the plants and berries. My *uppa*, my grandpa, he was always smiling, he told me to do that once. He said, 'Look down there, get real near the ground and see all that life. All those little tiny flowers, and moss, and lichen, the berries, the mushrooms, so many special things in one little space—then look up and out across the tundra and see how much there is out there. Don't ever let no one tell you this is a land of nothing,' he said, 'never let them tell you that. Everything you need to survive is right there.' He said that to me, and I'll never forget."

John added another handful of snow. The pot began sizzling and the snow melted quickly. His mouth seemed to be drying out faster than he could melt the snow. He wondered if they shouldn't just camp there since they were out of the wind and near a good source of firewood. He didn't like how exposed they were, though, no real shelter or cover from anyone approaching.

"He died before I couldn't see any more," she said. "So I remember that, too. I remember his body in our house before they took him to the church. They had him on a bed in my mom's room. Just dressed in black jeans and his church shirt, a white shirt that was too big for him. He was still kind of chunky when he died, but he looked happy. No smile. I remember wishing he was still smiling. He was the first dead person I ever had in my house. For a while I wouldn't look in her room because I was afraid I would still see him on that bed, even though they buried him. That was the mattress you found me under."

One of the sticks in the fire popped and a large piece of ash dropped into the water. He pulled it out with his fingers and the lukewarm liquid made him suddenly wish he could bathe. He glanced down at his icy brown beard and wondered just how awful he really looked and smelled.

A chill began to settle into his bones. Not enough food, and not enough water, he thought. He'd overexerted himself and could feel the chills taking hold. He clenched his fingers and began to move his toes inside his boots. Somehow during the day he'd quit paying attention to the signs from his body and now, as if his heart pumped ice water, everything began to constrict. He could feel the chill enveloping him right down the back of his spine to his testicles.

"Maybe you should get into your sleeping bag for a while," the girl said, as if she could hear his shivering, his front teeth beginning to tap lightly. "You can warm up with me. If you need to. If you want," she said.

He couldn't.

"I'll be fine," he said. "Let's get moving. I just need to keep moving."

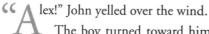

# 30

"Alex!" John yelled over the wind.

The boy turned toward him. His body swayed. He could hardly stand.

"Wha-choo-want?" His speech was slurred and he struggled to remain standing.

John held his pistol at his side and approached slowly. The wind gusts carried thin sheets of snow knee high across the drifted roadway.

"Alex, it's me. John. Your teacher. John."

He moved closer, slowly toward John, like the ground beneath might give way.

"It's okay. I'll help you!" John yelled.

John was too far away, but he reached out his hand anyway. When he did this, the boy started to laugh. He giggled and reached into his inside jacket pocket.

"Don't do that," John said. "Keep your hands out."

"You're too late, *kass'aq* man. Way too late."

His hand slid into his jacket and John raised the Glock. The boy pulled his hand out and John aimed.

The boy held up a narrow-necked yellow plastic bottle. John recognized it. He didn't need to see the blue lettering. HEET. Isopropyl alcohol.

The boy turned his head and stared out into the darkness. John followed the boy's stare into the approaching blizzard. The boy dropped the bottle and began staggering into the wind.

"Alex, is that you?" John lunged forward and with his free hand grabbed the boy by his jacket. The boy's black hair was long and tangled and his face was sunken, the skin stretched taut across his cheeks. His lips were cracked black and bleeding, most of his teeth missing. The air around him reeked of chemicals and death.

He called for him again, but it wasn't Alex. He looked like the boy he had taught, but older, worn. The person, barely able to stand, wasn't Alex. At least he hoped not. The boy's eyes were lifeless, as if what they had seen had burned the shine away.

"Death is coming for you, too," the boy slurred.

He tried to pull away. John held him tight. The boy stared out at the darkness, and turned his eyes back to John. For a moment, the boy's eyes seemed to clear, to connect.

"I seen the ghost of an old woman out there, John," he said.

"Yes, it's me. It's okay. It's me, John. I'm your teacher, Alex."

"Alex? My brother? He was one of the lucky ones in Kuigpak."

John let go of the boy and took a step back, his mind racing through his memories of the dried and withered faces in gym.

The boy swayed like a thin tree in the wind and pointed his middle finger at John as he took another step away, "I'm not like my brother. I wanted to watch it happen. And now I seen everything."

JOHN AND ANNA were the last of the school's five teachers into the principal's office. Dave shut his door, pointed to the remaining two seats, and then sat in the oversized chair behind his desk.

"I'm sure you heard about the flu virus spreading through the Yukon villages," he began and then took a drink of a diet cola and cleared his throat. "From what the District Office has told me, this flu thing has hit the schools pretty hard. We're trying to be proactive and head this off at the pass."

"What kind of flu are we talking about?"

The question came from Sandra, a frumpy middle-school teacher in sweatpants, who overreacted to every announcement that had ever come from the principal's mouth.

"They aren't sure. Two years ago we had a really bad RSV outbreak. Half a dozen medevacs of babies and toddlers from just about every village in the area. This sounds similar. They've sent twenty or thirty folks from Hooper Bay to Bethel for treatment. A few villages on the Kuskokwim side have sent in a few kids, too. I'm sure you've been listening to the news on the radio."

"What are we supposed to do?" Anna asked.

"Good question, Anna. For now the D.O. wants us to promote hand washing and keep an eye out for kids with runny noses and coughs. Any sick kids are to go straight to the clinic. If you can also try to wipe desks and keyboards and doorknobs, that will help, too."

Sandra chuckled. "You're kidding, right? Promote hand washing? These kids don't have running water at home! Half of them have coughs and runny noses at any given time. We're supposed to send them home?"

The principal nodded. "For now," he said, "send them home."

"That's the plan?" Sandra said. "No offence, but that's ridiculous."

John felt like telling her to shut up. Anna gently patted his knee.

Dave made circles on his desk with a black pen, rubbed the top of his shiny head with his other hand, and then stood up and paced behind his desk. He stopped in front of his office window, which looked out across the open tundra plain to the west. He tapped the pen against the window. "There's something else," he said, "probably nothing, but my wife's friend at the hospital in Bethel said if this outbreak comes back as a possible strain of bird flu to expect quarantine for at least a couple of weeks. Minimum."

Sandra gasped and pushed back from the table. "Bird flu? Bird flu? Quarantine? What do you mean?"

"Now relax, Sandra. I said it's probably nothing."

"Nothing? I'm not staying here to find out. I'm taking sick leave and heading to Anchorage. I'll wait this sickness out somewhere safe with adequate medical facilities, running water, law enforcement. Half of the men in the village are away at war. We'll be helpless quarantined. I refuse to be put in such a compromising position."

"I think you're overreacting," the principal said.

"Do you guys think so?" she asked and turned to the other teachers. John looked away. The woman annoyed him to no end.

"I hardly think this could be bird flu," Anna said. "Plus, none of my students seem sick. A few snotty noses, but that's at any school. I don't think it will hurt to stress some hand washing habits."

"Well, I'm not waiting around to find out," Sandra said. "I'm not comfortable waiting to see if we all get quarantined. What sort of plan is that?"

The principal turned, sat back down in his desk, and jotted down some note on a yellow legal pad. "You know what? I'm not going to argue with you, Sandra. I've tried to run this school with a team approach, and if a little bump in the road is going to be too much for you to deal with, then maybe it's better if you're not around while this bug runs its course."

"Good!" Sandra said and stomped out the door.

"Was I wrong there?" he asked.

"If anything, you were too kind, sir."

"Thanks, John," Dave said. "Listen, I didn't mean to scare any of you. I just wanted to pass on what was passed to me. If any of you think you need to join Sandra, go right ahead. Those news reports on KYUK have been enough for me to think about bailing, too. I'd hate to see my wife or daughter get that sick."

"PLEASE," THE GIRL whispered again. He tried not to look at her face, but when he did he saw that her white eyes couldn't carry the emotion her voice held. Her eyes seemed to search for an answer, but her white irises stared right into him.

"Just for a little while," she begged, setting her grass bundle aside. "I'm too cold. So cold. I don't want to freeze to death."

When he didn't answer, she took the silence as acquiescence and moved toward him. She felt for his sleeping bag and pulled it down enough for her to slide her feet in. She was shivering, and breathing hard. So was he. He closed his mouth and held his breath. She lifted his arm and put it around her and poured herself into him, nuzzling her face into his neck.

She lifted her shirt just a few inches and pressed the warm flesh of her stomach and hips against his. She touched her lips to his ear and whispered again.

"I'm sorry. I'm so cold. Just hold me, please, John? Just this once," she asked.

His mouth felt dry, his arms too weak to pull her in and just allow himself to return her embrace. The sleeping bag shrank and tightened to the point where he didn't know if he would be able to take another breath.

Her warmth, her skin against his skin.

He tore out of the bag and stumbled away from their camp into the dark. He dropped to his knees and felt like he had to vomit. When nothing came he just knelt in the snow and then took two handfuls and buried his face in the icy powder.

After a while he got up and slowly made his way back to camp.

"Are you okay?"

"I'm fine."

"I'm sorry," she said.

"There's nothing to be sorry about."

The girl was back in her sleeping bag, shivering. Anna's old sleeping bag. He looked at his own bag and his stomach turned again. At least they had been in his bag. He sat down on the tarp and closed his eyes and tried to clear his mind.

They had done nothing, just held each other for warmth, he told himself. But even that felt wrong.

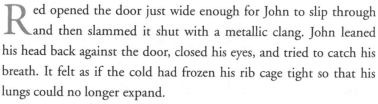

# 31

Red opened the door just wide enough for John to slip through and then slammed it shut with a metallic clang. John leaned his head back against the door, closed his eyes, and tried to catch his breath. It felt as if the cold had frozen his rib cage tight so that his lungs could no longer expand.

"Should have put the kid out of his misery," Red said.

John opened his eyes. The girl sat on the bed, her head in her hands. For a moment he was worried she thought he had left her, but then he noticed the old woman was gone.

"I tried to tell her to wait until you got back," Red said. "Even showed you on the monitor."

John looked down at the spot where the old woman's makeshift sled had been.

"Why did she leave?" he asked.

Rayna raised her head. Her white eyes glared at the two of them. "She knew you were drinking. You were getting drunk, so she left."

"Getting drunk?"

She stood up and walked to the table. She sniffed the air and picked up the glass that had held his gin.

"She smelled you guys. Said she wasn't going to be around drunks with the hunter coming."

"Did she say where she was going? Did you let her get her shotgun?"

Rayna shook her head. He looked at Red.

"You had the key to the cabinet outside. She wasn't having nothing to do with me, anyways. I don't think she would have taken one of my guns if I'd offered. And who the hell is the hunter?" Red asked.

John took the glass from the girl, slammed it on the table, and sat down on one of the folding chairs. He sat for a few minutes with the girl standing beside him. He stood up and looked at the monitor, half expecting to see the old woman, or the boy he had mistaken as Alex struggling against the blizzard picking up outside.

"You're not going to drink more and get drunk, are you?" she asked in a quiet whisper.

He pulled his parka back on and stood at the door. "Let me see if I can catch up with her," he said. "We're not getting drunk. Don't worry."

He put his arms around her. He'd never held her that way before, tightly in his arms; he'd never tried to comfort her like that.

"I'll find her," he said.

ANNA AND JOHN hid out in their home, listening to the AM radio and waiting for the all-clear sign.

"I wish we had a goddamn phone," Anna said, while she heated up the teakettle. "I just want to call Mom to tell her we're okay."

"She knows you're fine."

"It's just sort of ridiculous that we don't have a phone, you know. In this day and age. It didn't bother me until now."

"Or running water. The bucket is about full, and I'm not exactly thrilled to go dump it with everyone sick like this," he said.

"Do you think I could just run over to the school and call her?"

"No. Why don't you just email her?"

"The stupid internet isn't connecting. Plus, that's not the same, John. She needs to hear my voice. She needs to know this is just temporary and that we're okay."

"Shh—news time."

John turned up the volume on the radio he had brought home from the school.

The reporter's voice sounded thousands of miles away through the radio's single speaker. "For KYUK News, I'm Shane Keller. Here is a look at our top local stories. Army guard troops from the region may have their deployment extended. Lower Kuskokwim School District has cancelled class district-wide in response to a respiratory infection that has hit many area villages. Local health officials call for help from state and federal agencies to respond to the growing number of sick infants. And the controversial free fuel program from Venezuela will continue this year, but an announcement that fuel will be delayed until spring is drawing concern from local leaders who say supplies are already too low. All this and more for your KYUK midday news report."

"Turn it off," Anna said. "I can't listen to it any more. How many more ways can they say more people are sick and nothing is being done? No one is doing anything to help! How can they just sit back and do nothing?"

John shrugged. He turned the radio off and looked out the window. The village was a picture of lifelessness. Nothing moved outside except for a few thin golden grass stalks poking out through the snow. The winds shook the small dead stalks. No children played. No snow machines zipped past. For all he knew, the entire village had disappeared during the night.

## 32

When he returned without the old woman, they ate their dinner in complete silence. When he was done, John ran a finger around his bowl and licked it. The curry powder had given the canned chicken a strangely exotic flavour. That or his tongue had stopped working the way it was supposed to. He set his bowl down and picked a piece of meat from between his teeth with a fingernail.

"Which way did she go?" the girl asked.

"Toward the river," he said.

"She'll be okay," the girl said. "Maybe she'll go—where we talked about meeting up if we needed to, or somewhere else, somewhere safe."

John looked over to the girl. She hadn't touched her dinner yet.

"Maybe," he said. "I wish you'd made her stay. I'm worried. She's unarmed."

"Good luck making that old woman do anything you say," Red said.

"I tried," Rayna said. "I really tried, John."

"Well, I guess I can't sit here and worry about her. I can't. I mean I tried, but the wind. Her tracks were disappearing and I didn't know if I could find my way back. We've got enough to worry about. I can't worry about some old woman," John said.

"The hunter," Red said, in a half statement, half question.

John rested his head in his hands. "She kept talking about some man she thought she saw. Someone in all white, travelling downriver."

"Not an outcast. Someone else," the girl added. "Tell him about the hunter, John."

"It's probably nothing. We cut some ski tracks at the mouth of the Johnson River."

"Ski tracks? Like cross-country skis?" Red bit at his lip and stood up. He turned to the teapot and pressed his hand against the metal to see if the water was still warm. He turned the burner on and sat back down. "I don't like that news. Not one bit," he said. "Ski tracks? Are you sure? Not a dogsled or something?"

John nodded and took a drink of water and then reached over and took Rayna's right hand. He opened her fingers and slid the spoon between them. He lifted her hand and guided the spoon into the curry broth. She didn't resist as he brought her hand to her lips. She opened, and sipped the warm curry. He let go and she slowly dipped her spoon and began feeding herself.

"I want to check out what's here in town. See if I can salvage anything that will help us head upriver. Something to make travel a little easier."

"To help us find my cousins and the other kids," Rayna said. "And Maggie," she added.

"What cousins are you looking for?" Red asked.

"In Kuigpak, most of the kids disappeared. My cousins. I think they are still alive somewhere. I'm going to find them."

Red looked at John and John lifted a finger to his lips so that Red knew the girl didn't understand there were no cousins, no survivors.

"We're going for help first," John said. "We need to get help."

"Well, I can help you with that conundrum. There's nothing worth salvaging in this town. And no reason to head upriver."

"What do you mean?"

"Bethel's been picked clean. You've got more food on that sled than you'll find in this whole region. As far as fuel, snow machines— whatever you're hoping to find for transport, you've got to be crazy to think you're the first one to have looked. I can tell you that first hand. And then there's the others. Two groups of them so far as I can tell. Not sure how they're getting by, not sure I want to know. Bethel's version of her outcasts. They pretty much took over town, month or so after the bug hit bad, but I don't know what's become of them. Bad has a way of burning itself out."

"What about heading upriver? Seems like the only way to go."

"Way to go? Boy, I'll say." Red stood up and collected John's bowl. "Way to die, maybe." He went to the pot and divvied up the remaining chicken and curry and handed his bowl back. He poured a scoop into Rayna's dish.

"There's chicken in there—you can use your hands for that leg," he said to her. "It's on the right side of your bowl."

"Thanks," she said. "It's yummy. It's really good, Red. I never thought I would eat real food again."

Red sat back down and sipped a spoonful and then licked his lips.

"You're talking about travelling a helluva long ways, through some damned unforgiving land, for what? To find out if the rest of the world went to shit, too? Let me guess. Your plan is to make it to McGrath, then cut across the Iditarod Trail and head east through the mountains to Anchorage, the cradle of civili-fargin-zation. How long has it taken you to get this far? What, thirty or forty miles?"

"A while."

Red nodded. "A while, right. How long do you think it will take you to just get to McGrath, five hundred some miles? And with that heavy food supply and no skis or snowshoes? No trail? Not to mention the snow gets deeper and the ice gets thinner each step that direction. Best bet is to stick here with me. If there is a hunter out there, you're safest here, with me."

The strange man stared across the table at him. John shifted in his chair and turned his eyes toward what was left in his bowl. He could feel Red's gaze still on him.

"I don't mean to take away your hope, John," Red said. "But your plan ain't in the least bit realistic—especially not when you're already malnourished and toting a blind girl with you to boot—no offence, Rayna. If you could even get there, what do you expect to find?"

John shrugged.

"It's like being stuck in an old rusty leg trap. You can gnaw your leg clean off and get free, but you're still going to be out one leg. Say you make it. Say people aren't sick. That means they accepted this mess. They quarantined us and never came to help. Never made a food drop. Nothing. Who could live with people that would allow us to suffer like this? Or let's say you make it there—you travel damn near a thousand miles only to find it hit them, too. Then what? Keep travelling toward Seattle?"

John suddenly felt full. His body flushed hot. His stomach rolled. He felt trapped inside the tank. He slid back his chair from the table and stood up. He walked to the door, unbolted it, and cracked it just enough to stick his nose and mouth out. He took a deep breath of the cold racing in.

He shut the door, bolted it, and rested his cheek against the cool metal. He clenched his abdominal muscles and tried to will them to hold his dinner down.

"You okay?" Red asked.

"Just not used to being so full," he said, sitting back down, and then standing and walking around the room.

Red let out a long, low belch. "Me neither."

The girl finally took one of the pieces of chicken from her bowl and gently began to pull the meat from the bone. The two of them watched her and sat in silence while she ate.

She finished chewing the end of a bone and set it into her bowl. She reached across the table and took John's hand. "We should find Maggie and the kids and make sure they are safe first," she said.

THE LIGHTS FLICKERED and Anna posed a terrible question that he hadn't considered. "What happens if the power goes out?" she asked.

They were lying in bed, reading. The lamp beside their bed flickered again. She closed her book and rolled over and rested her head on his chest. Her skin felt too warm against his, but she always felt warm against him.

"What if the person who runs the village's power gets sick? Or his family? What then?"

"Don't be such a doomsayer, Anna. You're always giving me crap about my unholy statements. Where's your hope?"

"I'm serious. What if the power goes out? How will we stay warm? It's not like we have a woodstove, or any other options. If the power goes out, we won't have heat, John. No communications, nothing. Nothing!"

"It's not going to go out. Besides, if it did, we've got good sleeping bags. We can always generate our own heat, too, you know."

He thrust against her with his hips.

"Don't! I'm serious!"

She rolled over on her back and stared up at the ceiling.

"If this gets really bad, how long do you think it will take for someone to come help? I mean—they won't wait too long, will they? What would we do? We're so screwed, you know? We're helpless, aren't we? We might as well be on a desert island. What are we going to do? Walk out of here?"

He shrugged and pretended to read his book. He was worried her questions were building to some sort of hysterical breakdown again. She wasn't dealing well with being cooped up, and neither was he, and her constant fretting didn't help anything.

"I feel funny. Not sick. Just funny. You know? Probably dehydrated. We're going to have to get water tomorrow from the school. No matter what."

The light winked out for a moment and then popped back on. The power often fluctuated in the village, but the brief flicker felt ominous.

She turned away from him, curled up into a ball, and began to sob. He didn't know what to tell her, so he said nothing and just rubbed her shoulder with his palm; then he turned off the light and put his arms around her.

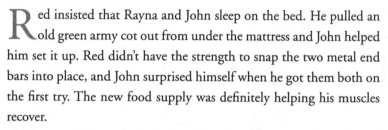

# 33

Red insisted that Rayna and John sleep on the bed. He pulled an old green army cot out from under the mattress and John helped him set it up. Red didn't have the strength to snap the two metal end bars into place, and John surprised himself when he got them both on the first try. The new food supply was definitely helping his muscles recover.

They settled into the bed, the girl on the side against the wall, and John on the outside. The cotton sheets weren't exactly clean, but he didn't care. They were a nice change from the dirty nylon sleeping bag.

Red laid out a blanket on the cot, took an extra pillow from beneath the bed, and then stood by the small screen and took one last look at the images from the surveillance cameras.

"I still have a hard time believing that you have that system working, when there isn't power anywhere else around here," John said.

"Well, isn't much to it. As long as the wind blows, which it always does, and the turbines keep working and charging the batteries, I'll have my security system and my heat. What I should have invested in was a shortwave radio. Kilbuck Elementary had one a while back, but of course someone torched that place, like most everything else."

John pointed to the AM/FM radio sitting on the counter. "You pick up anything with that?"

Red reached over to the radio and flipped it on. He hit the scan button and turned the volume up. From the bed, John could see the digital numbers scrolling through the AM stations. Nothing but static.

"For the first few months I did this every night. Scanned all the frequencies. Back before all this flu shit, on clear nights we could get stations from Russia, Korea—hell, all over. Now there's nothing. But watch this. Watch how it hits some numbers and pauses—like there is a signal there. See that, 650? That's KENI, an Anchorage station. It pauses for a split second and goes on. But when it passes over 640, the local station, nothing. I don't know what it means. Might just be crazy me thinking it's something, but hearing about this hunter character only makes me wonder that much more. No one would be out skiing. Why would they send one guy? Makes no sense."

He turned the radio off, flipped off the light, and settled into his cot. Then he said, "We both know that KYUK quit broadcasting when the power went out. To me it's like there are stations out there, but we can't get them. My guess is they're being scrambled."

Rayna sat up and turned to Red. "Why would they want to keep us from getting radio?" she asked.

"I don't know if that's what they're doing, honey, but could be that this whole region is under a complete communication shadow. Nothing in or out. A no-fly zone to boot. I'm sure you've also noticed the lack of contrails from commercial jets, John? This whole frozen countryside is no-man's land."

"I don't buy it, Red. How do you answer for all of the friends and family and relatives outside who would want to know what's going on?"

Red coughed and turned his back on them. "I'm just telling you what I think," he said. "Believe what you want. Whatever helps you get through the day, buddy. But I'll tell you this: no one listened to those friends and families when they talked about conditions here *before* the outbreak. There are populations in this world who are the expendable people in the eyes of all governments. I know none of this for sure, but then again, don't really matter much if I'm wrong now, does it?"

John rested on his back with his eyes open and staring at the white insulated ceiling. The girl reached beneath the covers for his hand. She grabbed hold of it, turned toward him, and pressed it to her chest. She held his hand there and squeezed.

"Do you think he's right?" she whispered.

"I hope not," he answered.

"John, we have to find them before the hunter does."

IT TOOK SIX HOURS from the time the lights blinked out until Anna and John could see their breath. They huddled beneath every blanket they had. Both of them had runny noses, and he couldn't convince her it was just a reaction to the cold and not the actual flu.

"I'm starting to feel warm. Too warm," she said, just barely sticking her head out from under the covers.

"You're making yourself sick," he said. "I'm sure the power will come back on soon enough."

They heard the sound of a snow machine pulling up to their house. The machine stopped, the engine continued to idle, and the house shook slightly as someone ran up the steps.

John pushed the covers off and pulled on his pants.

The heavy thumping on the door caught them both off guard. The one thing he'd never heard anyone in the village do was pound on a door. Even the kids who visited would only tap lightly, if they knocked at all.

"Coming!"

A scared voice came from the other side of the door.

"John? It's Carl. Are you guys okay?"

John opened the door, and the look of fear and worry on Carl's face troubled him.

"What's wrong? Come in."

Carl, wearing only a thin sweatshirt, no hat, gloves, or snow pants, shook his head. "No, I can't. I just wanted to know if you had any medicine. Anything? My family. They're all sick. The clinic is closed. No one has anything."

"We don't have much. Just some cold medicine, I think. Hold on." John stuck his head into their bedroom. Anna had been listening. "We don't have anything except that nighttime stuff. Give that to him," she said.

In the kitchen, John opened a cupboard and pulled out the bottle of NyQuil. "Do you have some ibuprofen?"

"Don't really have anything," Carl said. "No one does. The store is all out of everything and closed. We don't even have Aspirin at our house."

John emptied half the bottle of ibuprofen and then put the pills and the bottle of cold syrup into a plastic bag.

"I wish I had more for you, buddy."

"It's bad," Carl said. "Real bad. People are getting really sick. Dying. I'm afraid for my little one. So sick, she is."

"Here." John handed the bag through the open door.

"*Quyana*," Carl said, nodding. "Hope this helps. Anna sick?"

"She's fine," John said. "Are you going to take your girl to Bethel?"

"They aren't letting any more patients go in the hospital. No planes can fly. Too many sick people, I guess. If she gets any worse, I might take her by sno-go anyway."

"Do you know when the power will be back on?" John asked.

Carl shook his head. "Maybe there's no one to check on the generator. I would, but my family needs me," he said.

John nodded. "Take care of them," he said. "This will be over soon."

"See you," Carl said, closing the door. John waited until he heard Carl's feet on the steps and the machine roar to life and race off before he returned to their bedroom.

He stopped at the window and looked out at the sun, a dull yellow-white disc sinking into the frigid white canvas of snow and tundra.

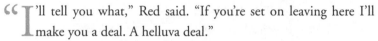

# 34

"I'll tell you what," Red said. "If you're set on leaving here I'll make you a deal. A helluva deal."

"I don't really feel like I have much to deal with," John replied. He looked over at the bed, where the girl was still sleeping. He was worried about what Red was going to say next. The man's attitude had changed once he saw they were intent on leaving.

Red stood up and rubbed his lower back with both hands. "Damn cot's not exactly comfortable," he said. He took the kettle and set it on the hot plate. "Tea?"

John shook his head. He didn't like Red's tone. His mood seemed different. Detached.

"The girl—walking the distance you aim to walk with her isn't going to be easy."

"I'm not leaving her," John said. "Not with you."

"Wasn't suggesting you should. I've got no use for a girl who can't see. I've got some MREs you can take. They would travel a little easier than those heavy cans. You need to know that the worst part of winter is on its way and travel will be hell, no matter how prepared you are." He sat down across the table from John.

"There's more. Under the tank here, in my storage bunker, I've got two snow machines. One's mine, the other was my wife's. You can take her machine and the two jerry jugs of gas. That's ten gallons. Plus the machine is full. That's enough fuel to get you a hundred fifty or so miles upriver or to find those kids she keeps talking about, wherever you want to go."

"What's the catch?"

Red leaned close and said, "There is no catch. I just need you to help me with something I can't do myself. Let's go look at those machines."

Red pulled the cover off the small yellow Ski-Doo. The machine had a long, narrow black seat with a metal basket at the back. Red pointed to a slender fibreglass sled with a heavy-duty aluminum hitch. "You can throw your gear and supplies in the sled, and put the gas cans here in the back on this rack. My machine is bigger and faster, but would burn twice the gas. I think my wife's rig here is the one to take. Plus, these damn Tundra Ski-Doo machines go forever, they're light, and if you get stuck, you'll be able to dig it out. No dude on skis is going to catch you."

Red spun around a few times and eyed all the equipment, lockers, and boxes stored beneath his tank. The space was just high enough that John barely had to duck his head. Red, with his slight stoop, walked around without any worry of bumping his skull on the metal tank above them.

"What are you using for a tent?" he asked.

"A tarp. Snow caves. Whatever," John replied.

"Not good enough. The girl deserves better. Here."

Red removed a ring of keys from his parka and counted through them. He found the one he wanted, and crawled over the snow machine that still had the canvas cover and began unlocking a blue gym-like metal cabinet. He opened the double doors and pulled out a heavy orange bag. He lifted the bag with a grunt and dropped it into the sled.

"There," he said, "the best winter tent money can buy. They call it an Arctic Oven. A winter bomb shelter. I love this thing. If that don't keep you warm, nothing will."

"Thanks," John said. And he meant it. He wasn't sure he could accept Red's offer, but it didn't really seem like an offer. The man wanted him to take the stuff. "Why don't you just come with us?" he asked. "Together, I know we can make it out."

Red sat down on the covered machine. He took off his black stocking cap and scratched at the top of his skull. He looked at his machine and the stuff around him. "No," he said, "I'm plumb tuckered out. You wouldn't understand it, but I spent a good majority of the last thirty some years planning and preparing for the world to end. When it did, I was going to be ready with guns a-blazing. Wasn't going to want for nothing. And I was about half excited when it came, to tell you the truth. But I didn't ever want it to just be me all by myself. I think I wanted people to be sorry they didn't listen to me. I imagined that they would flock to me and ask for forgiveness. Shit, I deluded myself into thinking that I would be like some gun-toting god of the tundra and finally get to have my say about how life ought to be. Turns out, I'm the one feeling sorry. Lonely and damn sorry about what I thought I wanted. This definitely ain't the outcome I envisioned. But I probably don't have to tell you about survivor's guilt."

He stood up and knocked on the metal tank above them, as if for good luck, or to test the strength of the steel. He manoeuvred around the sled and opened the cowling to the Tundra. He removed a spark-plug wrench from the black plastic toolbox inside and popped the spark-plug wire off and unscrewed the plug.

"Hand me that starter fluid," he said, pointing to a metal shelf loaded with cans of paint, lubricant, and cleaners. John found the starter fluid and tossed the can to Red, who sprayed a shot of liquid into the cylinder, and then began screwing the plug back in with his bare hands.

"She'll start now," he said, closing the cover and gripping the heavy plastic starter handle. He gave three quick pulls and the small motor roared to life, the sudden sound reverberating against the metal of the tank and the confined space. John winced at the harsh sound, realizing he hadn't heard a motor in a long time, and it sounded mean, angry.

Red let it run for a few minutes and then hit the kill switch.

The motor died and again they were surrounded by absolute silence. John's ears began to ring.

"Well, there you go. We'll pull this out of here, and the sled. Get you loaded, take care of some business, and you'll be on your way. No man on skis to worry about any more."

"What's the business, Red?"

Red sat down on the snow machine, briefly looked John in the eyes, and then turned his attention to the controls. He began popping the machine's kill switch up and down. He stopped and brushed some dust off the handlebars and lightly tapped the throttle.

"Before you guys showed up I thought I'd die alone out here. Probably deserved to. But you showing up changed that. Something of a miracle, John." He stopped and popped the switch up and down again. "I don't have to die alone now."

"I'm not liking your tone, Red. What are you asking of me?" John asked.

"Easy. You put me out of my misery." Red stood back up and smiled at him. "That's the deal. Take it or leave it. But I don't want the girl here when you do it. You can take her out of town a ways and come back for me. She doesn't need to know nothing about it. And she doesn't need to think she can't trust you, either."

"I don't think I can hold up my end of that bargain," John said. "I think you should just come with us."

Red shook his head. "Told ya, I'm spent. I'm like Chief Joseph said, 'My heart is sick and sad. From where the sun now stands, I'll fight no more, forever.'"

"Chief Joseph wasn't asking someone he just met to shoot him. You're going to have to just do it yourself, Red."

Red smiled and shook his head again. "Now, now, John, I'm afraid that wasn't the deal now, was it?"

THE TEMPERATURE IN THE HOUSE dipped to twenty below, according to the thermometer on his parka zipper-pull. When Anna coughed, bursts of steam erupted from her mouth. The coughing fits lasted four or five minutes, and she gasped and sobbed. She would sit, slumped in the bed, the blankets and sleeping bags covering her, her red knitted cap on her head, a heavy green fleece scarf wound around her neck. Frost covered her eyebrows, and small beads of sweat froze against her forehead.

John sat next to her, patting and rubbing her back, helpless.

"What's happening to me?" she asked, and then coughed up a tablespoon-sized glob of green phlegm. "I don't mean to be a baby. But I'm so cold."

He moved closer and wrapped his arms around her. "You'll be okay," he said. "We'll use the camp stove and get it warm. I'll melt some snow and make you some tea. Some tea will make you feel better."

"I don't want to die here, John."

"You're not going to die. What makes you say that?"

"My body aches. I've never hurt like this."

She began to convulse in another fit of coughing. Between coughs she heaved and shook uncontrollably. John slid his hand beneath her jacket, sweater, shirt, and finally touched his hand to her lower back. He recoiled momentarily from the heat, as if he'd touched his hand to a woodstove. She was burning up. He didn't know if he should undress her and try to break the fever. He pressed his open hand to her burning skin and rubbed her back.

When she stopped coughing, she leaned against him and sobbed in raspy, crackly breaths. After several minutes she pulled back the covers and looked at her lap. She gasped for air and pointed at the wet spot between her legs.

"I messed myself!" she cried.

"It's okay," he said, getting up from the bed. "I'll get the camp stove going and we'll get you cleaned up. It's okay, Anna. Just try to relax, girl. Relax. Breathe. There you go."

Outside he heard another group of snow machines racing away from the village. He peered out the frosted window. He could barely make out the shape of several dark objects with their red tail lights racing east across the snow-drifted horizon. He hoped whoever it was would bring back help.

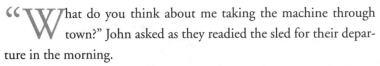

# 35

"What do you think about me taking the machine through town?" John asked as they readied the sled for their departure in the morning.

"Don't think it would make much sense," Red said. "No reason to go hunting for trouble, which you're sure to find. First sound of a machine running down the road will bring the guns. I'm worried enough about us firing up that Tundra for a few minutes."

"How many people do you think are left?"

Red pointed to a ladder attached to the side of the tank. "Want to take a look? Pretty good view up there."

John nodded and Red mounted the ladder. John worried that Rayna would get scared when she heard footsteps above her, so he poked his head inside. The girl stood near the sink, naked from the waist up, with her back toward him. She turned at the sound of the door, and he quickly closed the door to just a crack. "Sorry," he said.

"I'm almost done washing my hair," she said. "It feels so nice to be clean. You going to see if you can find Maggie?"

"Just going to look," he said. "I didn't want you to get spooked when you heard footsteps up top."

He shut the door and climbed the ladder. Red reached down a hand, and John grabbed it and eased himself over the edge. He stood beside Red and looked out over the city. The tank was just high enough that they could see most of the town. Two small tendrils of smoke rose from houses, one to the west of town, and one in the middle.

"With it being as cold as it is, and only two houses with heat, maybe a few others we can't see, I'd say there are probably less than fifty people living here. Most left. Fled by boat or snow machine, or on foot. The rest are dead. No fuel, no food. Don't make for easy living if you can't return to the old ways. See all those burned-out places? I think some of those fires are from people trying to burn the sickness out. They figured sick houses had to be burned. I think some of it was just madness."

John scanned the rows of houses and vacant buildings. The scene was not new, just on a larger scale. Hundreds of structures, blackened, broken, destroyed.

"I've been through the whole town, at night mostly. Just looking," Red said.

"For what?"

"I don't know. I guess for people who needed help, for supplies, for *anything*, mostly looking for meaning, probably. Redemption don't come easy."

Red pointed toward the high school. "They tried to set up a makeshift hospital. At one point, they had over a thousand sick people inside. All laid out on gym mats and cots. Then when the power went out and there was no water or heat, it all went to hell real fast. On the outside the building doesn't look half bad, but inside. You don't ever want to see in there. You ever see those pictures of the stacks of bodies in Rwanda or the killing fields in Cambodia? Like that—bodies just piled clear to the ceiling. Everywhere."

He lifted his hand again and pointed to the middle of town.

"And the hospital. Talk of Hades on earth. They quit taking patients early on, but people were forcing their way in. Total chaos. Too many sick people to help anyone. This whole place, this whole damn town just imploded on itself. Desperation brings out the best and worst in people, they say, but for the most part, what I seen wasn't the best. Fear. Pure fear."

Red coughed, and spit off the edge of the tank.

"You're welcome to take a little spin through town, but nothing good will come of it. I can pretty much guarantee you that. You're better off firing up the machine in the morning. We'll say our goodbyes and you can get on up the river, quick as you can. The storm will have covered her tracks. Don't suspect you'll find the old lady." Red took his rifle off his shoulder and looked through the scope out across the tundra beyond the wind turbines. "I've been thinking a lot about the skier. White camouflage. That changes everything, John, don't you think?"

"What do you mean?"

"This is more than a government quarantine. This sickness was concocted. Man-made. Monitored. Maybe some government agency acting on its own under the guise of a pandemic."

"And the man on skis?" John asked.

"I don't know. Maybe he's here to finish the job. Make sure no one survives to tell the story."

John looked out toward the west to see what the morning's weather would bring. The skies were strangely clear. Like the day the two Blackhawks landed with Santa in the village. He thought of the entire village lined up across the gym floor for ice cream and oranges, like the stories of shivering Sioux grateful and unravelling warm wool blankets infected with smallpox and measles.

A crisp blue horizon told him the night would be bitter cold. He was glad to know they would have at least one more night of safety, warmth, and a bed.

"You're worried about what the girl will think about our deal," Red said.

"She's not going to understand, I'll tell you that. She likes you. And you're growing on me."

"Growing like a fungus. Listen, I can explain it to her if you'd like. She'll get that I don't want to be alone no more. That I can't leave this place. She knows more than she lets on, you know."

"I know."

"What am I not going to understand?"

They both turned and looked down at the girl, standing on the deck beneath them with a red towel wrapped around her black hair.

"Nothing, Rayna. Nothing."

"Red's not going with us, is he? He won't tell anyone about them, my cousins, will he?"

"I've got to stay behind, girl. In case someone else comes along and needs help like you guys did. In case that hunter dude comes along. You know old Red will take care of him, too. Bang! Bang! Now go back inside—it ain't safe out here for a beauty like you. Plus, your hair is soaking wet. You'll catch a cold."

"I think it's too late to worry about catching colds, Red," she said and disappeared inside.

Red waited for the sound of the door latch and then whispered to John. "Now don't you steal her hope that those kids are alive. You don't know that she's right. You do what you need to, but keep her hope alive. That's all she's got. Hell, she's the only one with any hope in this whole damn place. Leave with her tomorrow, then tell her you forgot something, tell her whatever you need to and come back. That's the deal. Got it?"

The man's eyes showed no sign of conceding. John started down the ladder without giving him an answer. He had no intention of returning.

Once they were back inside, the two men watched in silence as Rayna combed and then braided her long black hair. The thick single braid reached down to the middle of her back when she finished. Red handed her a fat blue rubber band to hold it together. John stared at the collection of figure eights running down her back and tried to remember if Anna's braids had been the same. He didn't remember ever looking closely at them. They were just braids then; he hadn't paid attention. He looked at her braids and then at the girl's grass creation. The braids were similar, three strands that tapered to two, and then one, and he wondered how the girl could weave the strands so perfectly without seeing.

"Are we going to eat tonight?" she asked.

"Of course we're going to eat tonight, kiddo," Red said, standing up and stretching out his lower back. "We've got to have a little going-away party. We should eat something special, don't you think? Maybe I should order us a pizza."

The girl covered her mouth with both hands and giggled. The giggle turned to a cough. She coughed twice and cleared her throat. "Maybe you could order some Chinese food, too. I always ordered sweet-and-sour chicken when I came to Bethel," she said and giggled some more.

Red chuckled. "And Greek! I'll order us one of them gy-ros and a cal-zoni!"

They laughed together at his awkward pronunciation and John began to chuckle, too.

Red reached over and picked up a cordless phone sitting by the computer. John hadn't noticed it sitting there, useless. "Here's the phone," he said, handing it to the girl. "Order me some Pad Thai from Stinky Fingers, with some mango coconut rice."

The girl put the phone to her ear, laughing, and rolled back on the bed. John stood up from his chair and walked over to her. "Let me see that thing," he said. She stopped laughing and she held the phone out. He snatched it up and for a moment Red and the girl thought the fun was over, but then he put it to his own ear.

"Hello? Is this Impossible Hut? I'd like to place an order. Yeah. One order of new jeans, yeah, mine aren't fitting so well. I've lost a couple of pounds on this crazy diet. And a jet to pick us up and take us somewhere tropical, somewhere warm, yes, with a side order of cheesy fries. What do you want, Red?"

The girl held her stomach and rolled around on the bed, laughing and gasping for air.

"From Impossible Hut? I'll take some king crab with drawn butter, a bottle of Johnnie Walker Blue Label, and a Blackhawk chopper, fuelled and fully loaded for ass kicking."

"Did you get that? Wait, one more order. Rayna, what do you want?"

She stopped laughing and sat up. Her face got serious. "I can get anything I want?" she asked.

"Anything. Red's buying."

"The hell I am!"

"Okay, I'm buying. Order whatever you want, girl."

"Well, I'd like some ice cream. Chocolate with whipped cream on top. And I never had Japanese food before. What do they call it?"

"Sushi."

"Yes, sushi. I want to try that."

"Is that all," John asked, still holding the phone to his ear. "You want anything else?"

The girl thought long and hard for a moment, turned her face up toward him, and smiled. "Just ice cream," she said. "Chocolate ice cream."

HE LOST COUNT of how many days Anna had been sick, how long they had been without power, how many snow machines had raced away from the village, and how many groups he'd seen carrying corpses out to the cemetery at the north end of the village, just past their house. At first there had been a few crude plywood coffins. He suspected those had been hand cut. Then the bodies were wrapped in sheets. And finally, he would watch as just one or two people used all their strength to lug a body, no coffin or sheet, to a snow machine with a sled.

One night, while Anna slept, he walked out to the cemetery to stretch his legs, but also to see what they were doing with the dead. He didn't want to waste the batteries in his headlamp, so he kept the light off. He could see well enough with the snow reflecting the light coming from a waning half moon.

Each step through the snow zapped his strength. He'd started to ration their canned food. He figured help would be coming soon enough, but he didn't want to take any chances, and he worried what extent people would go to if they started running out of food and fuel to hunt and fish.

He took several steps backward at the sight of the dead. The rows and rows of bodies stood out against the snow. Behind them the white wooden crosses from the old graves stood leaning like weary soldiers on guard. He didn't count the corpses. There were too many to count.

In slow, short steps he backed away from the frozen, lifeless faces. Then he turned and sprinted home. He wasn't close enough to see their expressions, but he knew some of them were his students, and from the size of the smaller corpses, some of Anna's too. He wouldn't be able to live with himself if she joined them.

## 36

"See you, Red," Rayna whispered over the rattle of the Tundra's motor. She held his face with her bare hands and kissed him on the forehead. "*Quyana-cakneq.*"

Red's eyes welled as he watched the girl slide her hands into her mittens.

John was glad the girl couldn't see the tears beginning to stream down the man's weathered cheeks. He wished he couldn't, either.

"You travel safe, kiddo. You'll find gold where you're going, girl," he said. "And keep an eye on this goofy guy."

She laughed. "So funny you are, Red. *Piuraa.*"

John took off his glove and shook Red's hand. He gave a firm squeeze and nodded his head. He didn't need to say any more.

"Got everything?"

"I think so," John said.

"Well. If you need something else, don't be afraid to come back and get it."

John nodded again.

He swung his leg over the machine's black seat, and the girl crawled on behind him and wrapped her arms around him. "I've never been so happy to be on a sno-go," she yelled to Red.

Red grinned and patted her on the back, and then tapped John's shoulder. "Go on," he said, "you don't have all day. Cut across that way toward the bluffs, then drop down on the river. Watch out for open spots and overflow on the river ice. Good luck, you two."

John grabbed the rifle leaning against the cowling. He slid the weapon beneath his thighs, crossways, and gave a two-fingered salute. Red winked at him, and John squeezed the throttle and the machine and sled lurched forward.

He aimed the machine northeast, following the edge of town, in the direction Red had pointed out. He travelled at half speed, just fast enough to make them a difficult target to hit, but not so fast as to waste their fuel.

They cruised past the dump, where the ravens circled by the hundreds, riding the breeze that whipped up against the ridges of dirt and trash. The birds dove and swooped, and tucked their broad black wings, plummeting toward the ground and then opening their wings at the last moment to sail up into the grey sky again. He watched the ravens as he passed, and not once did one of them roll over and dump luck in his direction. Had Red not stocked them with everything they would need, he would have considered stopping and picking around the black-speckled expanse of snow, garbage, bones, and ravens.

Just before the looming river bluff east of town he stopped the machine and killed the motor. He sat for a moment, and then turned back to look at the city behind them.

"Is everything okay?" she asked.

"Just stopping for a second, that's all."

"You don't have to do it," she said. "Nobody should have to do something like that."

He wanted to know how she knew, but there was no point. She knew, just as she knew most everything he thought or said. He wondered if she knew about Red's tears, and then he wondered if those tears were because Red knew John didn't have it in him.

"I think we owe it to him," he said.

The girl thought for a while and nodded.

"He would do it for us," John whispered.

A bent figure emerged from the brush near the base of the bluffs. John lifted his rifle, but then realized the person was small, old, hunched, and carrying his ice pick the way the old woman carried her shotgun, in one hand like a cane.

"I'll be damned. There she is," John said.

"I knew she would wait for us," the girl said.

They both still sat on the machine, the girl's arms still wrapped around his waist, her body pressed against his back. John took off a glove and held his fingers against his cheek, where the icy wind burned at his skin. "You start walking. That way," John said, turning and touching her cheek with his fingers. She turned her head in the direction of the old woman.

"It's okay if you don't go back, John. Red would understand."

John slid his rifle back under his legs and squeezed the handlebars as tight as he could. He leaned forward and rested his head between the bars and with his face turned sideways, relaxed his eyes until the ocean of pallid flat earth to the north of them blurred. He felt Rayna lean forward as well and rest her head against his back, her arms still around him.

They sat that way for a while, and then the girl let go and slid off the seat. The cold air rushed to fill the space against his back where she had been. She pulled off her glove and put her hand on his back, followed his spine to his neck, and then knelt down and held her warm palm to his face. Her icy irises seemed to search for his eyes and then stopped, as if they had found something important. The bright sunlight against the snow turned her pupils into two black pinholes, smaller than any he had ever seen, but at the same time he felt as if he could crawl into one of them and hide himself from the world.

"I made a promise to her," he said, not sure if his voice was audible over the wind. "And I made a deal with Red."

He felt his voice wither and he blinked hard and felt his tears beginning to freeze against his cheeks. She wiped away a tear with her thumb and then leaned in and touched her lips to the freezing tear, and then kissed the new pools forming at the edge of his eyes.

"My grandmother used to tell me to never ask for a promise if I knew it wasn't fair. Maybe Anna made you promise something, but Red didn't. He doesn't expect you to return."

She kissed his cheek again, and then stood. He sat up and gave the starter handle a quick tug. The machine fired, and he pumped the throttle lightly and let it idle.

"I'll be back. I need to at least tell him I can't do it …"

She lifted her eyebrows slightly and turned in the direction of the old woman, who had covered half the distance to the bluff.

John gunned the machine, turned in a wide half arc, and eased the sled back toward the ravens circling Bethel.


ANNA HADN'T SLEPT SOUNDLY in days, and when she finally did, she moaned and cried and muttered in her sleep. When she finally fell silent, he took out his pistol and rifle from the closet and set them within reach of the bed.

The fever was only getting worse. Day and night she would sweat until her clothes were damp all the way through. He had worked tirelessly to keep her clothes changed, her water glass ice free, and as best he could, her nerves calm.

He wasn't sure why he felt the need to have a weapon close by, but the night before he was sure he'd heard shots. He'd started locking both doors, the door to the entry and the inside door. If someone came thinking they could do anything other than help Anna, they would be staring at the business end of his guns.

Suddenly Anna sat straight up and pointed toward the bedroom door. John squinted in the dark, trying to see what she was looking at. "He's here," she whispered. "He's here, for me."

John reached for his pistol and light. He flipped the light on, the beam cutting through their breath which hung above them in the freezing room. Anna slumped back on the bed, mumbling. He sat there waiting, almost wishing there was something or someone to unleash on. Trembling, John took a deep breath and leaned back, holding the pistol in one hand and turning off the headlamp with the other.

He didn't know how much longer she could hold out, but it couldn't be too much longer before help came. It just couldn't.

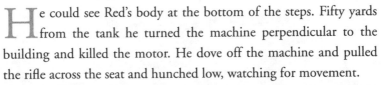

# 37

He could see Red's body at the bottom of the steps. Fifty yards from the tank he turned the machine perpendicular to the building and killed the motor. He dove off the machine and pulled the rifle across the seat and hunched low, watching for movement.

The gate to the storage area beneath the tank was open and Red's snow machine gone. He could see that the tracks from the other machine were headed toward the middle of town. One of Red's legs kicked, and John dashed toward the tank, rifle in hand.

Red's body was still, but his eyes were moving, and they tracked John's approach. John knelt down and cradled his head in his lap. He could see two quarter-sized bloody holes in Red's chest.

"I bought you a little time," Red gasped. "He's got my machine. But he's only got a half tank of gas." Red convulsed and spit up a mouthful of blood. "You don't have much time. Go. Save the girl. He knows about the gym. The kids. I told him the surviving kids are here in town, but he'll be coming for you when he doesn't find them. Sit me up, John. I want to be ready if he comes back."

"Who is he?" John asked. "What does he want?"

"Blood," Red said, lifting his hand to a dark, wet crimson smear on his neck. "He's here for the blood of the survivors."

"YOU CAN'T GIVE UP ON ME," he said. "Don't quit fighting. You can beat this," he said, trying to convince himself as much as her.

Anna's green eyes had already lost most of their life, the shine gone, replaced with a dull, listless stare, as if her spirit oozed from her body with each sniffle, each cough, and each glob of bright green phlegm spotted with droplets of blood.

"Just hold on until help gets here. It's on the way," he said, knowing no one would make it in time. It was already too late. He hadn't done enough.

He cuddled beside her and spoke to her while running his fingers through her hair, not sure if she could even hear him or if she was asleep or in some feverish coma-like state. There was lifelessness about her. Even her hair felt wrong, thin and dying.

"If anything happens to you, I won't leave you. I'll never leave you," he whispered. "I'll just stay right here until I'm gone too. I won't live without you, Anna. Don't give up. Please. You get a little better and I'll get us out of here. I promise. I'll take you home. Back to the warm and sunshine. I'll find a way to make everything all right. Just stay with me. Stay with me. Fight it. Come on. I'm right here, girl. I'll always be here."

He said it, and he meant it. Life as he knew it wouldn't be the same. It didn't make sense to even consider going on without her. She alone had kept the world from crushing him.

He slowly and quietly lifted the covers and slipped out of the bed. He pulled on his parka and boots, tucked the pistol into his waistband, and grabbed the rifle. He had to go check out the clinic to make sure there wasn't something there that could help her.

He was too late. Every possible medical supply had been taken. When he returned to her, empty-handed, she saw the look on his face and instead of crying, as he was so sure she would, she transformed. Right there on the bed, in front of him, she changed.

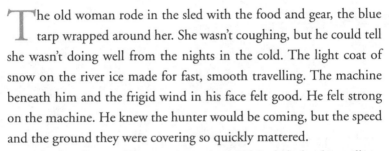

# 38

The old woman rode in the sled with the food and gear, the blue tarp wrapped around her. She wasn't coughing, but he could tell she wasn't doing well from the nights in the cold. The light coat of snow on the river ice made for fast, smooth travelling. The machine beneath him and the frigid wind in his face felt good. He felt strong on the machine. He knew the hunter would be coming, but the speed and the ground they were covering so quickly mattered.

As he put distance between themselves and Bethel, the thin willows and sporadic patches of black spruce along the wide, meandering river's edge gave way to thicker stands of spruce and birch. The mountains seemed to grow up out of the tundra with each mile.

Broken-down snow machines and stripped four-wheelers abandoned along the riverbank made ominous trail markers. Each bend in the river revealed something more of the panicked flight from Bethel. Between the broken vehicles he spotted the occasional piece of clothing. A single red boot. A black glove. A pair of blue jeans flapping in the willows.

The darkened eye sockets of half-buried skulls stared out at them from the passing snowdrifts. At one point he thought he saw a hand reaching up out of the ice. He slowed and saw it was just a stick with branches.

A frozen River Styx, he thought to himself as the river turned north and then east and then west. Winding and winding, circling and circling, the underworld somewhere in the distance.

John kept looking back. Checking to make sure the old woman was okay, but also worried about the other, faster machine that would be coming for them.

The roofs and hoods of several pickup trucks and taxi cabs poked through the river ice in places they'd gotten stuck or run out of gas on the frantic arctic exodus from Bethel. He passed a set of four tires poking up through the ice, the ridiculous long undercarriage of a stretch limo.

The sun moved across the southern sky as he manoeuvred carefully around the metal corpses that stretched for as far as he could see from each twist in the river. He expected the steel carnage to begin thinning out, but then wondered if the wreckage stretched on forever.

ANNA JUST SMILED her lovely smile. She knew. He didn't know if she knew it would be that night, or if she just knew there was no reason left to hope. She knew.

"Come here," she said. "Hold me."

He pulled off his parka and crawled beneath the covers and wrapped his arms around her. The cool air burned at his nostrils and his breath froze against the nylon sleeping bags over them.

"I'm sorry," she said.

"Sorry for what? I should be the one who's sorry. I should have found a way out."

"I'm sorry for bringing us here," she said. "We shouldn't have come. We didn't belong here. I didn't belong here. I just thought maybe we should connect with your heritage for our children. I was wrong, John."

"That's not true. The regular life isn't for us. And don't give up on me. I don't like your tone. You can't give up on me, okay? Okay?"

"You're not mad that I made the decision to bring us here?"

"That was our decision. We made it together," he said.

"Yeah, but I was the one ... I just wanted you to know where you came from."

She stopped and coughed. The air crackled deep within her chest and the phlegm and mucus seemed too thick for her to bring up. She coughed again, harder, and then rested her head on the pillow, her eyes wet with tears from the effort.

"I was the one," she whispered, "who pushed for it."

"It's okay. Who is to say this isn't happening everywhere? This could have happened to us anywhere. No matter where we chose to live. Besides, where else could we live?"

"Do you really think it's like this outside?"

"I don't know. I hope not."

"John?" she asked. "I want you to promise me something. You've got to promise me this one thing, okay?"

She pulled him close and whispered her impossible demand into his ear. He closed his eyes and tried not to listen, but it was too late.

"Promise me," she cried. "Promise."

"Promise," he said, trying to forget what she'd asked him. "I promise."

He wrapped his arms around her and held her sick, frail frame against his, hoping that her coughing, the snot, the tears, her breath—anything—would find its way into his body as they slept so that in the morning he would wake with his own shivers and chills, sick.

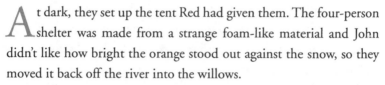

# 39

At dark, they set up the tent Red had given them. The four-person shelter was made from a strange foam-like material and John didn't like how bright the orange stood out against the snow, so they moved it back off the river into the willows.

Rayna didn't ask him what happened when he went back to Red, but he expected she would, and when she didn't that night, he wondered if she knew how scared he was or if she had sensed him looking over his shoulder all day—if somehow she could see into his head and watch the scene that kept playing and replaying in his mind. Over and over. Red lying at the steps of his bunker, a pistol in one hand, the AR15 at his feet in the blood-clumped snow. If she could see it the way he had, she would know Red did all that he could for them.

She cuddled close, but stayed in her own sleeping bag. He half wished she would climb in with him so that he could just hold her, but she didn't. He wondered if it was because it was almost too warm with the miniature aluminum woodstove and narrow chimney pipe. Or if it was because she sensed him struggling for air. Or perhaps she could see in her mind's eye Red lurch forward and then topple into the snow, the shadow of the hunter, of a wind turbine spinning over his body, blood trickling from Red's nostrils, and his blue eyes trying to fix themselves on the Colt revolver's barrel lodged in the snow near his face.

The old woman had said little except that she would have only waited one more day for them. And then she told them about a strange dream. "During one of those nights," she said, "I made a shelter in the brushes, and was sleeping on a bed I made from willows and my caribou skin. I got real cold and started seeing a man and a woman walking across the tundra. They were the only two people left in the world, and they were so sad."

John sat up and opened the shoebox-sized stove, slid in another piece of driftwood, closed the door and shut the damper down. It was dark, so he felt smoke wouldn't give them away any more than the snow-machine tracks leading straight to their tent. If the hunter hadn't caught them by now, then maybe he wasn't going to bother following them. He checked the airways to make sure the tent could breathe, as Red had insisted. Then he stretched out on his back and stared at the peak of their warm new shelter.

The old woman coughed once and continued her story. "The man wanted to maybe turn into animals and quit living like people, but that woman, she wanted to have a family and start a new village. Then they met a thing, the thing was part wolf, part bear, and part human. That thing told them he was once human and life was too difficult so he wanted to become a wolf, and then when he was a wolf he was not happy and he wanted to be a bear. As a bear he was too lonely and wanted to become human again. That was how he became that horrible thing. He never was happy with what he had or where he was. The thing went away alone and that man started building a new house and the woman started collecting grass to weave their new bed."

The old woman fell silent. John felt as if she'd been talking directly to him, but he didn't know what she meant. He wanted to ask, but didn't know where to start. How long had he been like the *thing*?

The girl rolled on her side, facing him. She pulled her sleeping bag down and slipped her hand into his. She gave a soft squeeze and he closed his fist and held her hand tight.

"It's almost ready," Rayna whispered.

"What is?" he asked.

She said nothing and closed her eyes.

He wanted to lie and to tell her that he rode back and told Red he couldn't do it. He thought that might help her not think of him as someone who could kill a friend. But then again, he still didn't believe what Red had told him before he died. What bothered him most was that after all Red had done for them, he still couldn't believe his story.

"It's okay," she whispered.

"You know?"

"I couldn't smell any gunpowder on your gloves. But he's dead. The blood. Red hurt himself?"

"No."

"The hunter?" she asked, in whisper he could hardly hear. "He's coming for us."

"I don't know," he said. "Probably."

"I know," she said. "I know he is."

She squeezed his hand back and rested her head on his shoulder. Her hair smelled clean, and he nuzzled his nose and lips against the top of her head and inhaled deeply through his nostrils. The scent of apple shampoo brought back a flash of almost foreign memories of Anna and carefree college days, cheap shampoo and long hot showers, but then the memories were gone and he only smelled Rayna.

He thought of Red again and wondered why he'd left the safety of the tank. Why he had sacrificed himself like that for them.

The girl turned her face toward his, as if she could hear the tears building at the edges of his eyes.

"Did he tell you?" she asked.

"Tell me what?"

"Where they are hiding," she said.

"No. Rayna, I don't think your cousins are alive. I'm sorry."

"But they are, John. I think he told me where."

John sat up on his elbow and from the small bits of light coming from the woodstove, he could see her white eyes. "He told you?"

She nodded. "He gave me an idea. If we're lucky, we'll take the sno-go there tomorrow," she said.

"Where? What did he tell you?" John asked, suddenly feeling strange. Warm. Something that felt like hope flooded his body.

"He said I would find gold where I'm going. There's only one place where the kids here ever went to find gold."

"Where? Tell me where," he whispered.

"I said I would never ask you to promise me anything," she said.

"WILL YOU GET something for me?" Anna asked in a hoarse whisper. "There," she said, weakly trying to pull a hand out from beneath the covers to point to the one-drawer nightstand on her side of the bed. "In the back, a plastic bag," she wheezed, using the last bit of her energy before she collapsed on the pillows.

He pulled the drawer open and dug through the letters, photos, lotions, and massage oils. Behind all of it he found a sandwich bag, with a white plastic object inside. He held it up to the last of the evening light coming in through the frosted window.

She watched him as he opened the bag. As he began to pull it out, his hands started to tremble. He turned the thin white plastic device over and over in his hands, but he didn't need to see the blue + to know what it was, or what it meant.

He sat beside the bed and held her.

"I wanted to wait to be sure," she said. Tears streamed down her cheeks and her sobs turned to coughing that came from somewhere so deep inside her chest he thought she might burst in his arms.

He didn't know why she had bothered to tell him. Or why she'd waited to tell him. Or why, when they had the chance to leave, she didn't say something. Now it all meant nothing. It could mean nothing. He couldn't think of it, or allow himself to be angry with her. Not now. Not ever.

The white plastic cracked inside his trembling fist.

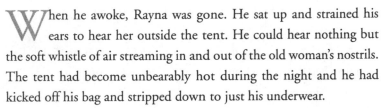

# 40

When he awoke, Rayna was gone. He sat up and strained his ears to hear her outside the tent. He could hear nothing but the soft whistle of air streaming in and out of the old woman's nostrils. The tent had become unbearably hot during the night and he had kicked off his bag and stripped down to just his underwear.

He felt for the pistol near his pants he'd used for his pillow the night before. It was gone. The girl's parka, clothing, and boots sitting at the entrance to the tent made his mouth suddenly dry, and his pulse quickened. Far off he could hear the whine of an approaching motor.

He gave the old woman's shoulder a rough shake. She was sleeping with her parka pulled over her. "Wake up," he said, "he's coming."

When she opened her eyes, he pointed to the girl's boots. She sat up, coughed out a mouthful of phlegm, and wiped it away with the back of her hand.

"How long she been gone? Where's my caribou hide?" the old woman asked.

He shrugged and tried to listen for her, hoping she was just outside. The machine drew closer. Closer.

"She took my pistol, too," he whispered.

"What you done to her?"

"Nothing. I would never hurt her."

"Maybe she thinks you don't need her no more. You'll leave her."

"No. She knows I do. I won't leave her."

"Go, then. See where her tracks take you. I'll wait for that man."

He pulled his down parka over his naked back and reached for the rifle leaning against the wall of the tent. He slid his boots onto his feet, not taking the time to put on his pants or socks. The sound of the zipper angered him. He stuck his head out and took a deep breath of the cool air. He couldn't believe he had slept so deeply and he hadn't heard the girl open and close the tent door.

As he zipped the door of the tent all the way open the old woman opened the breech of her shotgun, checked the shells, and spoke again. "When you find her, maybe he'll have found me and maybe not. *Piuraa,* John."

"*Quyana,*" he replied and stepped out into the pale dawn light. The air burned cold and a sick sinking feeling spread through his gut. The snow machine wasn't far now. To the east, the sky glowed pink, the arctic sunrise minutes away. Her tracks, small, soft prints of bare soles, headed away from the river, through the birch and black spruce.

He followed them quietly, with quick, sharp strides, watching each track, noticing their deliberate pace, the distance between each step, and how she allowed the whole bottom of her foot to sink into the snow, as if that solid connection with the earth would allow her safe passage through the woods.

In places he could see where she had bumped a branch, knocking the snow free. The motor drew closer. Closer.

At one point, he found where she stopped, long enough to pick up a stick to help guide her. He knew this from the small, round black holes spaced evenly between each barefoot track.

He wanted to call out her name again, but the sound of the snow-machine motor racing closer and his heart drumming against his chest was already too much.

# 41

The trees thinned and turned to willows. The remaining spruce were black and leaning. The distance between her footsteps had increased and she had abandoned the stick she had used for walking. He picked it up and wished it was still warm where she had held it. In his mind he imagined her running now with the pistol, through the willows, the thin branches whipping against her face.

The motor had died and he suspected the hunter was making his stalk on their camp. He hoped he would spare the old woman.

Where was the girl going? Why was she running? What was she running from? Did she know he was coming? Did she know the hunter had found them?

He pushed his way through the willows until they opened up to a steep tundra bluff that rose above a long, frozen oxbow slough. Her tracks made a straight line across the ice, up the fifty-foot slope, and out of sight.

He squatted down and put his bare fingers to a footprint. He touched each toe impression, the ball of her foot, traced the arch, and then stopped at her heel. The track had a small spot of blood. The ice beneath the snow was beginning to cut her feet. If she was still alive when he found her, he would tend to her feet and tell her everything. They would make a stand and he would protect her.

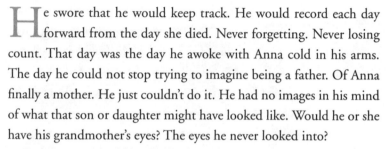

# 42

He swore that he would keep track. He would record each day forward from the day she died. Never forgetting. Never losing count. That day was the day he awoke with Anna cold in his arms. The day he could not stop trying to imagine being a father. Of Anna finally a mother. He just couldn't do it. He had no images in his mind of what that son or daughter might have looked like. Would he or she have his grandmother's eyes? The eyes he never looked into?

But worse, it would be the day he would have to start trying to keep his word to Anna.

And on that day, he knew in his heart, he couldn't keep it. She had whispered into his ear and asked him to do the unthinkable. And he said he would. He would have told her anything she needed to hear. And he did.

Anna whispered her dying wish in his ear, "Promise me you will love again, John. Promise me."

"Promise," he replied.

Asking him to promise he would keep on living would have been too much in and of itself, but to love again?

Impossible.

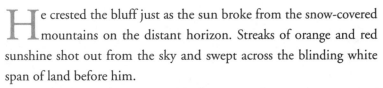

## 43

He crested the bluff just as the sun broke from the snow-covered mountains on the distant horizon. Streaks of orange and red sunshine shot out from the sky and swept across the blinding white span of land before him.

Somewhere in the light was the girl lying on her stomach. Covered only by the old woman's caribou hide, and beyond her, a herd of caribou stretched east and west along the edge of the mountains and out across the tundra plain as far as his eyes could see.

Rayna sat up and waved for him to join her.

Relief swept through him.

The pistol sat in the snow at her side. He crouched low, worried the caribou closest might spot him, and he half ran, half crawled to her. The snow crystals cut against his bare knees. When he reached her, he held her two frozen feet in his hands. Spread out beneath her naked body was a wide, tightly woven grass mat.

"What are you doing? I was worried. You're going to freeze to death," he whispered as he ran his fingers over the grass braids.

"I heard the wolves howling in my sleep. I thought it was a dream. Then I heard them, the caribou. The tendons above their hooves, clicking. Lie down here. Listen. You hear them? You hear that clicking? Like the tundra's heart. A spirit drum. Close your eyes and just listen," she whispered.

"But the hunter," he whispered, "he's coming."

"Shh …"

He looked back in the direction of their camp beneath the bluff. Caribou were beginning to move around them. He lifted the caribou hide, took off his parka, and wrapped it around her body. He slipped beneath the hide and stretched out beside her and closed his eyes. He took a deep breath and held himself still.

Then he heard them. At first just a faint sound, like fingers snapping together. Click. Click. Click. The sound of a pistol firing on an empty chamber. The tap of a stick against the rim of a drum. The clicks grew louder and louder.

CLICK.

CLICK.

CLICK.

She pulled the caribou hide over their heads and eased herself closer to him, opening the parka, and pressing her warm naked body against his. She took his hand and held it against the frozen moss in front of them.

The soft clicking of the caribou hooves filled the world around the two of them. Above. Beneath.

"He's going to kill us," he whispered.

"You feel them?" Rayna asked, holding her hand over his, and pressing his palm down into the frozen moss and snow. "These are the tundra spirits," she said.

"I feel them," he said, "I can feel them through the ground. They are everywhere."

"Maybe this is how we became Yup'ik, how we became the Real People. We could feel the earth's heart beating and we would transform." As she said this she lifted one hand from the cool earth and pressed it against her breast and the other on the grass mat she'd woven.

"And here," she whispered. "I made this for us."

He opened his eyes and she held the parka open and he slid his arms around her naked body. She lifted the caribou skin just enough that the morning sunlight radiated brilliant gold against the snow and reflected against her irises, forcing him to snap his own eyes shut tight against the glare.

But even with his eyes closed he could still see the piercing light, as if in that single moment the morning rays had somehow snow-blinded him.

He felt the caribou around them, running above their bodies, and below through the ground. He could smell their earthy hides, their wet, mossy breath. He could hear them panting, clicking, eating. Living.

He imagined the two of them melting together, the grass mat weaving itself into their skin, the hide becoming their own skin, the herd surrounding them, engulfing them.

Protecting them.

He kept his eyes shut tight as the blinding white enveloped them, bathing their bodies in warmth. The clicking of the hooves, the rumble of the herd against the permafrost, and their breathing coalesced into a single steady rhythm, into one beat that filled the world around him.

"Just listen to them," he whispered, and he held her like he would never let go.

Beneath the heavy caribou hide the gunfire was muffled, the echoes and the sounds of a motor came from some distant place. The hunter would be coming and it didn't matter any more. The hunter. The cold. The outcasts. Or the hunger. None of that mattered.

Under the warmth of the hide, the cold frozen world beneath them fell away. The light around the edges of the hide was too bright for him to see. He held her close, and imagined himself rising, escaping, her hands wrapped around him, his arms becoming two wide black raven's wings. He flapped the wings once, rolled to his back looking down at the tundra below, and then lifted them into the sunlight.

# 44

The black snout poking beneath the hide pulled him from his sleep. In the space between the hide and tundra he could see paws and furry muzzles.

"Wolves," he whispered, feeling around for the pistol, "we're surrounded."

He found the pistol and readied to shoot the next snout that he saw.

"Wait," she whispered. "Listen."

Suddenly the hide lifted off them, and John pointed the pistol skyward.

"Don't shoot, dude! Whoa, sorry!" the voice from above pleaded, and the hide was quickly dropped down on them again.

Darkness.

"Put some clothes on, man! What are you guys, animals?"

John knew the voice. He pulled the hide back and peered out. He squinted at the piercing sunlight that surrounded them. His eyes adjusted to the light and he saw the caribou were gone, and around them stood a team of panting sled dogs. The boy had levelled his rifle at them.

"Alex? That you? Alex!"

"John? Little Bug! No way!" Alex dropped the rifle to his side and knelt down and kissed Rayna on her forehead. She kept the hide pulled up to her neck. He looked at the old hide and then off to the south, the direction the caribou had gone. "Nice hideout. I thought you guys were a sick caribou. Free dinner for the dogs. Why you ain't got clothings?"

"My cousins, where are they?" Rayna asked.

"I'll take you to them. They're safe at Nyac Camp," Alex said. "Did like you said, John. Took care of myself, and then the others." He went to the bag on his dogsled and pulled out a pair of grey sweatpants. "Put these on," he said, handing them to Rayna. "You can wear these, John," he said. "I have two layers." He pulled down his snow pants and tossed them to John. "And my jacket, for her."

"Our stuff, back at the tent," John said.

"Burned. Looks like Maggie used gas and torched the tent and the sno-go. Maybe she wounded him. I took the ice pick and food from the sled, though. Lots of food you guys had. His tracks went that way, followed the herd like a wolf. He thinks you're hiding in the caribou."

"We were hiding, just like she told me to," Rayna said, with a sad smile. She turned her face away from them. "She said I would know when it was time. She was right. Is she gone?"

"She is, but she died fighting."

"Before I left her she said a word," John said. "*Be-you-gaw*. What is that?"

"*Piuraa?* I'll see you," Alex said. "We say that and not goodbye. We don't say goodbye."

"That's what we say," Rayna said, "but that's not what it really means. My grandpa told me why we say *piuraa*. It means stay as you are. She was telling you to stay as you are, John."

Alex laughed. "Maybe she meant she'll see you, and you naked ones will bring her spirit back with a baby, ah? I jokes." He pointed to the west. "We don't have long. The good news is that bad weather is coming to cover our tracks. The bad news is that bad weather is coming and if we don't get moving it will cover us. Get in the sled. Holy cow, the kids are going to be so excited to see you, Rayna. You too, Teach," Alex said. He extended his hand and John shook it.

John pulled on Alex's snow pants, his own jacket, and then crawled into the sled first with the rifle and the pistol. Rayna sat down on his lap and Alex rolled up the grass mat and stuffed it behind John's back. Then he tucked the hide around the front of them to keep out the cold.

Alex lined out the six dogs and yelled, "Haw! Haw! Let's go home, pups. Hike!" The leader started pulling left, and the team turned and followed him. Alex hopped on and off the sled runners and John could feel him pushing and running, jumping on and off the two thin rails jutting out the back of the sled.

The dogs moved silently, effortlessly, toward the low, rolling snow-covered mountains looming ahead of them. The plastic sled runners beneath them made a soft hiss and they picked up speed.

"I was just going out hunting. Lucky I found you guys," Alex said.

"We would have found you anyways," Rayna said.

"How many of you?" John asked.

Alex patted John on the shoulder. "Two groups. One at Nyac with twenty-two. They didn't want us to know where the other group was going. Somewhere on the coast, I bet."

"How did you guys get away?" Rayna asked.

"The village met in the gym and decided who would take the kids and hide in the mountains. Three dog teams and four sno-gos. The rest had to stay behind. I guess I was one of the lucky ones," Alex said.

"We all were the lucky ones," Rayna said. "Right, John?"

John wrapped his arms around her and held her close. He put his head on her shoulder and she turned her warm cheek and rubbed it against his. She pressed her lips against his ear and whispered, "I'm sorry if I made you break your promise to her."

"You helped me keep my promise, Rayna."

He tilted his head and looked up into the sky. Anna's sky. He closed his eyes and could see her face, healthy, vibrant, her green eyes full of life, her smile bright and wide.

He kept his eyes closed as the sled raced forward. With the cold wind in his face, he soared with Rayna, into the air, becoming a raven again.

Far below he could see the snow-camouflaged hunter searching the herd, and in front of him raced two sleek wolves, one black and one grey, galloping shoulder to shoulder at the edge of a brown and white surging sea of thousands of caribou.

# AUTHOR'S NOTE

In July of 1881, the *Corwin* set anchor off the coast of St. Lawrence Island in southwestern Alaska to investigate "reports of massive deaths." What Edward Nelson, the Smithsonian Institution's premier field naturalist, discovered and documented was horrific. In *The Eskimo About Bering Strait* he estimated that over a thousand Yup'ik people on that island alone were dead from disease and famine. Nelson describes corpses "stacked like cordwood" in one village and in another, "bodies of the people were found everywhere in the village and scattered along in a line toward the graveyard for half a mile inland."

I was haunted and angered by what I read. I grew up in south-western Alaska. As a student of the amazing Yup'ik culture around me, I had heard the elders' stories of famine and sickness, but I'd never learned of the magnitude of the death and destruction. I was in my early twenties when I first read Nelson's book. Armed with this knowledge, I dove into the important works of Ann Fienup-Riordan, a local anthropologist. Ann's work included historical information that wasn't taught in our schools, and she also worked diligently to record the stories and wisdom of the remaining elders. Years later I encountered Yup'ik writer Harold Napoleon's *Yuuyaraq: The Way of the Human Being*. Napoleon's book argues that the epidemics and famine led to generational post-traumatic stress and a widespread loss of cultural knowledge and tradition. I realized then that my friends and students were dying because they grew up as their parents and grandparents had, immersed in a constant struggle for survival. The substance abuse, the suicides, and the violence were symptoms of an indigenous culture battling to maintain cultural identity in the face of a new and often oppressive and soul-consuming way of living—a new paradigm that at once demanded adoption of our consumer culture and rejection of a traditional way of life that had worked so successfully for millennia.

Napoleon's book helped me understand the continual tide of trage-dies sweeping across the Yukon-Kuskokwim river deltas. What I didn't understand was why, at the very least, Alaskan youth weren't learning about the history of contact. Why didn't we learn about the destruc-tion and disease brought by the Russians, the whalers, the gold miners, or the missionaries? Why did our Alaskan history studies begin with the struggle for statehood?

As a student of history and as a teacher, I was worried about being condemned to relearn the lessons and repeat the horrors of another epidemic and famine. For years this simple question kicked around in my head: What if?

Then in 2003, the Centers for Disease Control and Prevention began tracking H5N1 ("bird flu"), and fears of a global pandemic became nightly headlines. Very quietly the Alaskan government began making plans and asking area hunters to bring in dead birds they found while afield. Plans for quarantine and protocol were posted online. Meetings were held. But no one mentioned the epidemics and famines of old.

Suddenly my hypothetical "What if?" turned into a more ominous "When?"

This book is my attempt to share the stories that I grew up with, and to pass along the knowledge of survival in the face of disease and famine provided to me by my friends, their families, and the elders. The ancient stories the elders tell are all about survival. They provide clues not just about how to survive the elements but about how to live on this planet as human beings. The stories and the knowledge contained in them will prove to be as powerful and important today as they were thousands of years ago.

In "Homemade Remedies," Yup'ik elder Marie Nichols, from Kasigluk, reveals the importance of learning the ancient stories: "They also taught us how to live. One person can never erase what another has learned, can never steal what he knows ... If a person has none of these teachings, he will be like someone lost in a blizzard. But the person who has the teachings will derive strength from them and use them like a walking stick to prevent himself from getting hurt."

The process of writing this book has been magical. Perhaps that is the nature of working with ancient and powerful stories. They exist so that we may continue to exist.

Revisiting Edward Nelson's work provided me with one of the most powerful and profound experiences I have had as a writer and researcher. Nelson wrote many ghastly descriptions of the villages destroyed by the 1880 plagues that struck southwestern Alaska, and the most haunting of all has continued to trouble my mind a full fourteen years after I first read it: "The total absence of the bodies of children in these villages gave rise to the suspicion that they had been eaten by the adults; but possibly this may have not been the case."

I hold on to the hope that "possibly this may have not been the case," just as I hope that this story isn't a vision of what is to come, or a simple metaphor of what is happening right now in rural Alaska. I hope this story is a shared vision of what we can do to save a culture, and perhaps ourselves along the way.

We start by saving the children.

Don Rearden
Bear Valley, Alaska
May 13, 2010